TAMING
GEORGIA

TAMING GEORGIA

ELLIE WADE

everafter ROMANCE

EverAfter Romance
A division of Diversion Publishing Corp.
443 Park Avenue South, Suite 1004
New York, New York 10016
www.EverAfterRomance.com

For more information, email info@everafterromance.com

Visit the author's website at www.elliewade.com

Cover design by LJ Anderson, Mayhem Cover Creations.
Book design by Pauline Neuwirth, Neuwirth & Associates.

First EverAfter Romance edition May 2019.
Paperback ISBN: 978-1-63576-568-7
eBook ISBN: 978-1-63576-630-1

Jen Jones, you are such a beautiful person. Thank you for making me feel like a superstar. As long as you continue to read my words, I'll continue to write them. I love you, my friend—always.

PROLOGUE

GEORGIA

*"True love is a concept only valid in storybooks.
A boy will never save me—only I can do that."*
—*Georgia Wright*

I've never believed in fairytales. I'm not waiting for a prince to come to sweep me off of my feet. Sometimes, I wonder if true love—the kind that lasts a lifetime—is even real. Is it possible to love someone so much that their mere existence is enough to fill one's soul until their lungs take their last breath? When my heart ceases to beat will its last fatigued movement be bursting with unyielding adoration for the love of my life? Or will it just stop because it's tired?

Happily ever after is a big commitment. *Ever after*, that's like always. It's huge. But is it attainable?

Most days, I think not.

And it's not because I haven't had a good example. My parents claim to have that kind of love. My mom is always boasting about being one of the lucky ones to have found her soul mate. There's a part of me that's not certain if she even knows what true love means. I know that they love each other, sure. Yet sometimes I wonder if it's more valid to say that they *need* each other.

My mom worships my dad. She's his cheerleader, his stunning partner always ready to look good on his arm. She's there to encourage him and tell him how great he really is. He eats it up too. I'm not saying that my dad isn't great, because he is. He works hard and has made a lot of money in the business world doing so. He deserves someone to love him the way my mom does.

In turn, he makes my mom feel beautiful, needed, special. As a handsome, wealthy man—he could've chosen anyone, but he wanted her. He decided that she was the woman that was worthy to be by his side, to raise his kids, to spend his money.

If his job, title, and money went away tomorrow, would their love remain as strong? I can't say for sure, and that's why I question it all. True love isn't fostered by circumstance, it's steadfast—impenetrable through any storm that life throws its way. It's two people that love each other so deeply that the entire world could fade away and as long as they had each other, they'd be okay. That's a tall order to fill.

Even though it goes against my beliefs, sitting here now on this hard stool, I want to be proven wrong.

It's insane that one boy can make me want to throw all of my principles out the window.

But he does.

My fingers tap the cool tabletop as my gaze darts toward the door—waiting for him. In my mind, I know that I'm too young to understand what true love feels like. The rational part of my seventeen-year-old brain knows this is just hormones. But the small sliver of my conscience that dares to listen to the tales of Cinderella and Snow White wants him to be my prince charming.

I've only been in contact with him in this classroom and yet he holds a permanent residence in my nightly dreams.

I want him to be the one that would search the world until he found me to return my shoe. I want his love for me to be so incredibly powerful that with one kiss he could wake me from the deepest sleep. I wish it so entirely, though I know it could never be.

Fairytales aren't real.

Our eyes meet, and I take a sharp breath, quickly pulling air into my lungs before holding it in. He shoots me his signature grin. Lips full, smile wide—the joy that radiates from his face causes me to feel sick with happiness.

Wyatt Gates strolls across the room toward me. His hair is a deep brown and short with a few random chunks styled up framing his face. The contrast of his dark hair and bright blue eyes is a combination that drives me insane. Though it's now November, he still holds onto his summer tan, making his eyes shine brighter.

At this moment, my heart breaks at the sight of him, as it does every day. How can someone so perfect exist if not for me? The thought is selfish, I know. But I don't care. Wyatt makes me want to believe in true love.

Surely attraction has something to do with my obsession with this boy. Would my heart pound such erratic beats if he weren't as beautiful as he is?

Maybe.

"Hey, Peaches," he says, taking a seat on the stool beside me.

I'm going to faint.

"Are you all right?" he asks when I don't respond.

Breathe, Georgia.

I take a breath. "Yeah. I'm fine. How are you?"

"Good. Did you finish the worksheet?"

"Yeah. Did you?" I grin, lifting an eyebrow.

"Not all of it." His lips purse into a slight pout.

I let out a quiet chuckle as I pull the homework from last night out of my folder and place it on the table.

"You better hurry. The bell's about to ring," I tell Wyatt as I watch the door for Mr. Williamson.

Fourth-hour biology class is my favorite part of the day.

Wyatt is my favorite part of the day.

He finishes scribbling down the last answer as our teacher walks into the room at the sound of the bell.

"Good afternoon," Mr. Williamson says. "Please pass your homework up to the front."

"Just in time," I whisper to Wyatt as we hand our papers to the students sitting at the table in front of us.

"I wasn't worried. I can always count on you to save me," he says softly in my ear. His warm breath against my skin causes an epidemic of goosebumps to explode over my body.

Wyatt turns his attention to the front as Mr. Williamson starts his lecture, and I'm hoping he missed the reaction that his words had caused.

It's a miracle that I retain enough from class to even complete my homework so that Wyatt can copy it daily, as the entirety of fourth period is spent stealing subtle glances of him. At least, I hope they aren't obvious.

Truthfully, I've taken biology before—in another city, at a different high school. This is one of the times in my life that the fact that we move a lot for my dad's work has benefited me.

I doodle small daisies on my folder as Mr. Williamson talks about an upcoming project. I'm barely listening as I pretend each flower is a heart, one for each of Wyatt's features that drives me crazy.

His hands. They're tan and strong. The veins from his hands extend up the muscles of his arms, and that makes them irresistible to me somehow.

Since when do veins do it for me? I have issues.

He's writing something in his notebook now causing the firm muscles of his arms to flex. He must work out. I can't imagine that forearm muscles are naturally so defined.

His voice breaks my stare. My eyes meet his, and I blink. "What?" I ask.

Wyatt grins, and it's magnificent. "I said, whatcha think? Want to be my partner?"

"What?" I say again, this time the question comes out airier as all the oxygen leaves my lungs.

"For the project," he eyes the information on the screen at the head of the classroom. "We need to pair up."

"Oh," I quickly glance at the project parameters on the screen. "Right, partners. Yes, sure."

"We should plan to get together soon to outline our project. When are you free?" he asks.

"Anytime," I answer.

"Do you have a few minutes today after school? We can meet in the library and just pound out the rough draft really quick."

I swallow hard. My spit seems to stick in my throat. "That works."

"Great. See ya then." He taps my hand as he stands to leave.

The students file out of the classroom as I remain; my stare remains focused on my hand where Wyatt Gates touched me. *Because...OMG...he touched me.*

After a quick stop to the girl's bathroom after last period to spritz on some body spray, check my hair, and touch up my lip gloss, I rush to the library and check out a study room. Mrs. Jacoby, the librarian, has just unlocked the room when I feel Wyatt behind me.

"Thank you," I tell her as she leaves us.

We sit on opposite sides of the table and pull out the project rubric and our notebooks, placing our backpacks on the empty chairs beside each of us.

"Are you going to the game tonight?" I ask him. I've never seen him attend a Friday night football game, which is odd because everyone else from our high school is there.

"No, I have to head to work in a bit. So let's make this quick. Okay?"

His tone is kind but the abruptness of his response throws me off. I bow my head and focus on the paper from class. "Right, quick. Sure."

"Sorry, I just can't be late."

I lift my gaze to meet his. "It's fine. I understand."

I want to ask him where he works. Our high school is located in a very affluent area and I don't know many students my age that have jobs. But I don't ask. He doesn't seem like he's up for small talk.

We get to work outlining our presentation and splitting up who is going to research and talk about what.

"So we have two weeks before our presentation?" His question is rhetorical because he continues. "We should probably meet up here again before we're due to present so we can go over everything and practice at least once. Does that sound good?"

I nod, "Yeah, that sounds like a plan."

Wyatt stands from the table and shoves his work inside his backpack. "Thanks, Peaches. Sorry to study and run but I gotta go."

I quickly place my work in my bag and step out around the table toward the closed study room door. "No problem."

Wyatt steps toward the door and I hastily step back in an attempt to get out of his way. My foot gets caught on my chair leg and I start to wobble. Wyatt places a hand on either side of my arms stopping me from falling.

"Whoa. You okay, there?" His beautiful blues peer down toward me.

"Yeah," I point toward my feet. "I just tripped."

He doesn't loosen his grip on my arms. I tilt my chin down to stare at his hands on my arms and then lift my eyes back to his.

He still he doesn't let go.

The hue of his irises seems darker now, like the blue of the ocean before a storm. He leans in closer, his expression almost somber. The corners of his eyes pinch together as he takes me in. His focus lingers on my eyes dropping to my mouth and then back up again.

I notice him swallow, the skin of his throat flexing with the motion. Suddenly, I'm very conscious of the heat in his stare. My mouth feels dry and my tongue peeks out to moisten my lips as I pull my bottom lip between my teeth.

Everything is happening in slow motion, yet I feel each small movement with such an intensity that my entire body aches. It's a delicious ache. It's new, this sensation, and I like it.

His hands continue to hold my arms. Our breaths are deep. When he exhales tingles race down my spine, and I shiver. He leans in slowly, his eyes never leaving mine—until they do.

I mirror his action by closing mine as well. Then I feel it— his lips on mine.

They're soft, warm, and utterly intoxicating. A soft moan escapes my throat without warning, but I'm too turned on to care.

Wyatt Gates is kissing me, and it's everything I had hoped it would be.

His tongue gently requests entry as it runs along my lips, and I open my mouth inviting it in. *God, yes.* Wyatt deepens the kiss. His fingers are gripping the nape of my neck, threading into my hair, pulling my mouth into his. I wrap my arms around his neck and hold him close to me.

We kiss until my head is light and dizzy. I sigh when he pulls away, immediately missing the contact.

Wyatt leans his forehead against mine as we both catch our breaths.

"I have to go," he says, this time with quiet remorse.

I know he wants to kiss me again just as much as I want him to.

"Okay," I whisper.

He steps back, tucking a piece of my hair behind my ear. "Can I see you this weekend?"

My heart beats wildly within my chest. "I'd love that. Yes."

"Do you know where Gallop Park is?"

I nod.

"I can meet you there at six. At the bench beneath the overpass by the river at the far entrance. Do you know where that is?"

I know exactly where it is. My sister and I have ridden our bikes past that bench many times.

"I do," I answer him.

"Okay, then I'll see you tomorrow." He smiles, and it sets my soul on fire.

"Six o'clock," I say.

"Six o'clock." He squeezes my hand before opening the study room door and walking out.

I let the door close behind him and lean against it.

I just kissed Wyatt Gates and I want to do it again and again.

That was the best first kiss in the history of first kisses. I'm sure that I'm one of the last juniors in high school to experience a first kiss, another downfall of always moving around. I suppose I've never gotten close enough to someone to want them to kiss me. But now I know it's because I was waiting for Wyatt.

His lips were meant to be the first ones to kiss mine, and he was worth the wait.

A warm breeze rustles the multihued leaves of the trees. Some of them drop from the branches, swaying to the ground like yellow, red, and orange snowflakes. The sun sits low in the sky, its rays giving the leaves that remain in the trees a golden glow.

I've lived in a lot of places, and I can honestly say that autumn in Michigan is absolutely incredible. When I grow up, I want to live somewhere that has a fall season.

My toes tap anxiously against the ground as I pull out my cell phone to recheck the time.

6:30.

He's late, and it's making me nervous. He should be here. *He'll be here.*

Taking deep breaths, I attempt to bring myself to center, to calm my nerves. I take note of the beauty that surrounds me, the running river that splashes against the gray rocks, the color of the leaves of the grand oak trees, and the refreshing warmth of the wind that's dancing halfway between summer and winter as it tickles my skin.

It's a picturesque day, and it's only going to get better when Wyatt gets here, which he will.

But he doesn't.

I meant to ask him for his cell phone number at the library yesterday, but somewhere between the deafening echo of my heart beats and the way in which his stare captured me so intensely stealing my breath after our lips parted—I forgot. Surely, if I had it I could text him and all would be explained. He would tell me that he was on his way.

Of course he's on his way.

I simply need to be patient and just stay right where I am, where he told me to be, until he comes.

I wait until the sun sets to the west and darkness takes over. I remain until the wind turns cold without the sun's warmth. I wait until I'm too chilly to wait any longer. And he still doesn't come.

He's not coming.

I can't believe it.

After a Sunday that would never end, Monday has finally arrived. I've scanned the halls between each period hoping to catch a glimpse of him, but I don't. I'm both relieved and nervous when I finally walk into biology. I take a seat at our table and wait. The bell rings, and there's still no sign of Wyatt.

Mr. Williamson begins his lecture, and my mind races thinking of all of the things that could be wrong with Wyatt. What if he's hurt? What if he was in an accident?

God, I wish I could text him. Why didn't we exchange numbers? My brain is torturing me with the worst possible scenarios when Wyatt finally arrives.

He's okay.

He hands a late slip to Mr. Williamson and begins to walk toward the back of the room. The closer he gets to our table, the more anxious I am to talk to him, to find out if he's okay. Only, he continues past me without so much as a glance in my direction.

I turn around and watch as he sits on an empty stool next to Clarke, the goth loner that usually sits at the back table by himself.

When it's clear that he's not going to make eye contact with me, I turn my attention back to Mr. Williamson. I'm so confused. I think back to the kiss we shared, my first kiss. My body hums at the memory. I'm finding it hard to process this reality. The Wyatt whose lips caressed mine a couple of days ago isn't matching up to the sullen boy seated at the table behind me.

After an hour of Mr. Williamson rambling about who knows what, the bell rings and I jump up out of my seat. As quickly as I exit the class, Wyatt is faster. I almost have to run down the hall to catch up with him.

I grab his arm. "Wait. What's going on?" I ask, desperation lines my voice.

Wyatt doesn't say anything; he simply glares down at me with what looks like hatred in his eyes. I'm not used to seeing Wyatt look at me this way, in fact, I've never seen him look so angry. He's different. I release my grip and drop my arm to my side.

"What is it?" I plead knowing that nothing good is going to come out of his mouth but wanting to know nonetheless.

I have to know.

Wyatt raises his hands in front of his chest in a stop motion. "Just go, Georgia."

I'm thrown off by his dismissal and the way in which he addresses me. He's never called me by my real name before.

I ignore his warning. "No." The conviction in my voice surprises me. "Why didn't you show on Saturday?"

He scans the hallway as other students hurriedly pass us on the way to their next classes. He shifts uneasily on his feet. I see the moment when he decides to talk. He stands taller, his body rigid as he peers down at me.

"I didn't meet you because I didn't want to," he says between gritted teeth.

"Why?"

He throws his head back and takes a breath before returning his gaze toward me.

"You're a spoiled, rich brat, Georgia. Your life is a fucking joke. I would never waste my time with you. Now, stop following me."

He turns on his heel and is gone before I can close my gaping mouth. Tears stream down my cheeks, soaking my shirt as they fall. But, still, I stay, frozen in this space in time where my perfect dream has morphed into a nightmare. At some point in this haze, the bell for the next class rings leaving me alone in this abandoned hallway.

My chest stings as my broken heart continues to beat. I thought I could've loved him. I thought maybe he could've loved me. Now I know what a fool I've been.

I drop my chin to my chest, unable to find the strength to hold it up anymore. My back shakes as I cry.

I knew better. This is my fault.

I let myself hope against my better judgment. I allowed my heart to dream of a prince charming with striking blues that was made to love me unconditionally. I fell victim to the false fables of my childhood. Because I've known all along, fairytales aren't real. Even if they were, why would the prince choose me?

Yet Wyatt Gates is no prince. He's an asshole, one that I refuse to waste another second of my life on.

I pull in a deep breath and stand tall, wiping the tears from my face. No way in hell I'm going to let a jerk like Wyatt break me. Maybe my first kiss didn't turn out the way I thought it would, but it taught me a valuable lesson—one that I'll never forget.

True love is a concept only valid in storybooks. A boy will never save me—only I can do that.

When I get home from school, my mom lets my sister London and me know that my dad has acquired a new company in California and unfortunately, we will be moving again. London is furious as this is her senior year in high school, and she wanted her last year to be one without a relocation.

Had this news come two days ago, I would've been devastated, too. Yet my mom's announcement only makes me smile. Six months was more than enough time here. Who needs autumn and multicolored leaves when one can have the beach and the ocean? After all, the leaves change colors and fall because they die. It's pretty morbid when I stop to think about it.

Wyatt can have this stupid place surrounded by death. I'll take sunny California. When I'm surfing in the blue ocean, I hope Wyatt knows that I won't be thinking of him. In fact, I'm never going to think of him again.

ONE

SEVEN YEARS LATER

"I may not be able to change the world, but I can make one person's day a little brighter. There's a euphoria that comes with that—it's unlike anything else."
—*Georgia Wright*

I wake with a start. A small yelp escapes my lungs as I sit up in bed. I hold my hand to my chest, my breathing ragged.

It's dark as I look around trying to get a handle on my bearings.

Where am I?

One might think that this sensation of not knowing where I am would be an uncommon one, but they'd be incorrect. I actually wake, quite regularly, not knowing where I am. That's one of the downfalls of moving around as much as I do.

It takes me a minute to realize that I'm in Paige's guest bedroom. I can breathe again. I allow my head to fall back to my pillow, but I don't dare close my eyes. I can't risk falling back into the nightmare I just awoke from.

I can still see the fear in Ye-jun's face as he sprinted across the border between China and North Korea fleeing the country which he served. The moss green military uniform he wore as he ran for his life said nothing of his loyalty, only of his desperation.

One might think that the soldiers in North Korea are treated well seeing that they are there serving their country, but they're not. Their service isn't a choice and their quality of life is an afterthought. They are starving just like the rest of their people.

Ye-jun's life was so miserable that he was willing to risk it as he dashed into China with the guns of his brothers firing at his back.

The organization that I worked with tried to save him, but his injuries were too great. I held his hand as he took his last breath. The part that haunts me is that I got the feeling he was happy to die. His life on earth was so bad that his looming death was a relief. *How sad is that?*

I can remember all of their faces, both of the ones we were able to save and the ones we weren't. And the overwhelming similarity between them is that they were all willing to die to escape North Korea. Mothers risked their baby girls' lives to escape. I can't begin to imagine how bad life must be in order to sacrifice everything.

Honestly, the world is a messed-up place. I've fed starving children. I've held people while they died from AIDS. I've tied myself to a hundred-year-old tree in the rainforest of the Amazon in an attempt to stop it from being chopped down. I've aided in rebuilding schools that were demolished from a hurricane. I've delivered clean water to people who acted as if it was the most amazing gift they've ever received. I've spent every free moment of my adult life trying to make the world better because I feel I have to.

I was born into money. I was given a trust fund amounting to hundreds of thousands of dollars simply because I exist. I did nothing to earn it. Truthfully, part of me doesn't even want it. My guilt overwhelms me.

I've had all that I've needed, always. So I choose to spend my money traveling to places where I can help people in need. Giving myself in this way alleviates some of my guilt, but not all of it. There is so much more to be done.

I should say that I chose, past tense, to spend my money on important travesties taking place. Though, at the present time, I no longer have access to my trust fund. My parents hate that I travel and put myself in dangerous situations. So when I came back from China a couple of weeks ago to surprise my sister London for her birthday, they seized their opportunity to cut me off so I couldn't leave again.

My dad still deposits a monthly allowance into my bank account so that I can afford my living expenses—not quite enough to travel the world—but more than enough to live comfortably. The concept of being cut off doesn't mean the same to me as it would to others—yet another privilege that brings me shame.

I suppose I don't blame my parents for wanting me to stay in the same country as them. If I had a daughter, I'm sure I'd feel the same way. I'd want to know that she's safe.

My sister's best friend, Paige, offered me her guest bedroom until I can figure out where I'm going next. I accepted her offer immediately. I love my parents, but I love them more when I'm not living with them. I'm sure I could've stayed with London as well. Yet she and her husband Loïc are still newlyweds, and they're trying to conceive a baby. I didn't want to cramp their style.

I roll out of bed and put my running gear on, making sure to wear my fleece-lined leggings as it snowed last night. Stepping out onto Paige's front porch, my face is assaulted with a bitter wind. The sun is just starting to peek up over the Eastern sky and it's freezing.

I'm not a fan of the cold, but then again, I'm not a fan of watching my mom and her Acroyoga coach bending their bodies into weird positions in the middle of the living room as I'm trying to watch reality TV. Nothing ruins a good episode of *Property Brothers* like seeing my mom's ass in the air.

Yes, Paige's place in Michigan is better than living with my parents, cold and all.

As I jog down the sidewalks of Ann Arbor, certain buildings and places bring back memories. London went to college in this town, and I visited her several times. Plus, once upon a time, I lived here with my family for a few months. There aren't many places I haven't lived.

Despite the cold, the fresh snowfall is stunning. A blanket of white covers everything creating a clean canvas to start the day. With each crunch of snow beneath my feet, I pull the brisk air into my lungs. The icy burn feels oddly pleasant and invigorating.

I turn the corner onto Main St. and see a homeless man huddled with his dog against a building. The two of them are wrapped in a tattered fleece blanket and my heart sinks.

"Come on, Georgia," my mom says from the sidewalk. I hop down from the car and shut the door, skipping over to meet her.

"Sorry, I couldn't get my seatbelt undone," I tell her.

"It's okay. We don't want to be late for our appointment. Unfortunately I couldn't get a closer parking spot, so we're going to have to walk for a few minutes," she says.

I love spa days with my mom. She usually takes both London and me, but today it's just me. We started a new school last week, and London made a friend. She has a playdate with her today. I was a little jealous when she told me that they were going to Chuck E. Cheese's. Mommy never lets us go to Chuck E. Cheese's. She says that the food is garbage, the games are germy, and the prizes are crap.

I don't know if that's true, since I've never been, but it sure looks awesome on the commercial on TV. But I stopped feeling jealous when Mommy told me that we were going to have a spa day, just the two of us. Mommy says we're getting our hair done, a manicure, and a pedicure. She even said that I could get designs on my nails if I wanted.

Mommy gets some other stuff done, too. But she says I have to be grown up for that stuff. Sometimes the salons have this yummy lemon water that they give me and sometimes they have cucumber water. I really hope they have the lemon today. I think the cucumber water tastes like grass.

I walk fast next to Mom as she pulls my hand. Her heels click against the pavement, and it sounds like small drums.

Sitting up ahead on the sidewalk is a man. His beard is long and his clothes are dirty. He has a bucket in front of him. When we pass him, I pull my hand from my mom's grasp and turn to face him.

"Hi," I tell him. "I'm Georgia."

"Hi, Georgia. I'm Stan," he says. He sounds nice. He seems like he's younger than my dad, but when I really look at his eyes they look older like my grandpa's.

I feel my mom pull my arm, "Let's go, Georgia."

I look down and see that in his bucket there's some change. There are a couple of pennies and a quarter.

"Mommy, can I have some money?" I ask as she continues to pull me away from Stan. "Mom, stop," I tell her. Doesn't she see that Stan needs money?

"Let's go now," she says in her mad mommy voice.

As Mommy pulls me away I look back at Stan and he smiles and waves at me. I don't know why, but I start to cry.

"Mommy, he doesn't have any money," I tell her through my sobs. Maybe she doesn't know. "He might be hungry. We need to give him some money."

"We don't have time for this, Georgia. We're going to be late. It's not polite to make Gretchen wait," she snaps at me.

"But it won't take long," I plead.

"I don't have extra cash! I need it for Gretchen's tip. Now, you stop acting like this right now, or I'm not bringing you next time."

Mommy never gets mad at me, so the anger in her voice makes me stop questioning her. When we get to the salon the receptionist tells us that we're a little early for our appointment and that we can have some cucumber water while we wait.

Our spa date isn't as fun as it usually is. I don't talk to Mommy and she doesn't talk to me. I keep thinking about Stan and wondering if his tummy is hurting. Sometimes when I don't eat, I'll get a tummy ache. When all of Mommy's procedures are finished, she pulls out her wallet to pay Gretchen. She has a big wad of bills in her hand and she only gives Gretchen two of the bills. The rest go back in her purse.

I feel like I hate my mom. I know I really don't and that I'm just mad. It'd be impossible for me to really hate her. Yet, right now, I do. She lied to me. I think Stan knew she was lying, too. I wonder how that made him feel? I hope he's not sad.

Maybe now that she knows she has enough money, we can give him some on the way back. "Mom," I say as we walk back to the car. "Can we stop by and give Stan—"

She cuts me off, "Stop. Not another word about the bum, Georgia."

"But we have extra money."

She stops walking and turns to face me. "Listen." Her voice is softer now, and I'm happy she isn't mad. "There are tons of homeless people in the world. I know you want to help them. I do, too. But we can't. If we give all of our money to the homeless people, then we won't be able to pay for our house and we'll be living on the street. Don't you see that if you help everyone, you won't have anything left for yourself?"

"I know, Mom. But I don't want to help everyone. I just want to help Stan."

"Did you listen to what I said? We can't help everyone, Georgia. It's just the way it is."

"But…" I start to protest.

"No more. I'm serious," she says sternly before smiling. "Now, where would you like to eat?"

I shake the memory from my head and stop running. Looking up and down the street, most places are still closed, but I notice a gas station open a block down.

I run to it.

The selection is pretty good for a gas station. I'm assuming this one is frequented by drunk college kids coming home from parties at all hours of the night.

"Can I help you find anything?" the clerk asks me as he stocks the shelves with canned goods.

"Do you guys carry dog food?"

"Yeah, two aisles over." He points in front of him.

"Great. Do you have an ATM?"

"Yep, back by the bathrooms." He sticks up his thumb and swings it behind him.

"Awesome, thank you."

I grab a small bag of dog food, some snacks, and some sausage and cheese sticks. The idea of unrefrigerated meat and cheese grosses me out, but there's not much in the way of protein in this store. Plus, they won't go bad if he doesn't eat them right away. I throw some more nonperishable food items into the basket and grab a six-pack of water. I withdraw two hundred dollars from the ATM and pay.

Arms full of supplies, I walk back toward the homeless man. The memory with my mom and Stan is still vivid. I'll never forget that day. I've thought about it a lot since it happened. It's honestly one of the saddest days of my life. It's the day that I realized that I didn't want to grow up to be anything like my mom.

That's a hard reality for a little girl to swallow. At that age, one's mom is their everything. But after that day my mom wasn't mine. It was also the day I first started to feel guilty for who I was, for the family I was born into.

I reach the man and say, "Good morning," softly, afraid to startle him.

He lifts his head up from his knees. "Good morning." His dog sniffs me a few times, and he must've decided that I'm cool because his tail starts wagging.

"I hope it's okay that I brought you some things." I set the bag down beside him.

"Oh sure. Thank you." He smiles up at me.

"Hi, I'm Georgia," I extend my gloved hand to shake his.

He reaches his hand out toward mine, "I'm Mark."

"Nice to meet you, Mark."

I bend at my knees and pet Mark's dog. He's a gray pit bull. His mouth is big, smiling with a long tongue hanging out the side.

"He's so cute," I say as I hold his big head in my grasp.

"Yeah, I don't know what I'd do without him."

"I brought you a small bag of dog food, but I can bring you more if you need it."

"No, that's okay. I get free food and vet care for him at Cooper's Place."

I'm happy to hear this sweet boy is getting cared for by a veterinarian. "That's awesome. What's Cooper's Place?"

"It's a local pit bull rescue. The owner's really great. He's helped me and Stanley boy here out a lot." Mark reaches out and pats his dog's back.

My eyes widen. "Your dog's name is Stanley?"

Mark nods, his eyes narrow slightly before answering. "Stan, Stanley, or sometimes Hey, You will work, too. Why?"

I shake my head and chuckle. "I just used to know a Stan. I was just thinking about him, actually."

He nods as if he understands. "It's a good name."

"Yeah, it is. Isn't it?" I smile and pull the cash that I withdrew from my account from my pocket. "I have this for you, too. I thought you might need a warm coat, boots, or another blanket or something. The gas station didn't have much in the way of those types of things, but hopefully this will help you."

Mark takes the money. "Wow, thank you Georgia. This is all too much."

I shake my head, "No, it's not. I wish I could do more. Is there anything else you need help with?"

"No, you've done plenty. Believe me. You're an angel."

"I don't know about that." I let out a laugh. "But I try to help out when I can." I pull Stanley's ears between my fingers. "Stan, huh?" I say more to myself than anyone. "Mark, do you ever get the feeling that you're exactly where you're meant to be?"

"I do. I was meant to be sitting here on this delightful, snowy day so that I could meet you, Miss Georgia." He smiles wide, and I notice he's missing quite a few teeth.

"You know, I normally don't believe in things like that, fate and such. But I have to say, I feel like I was meant to meet you and Stan today."

He nods, "I think you were."

"Well, I hope we meet again, Mark and Stan." I pet the dog once more before standing.

"I'm always here, so there's a good chance that we will," he replies.

"Have a great day," I wave.

"You too, Miss Georgia. Thanks again."

I turn away from my new friends and begin my jog back to Paige's house with a large grin plastered across my face.

My mom was so wrong.

Sure, maybe I can't help everyone, but today I helped Mark and Stanley and that's the best feeling there is. I may not be able to change the world, but I can make one person's day a little brighter. There's a euphoria that comes with that—it's unlike anything else. More than anything, I'm sad my mom doesn't get to experience it.

My dad may be able to keep me in the States for now by limiting my funds. But there's plenty of good I can do here.

I think Stan—the dog or the person—may have been trying to tell me that. My life has a purpose again, and I don't care who my parents are, they can't take that away from me.

TWO

"I'm paid in a currency that's much more important to me, self-worth."
—Georgia Wright

It's been a week since I met Mark and Stan downtown, and I haven't been able to get them out of my mind. I've been all over the internet trying to decide what to do with my life, but I keep coming back to the shelter. As much as I don't believe in signs, I know it was one. I can feel it.

So yesterday I finally broke down and called Cooper's Place to ask if they needed help. A lovely woman named Ethel answered. She told me that they are in desperate need of volunteers and asked if I could start today.

"So that's your plan?" Paige tilts her head to the side.

"Yep!" I put emphasis on the "p" sound, making it pop.

"You're going to volunteer at an animal shelter?" she asks again.

"Yes, Paige. A pit bull rescue."

"I didn't even know you liked dogs." She scrunches her lips together.

"Of course I like dogs. Who doesn't like dogs?" I pull the brush through my hair one last time before wrapping a band around my ponytail.

She pours the kale smoothie that she just made from the blender into a to-go cup and tightens the lid.

"There are actually many people that don't like dogs. Some are allergic to them. Some think they smell. Some hate drool." She shrugs.

"They only smell if you don't bathe them. Not all dogs drool. But yes, those who are allergic to them may not be too fond of them. Most people love dogs. I mean…dogs are adorable."

Paige grabs her purse from the table. "Hey, I'm not trying to rain on your thunder. I'm just saying that it's an odd choice of job. I never pegged you for one to shovel out dog crap."

"First of all, the expression is rain on my parade." I raise an eyebrow. One of Paige's most endearing quirks is her ability to mess up the most well-known phrases. "Secondly, I've done much crazier things to help someone or something out than shoveling a little dog poop. Have I told you about the time…?"

She raises a hand to stop me. "Please, no. I need to get this smoothie down without gagging. I can't hear one of your gross stories right now."

"Fine," I laugh. "I'm just saying, dog poop isn't that bad."

"Well, then you go girl!" She raises her smoothie as if to make a toast. "You go save the world, one dog at a time. Whatever makes you happy, chica. I have to go give a marketing presentation on summer trends." She starts toward the back door.

"But it's still winter. Why are you already working on summer?" I question.

"Gotta stay ahead of the curve, my dear. Time is money, my friend. Strike while the rod is hot."

I can't help but laugh. There is no one in the world quite like Paige. I completely understand why London loves her so much.

"It's strike while the iron is hot, and I'm not sure that fits what you're trying to say," I yell after her.

"You know what I mean," she calls from the back door. "Have a great day with your dogs, George."

"Have a great day with your rods," I say in response before the door closes.

I'm a ball of nerves as I approach the entrance of Cooper's Place. I had changed my jeans three times before making a final decision. It may be silly to fret over an outfit to volunteer at an animal shelter, but I'm just as excited to start here as I would be starting a corporate job.

I think the jeans and black V-neck shirt I'm wearing are perfect. I look presentable yet ready to work. I'm always proud to work someplace where I can help. Although I'm not making a six-figure salary, much to my father's displeasure, these kinds of jobs aren't without reward. I'm paid in a currency that's much more important to me, self-worth.

I get that I'm still viewed as the little rich girl who can volunteer instead of holding a paying job because she has her daddy's money to fall back on. I also know that there are a lot of people out there who wish they could help causes the way I do, but instead they have to work to put food on the table.

I've felt guilty about it my entire life. But helping others relieves some of the shame that comes with being the daughter of Mr. and Mrs. Wright who wouldn't give five dollars to a homeless man if it meant he wouldn't starve. There is an exception to their Scrooge-like ways, and that's donating a large sum at a fancy ball or benefit where others can applaud their generosity. My parents are all about that.

They give because it makes others think highly of them. I give because it makes me feel good about myself. Sometimes I don't know how I came from them.

I step into the brick building and a giant dog barrels toward me. My eyes widen and I freeze.

But as soon as he reaches me he bombards me with kisses, licking me incessantly.

"Cooper! Coops! Stop it, boy."

A plump woman in a bright blue sweatshirt with embroidered kittens all over it comes walking toward me. The cats on her shirt even have fuzzy yarn tails that sway as she approaches.

"You'll have to forgive him. He has no manners. Nicest boy you'll ever meet...zero manners. Isn't that right, Coops?"

The brown and black brindle pit bull turns toward cat shirt lady and licks her.

"Is he the Cooper of Cooper's Place?" I ask her.

"Sure is. The boss rescued him from a life of dog fighting in the projects of Ypsilanti. They've been inseparable since. Cooper here is why this place was started. I'm Ethel by the way." She extends her hand.

"Georgia." I shake her hand.

"Our new volunteer, Georgia? Well, just wonderful! So glad to have you here."

"I'm excited to start," I tell her truthfully.

"Let me give you a tour and get you started," she says.

I follow her with Cooper at my side. My first impression of this shelter is that it's pretty posh and not what I'd expect of a pit bull rescue. The building seems new, and everything is clean. The place is huge with tiled flooring throughout. A large abstract painting of a dog that looks a lot like Cooper hangs on the back wall of the first room.

"Is that Cooper?" I ask Ethel of the painting.

"It sure is. One of Kenny's creations. He was so talented, our Kenny." Ethel's voice is suddenly thick with sadness, and I get the impression that the artist is no longer living.

Ethel clears her throat and motions toward the burly dog prancing beside me. "Normally, you wouldn't find Cooper anywhere besides by his daddy's side. However, the boss doesn't take Cooper out on rescues usually. The dogs he's picking up are scared and confused. Cooper could get hurt if a fight were to break out. But as you can see he has the run of this place, and he's really good with all the dogs once they get used to his obnoxious charm."

"So he's out on a rescue now?"

"Yes. He got a call this morning about a starving pregnant girl out by the tracks in Detroit. The momma dogs are always the hardest to catch. They'll do anything to protect their future puppies. In the picture he received of her she was nothing but skin and bone and belly. Poor thing. I really hope he gets her."

The vast room where the kennels are located has a cement floor and painted cinder block walls. It's different than the previous room, starker. I'm assuming the bare simplistic quality of it makes it easier to clean. Yet, despite the hard surfaces, it's still about as cozy as a room with metal cages can get. Each kennel is made so that the dog has an inside space and a doggy door with access to an outside area.

"As you can see, all the dogs can be indoors or outdoors, but we still take them on walks twice a day and let them run in the open play yard as well. We try to get them as much exercise as possible. Pit bulls are terriers by nature and have lots of energy. They love to run, dig, and chew."

"So you only have pit bulls here?" I ask.

"No, we started as a pit bull rescue, but we can't turn away any dog that needs our help. We do have more bully breeds than not because they're hard to adopt out. There's still such a stigma around them. Also, we rescue a lot of pit bulls that are going to be euthanized in other shelters."

"Do you take in cats?" I ask, peering toward her shirt causing her to laugh.

"No, we don't technically take cats. Though, I've been unable to turn them down when asked, which is why we have a handful of office cats, much to the boss's displeasure. I also foster many cats at my house until I can find them homes."

I nod toward Ethel's shirt, "Well, then your shirt makes sense." I smile at her.

She throws her head back in laughter leaving me to wonder what I said that was so funny.

"Oh no dear. I'm wearing this hideous shirt to drive the boss man crazy. You see, he's a bit of a grump, and it drives him insane when I wear these obnoxious, gaudy outfits…especially ones with cats on them. So I've made it my mission to collect the ugliest feline related clothing I can just for work."

I can't help but laugh with her. "That's great."

"It is. Annoying him really makes my day." She shakes her head, grinning. "I'm going to be honest with you. Working in a rescue is really hard. Your heart will be broken more often than not. If I can do my part to break up the bad with a little tackiness, then I'm going to do it."

I can tell that I'm going to adore working with Ethel. She's one of those people that you can't help but love.

"Let's get your paperwork filled out and get you to work, shall we?"

"Yes. Do I get to meet some of your office cats?" I ask her.

She huffs out a laugh. "They won't let you avoid them, that's for sure. They're social little buggers."

The office is ample in space but simple. An old metal teacher desk sits in the corner with a large desk calendar, laptop, and phone atop it. There are a few filing cabinets, some storage shelves with labeled plastic bins, and probably a dozen cat trees—those tall carpeted scratching posts and resting areas for the kitties.

"There are a lot of cat trees in here," I remark to Ethel.

"Oh yes. Enough for each cat to have two of their own." She chuckles again. "Drives him crazy."

"He must really value you. I've had some cranky bosses that would've fired me if I set out to annoy them."

"He loves me. You won't ever hear him say it, but he does. I've known him since he was in diapers. I used to work with his mother. We were surgical nurses at the hospital in Ypsilanti."

I nod knowingly. "Ah, so he has to put up with you. You're like family."

"Exactly." She wiggles her eyebrows causing me to laugh out loud again.

She sets a stack of papers in front of me. "Here you are. Just says you won't steal, hurt the dogs, sue us if you get your hand bitten off, yadda-yadda…stuff like that. Though, if you wanted to take a cat, I'm sure he wouldn't press charges."

"I think I'm good on cats right now."

"Not a cat person?" she asks.

"Not sure. Haven't ever really been around them. But I'm also crashing with a friend right now, and I don't think she's going to want me bringing rescue animals home anytime soon."

"Probably a safe bet," Ethel agrees.

I sign the appropriate paperwork while a couple of fuzzy felines rub against my legs, purring loudly.

"You're lucky. Xavier and his team of guys were in early today and they finished cleaning all the kennels. So you can start with the walking, you'll be the dogs' new best friend. They love going out. It will give you a chance to get to know them all, too."

"Sounds great. I'm here to help any way I can," I tell her.

She grabs a leash off a hook on the wall and hands it to me. "I wouldn't broadcast that just yet." She winks. "Let's start you off slow. You seem like a tough cookie, but I'm serious when I say this job is really hard some days."

She introduces me to Skye, an all-white pit bull mix, first. "Skye was abandoned in Detroit with her eight siblings when they were just puppies. She's the last one left."

"She hasn't had anyone want to adopt her? She's so pretty."

"She's had plenty of applications. Everyone wants a white pit bull. But all of the applications have fallen through so far. They've all requested that we not spay her."

"And that's bad?" I wonder aloud.

"Oh yes. There is no shortage of this breed. You can go into any shelter in the United States and find whatever type of bully breed you're looking for. If someone doesn't want her spayed it's because they want to breed her, and there's no reason to breed pit bulls. There's already too many. They get euthanized at a very high rate daily around the United States. Also, unfortunately many people that want to breed pitties also want to use the puppies for fighting or bait dogs. So we never let a dog leave here that hasn't been spayed or neutered."

"What's a bait dog?"

Ethel looks down. "Unfortunately, you'll get to meet some former bait dogs today. You'll be able to tell by all of their scarring. It's a dog that's used to help the fighting dog build confidence and become more aggressive in the ring. They're basically bitten to death."

I gasp, "That's horrible."

"I'm telling ya, this line of work is not for the faint of heart."

She gives me a few instructions on Skye, and I take her outside. I walk her on the leash until we're in the fenced-in play area. After double checking that the fence is secure I let her off of her leash. She gallops through the snow like a bucking bronco, kicking her hind legs up like a bull. It's hilarious, and I just laugh. She dives her nose into the snow and flicks it in the air.

"They should've named you Snow," I tell her. She's one of the cutest things I've ever seen, so happy. Eventually, I take her back knowing that there are many other dogs that want a turn to walk.

Once inside the shelter, I see that one of the formerly empty cages is now occupied by a skeletal pregnant pup. *Poor thing.*

I get Skye settled into her kennel and refill her water bowl before latching the door closed.

"How was she?" Ethel asks from behind me.

I turn to face her. "She was incredible. She loves the snow. She couldn't stop dancing around. It was so cute."

"She does love it," Ethel agrees. "I wanted to introduce you to the man in charge. I don't know if you noticed the new addition since you've been back?"

"Yeah, I saw her. Poor baby."

"Yes, but the good news is that she won't go hungry anymore and her puppies won't be left to fend for themselves on the streets of Detroit. After I introduce you to the boss, I was wondering if you'd like to help me give our new addition a bath before taking the next dog out?"

"Sure, I'd love to help."

"Great. Bending over to wash the dogs really does a number on my back. I guess that's a sign that I'm getting old."

"Come on, you're not old." I nudge her arm playfully with mine as we make our way to the office.

"You're a breath of fresh air, Georgia. Promise you'll come back tomorrow?" She chuckles.

"Of course. I told you over the phone, not much scares me."

"Okay, you remember that." She shoots me a wink as she opens the office door. She whispers, "Remember, he can come off as a real ass, but he has a heart of gold. You'll warm to him, I promise."

The man standing behind the metal desk raises his stern stare to meet mine and says, "You've got to be fucking kidding me."

I'm going to have to tell Ethel that's one promise she won't be keeping.

THREE

*"I could spend the rest of my life never
interacting with humans again."*
—Wyatt Gates

"It's okay, baby girl. No one's going to hurt you." I make shushing sounds as I pet our new pup's head. She's ready to pop out a litter any day, and she's still just a puppy herself. She's also extremely malnourished, so she might be a little older than she appears.

Different day. Same shit.

I've been in the rescue business for years, and it doesn't seem to be getting any better. There doesn't seem to be any fewer dogs in need. I don't know what it's going to take for people to learn to take care of their animals.

After we've sat idle for a few minutes allowing the pregnant pup to calm her nerves a little, I turn off the ignition.

"Ready to go in, eat something, and get cleaned up?" I ask her in a soft voice.

"Easy, Coops," I say when I see my big boy barreling toward me. He immediately stops and allows me space to get the crate situated so I can let the new girl out into her kennel. Cooper is a bull in a china shop, that's for sure. Yet he's so good with other dogs. He knows when to back off.

After I've given the new girl some food and water and closed her kennel door, Cooper jumps on me knocking me to my butt while attacking me with his kisses.

"You're such a brute," I tell him through a chuckle. "Down, Cooper. Down." He sneaks one extra-long tongue swipe against my cheek before hopping off me. "I missed you, too, dude," I tell him.

I find Ethel filing paperwork in the office and give her a rundown of the rescue.

"You should've taken Xavier or one of the guys with you. You're lucky you caught her," she chastises me.

"Xavier was cleaning kennels when I left. There's too much work around here and not enough workers. I couldn't spare him. Besides, I knew I could get her."

"You only say that because you got her. Had she gotten away from you, it'd be a different story." She shakes her head. "Anyway, our new volunteer showed up today. I think she's going to be around longer than a day."

"You sure about that?" I laugh, thinking of the past dozen volunteers that never returned for their second shift.

"I am. She seems like a tough one."

"They all do...at first."

"She's different."

"If you say so. Where is she now?"

"Out walking Skye."

"Alright, well bring her up to meet me when she gets back. I'll play nice." I press my lips into a line.

"You better be nice, Wyatt. We have a hard enough time keeping good help around here as it is. I don't need you scaring the girl off."

"I said, I'll play nice."

"Well, considering that you don't have the best track record regarding your people skills, excuse me if I'm leery," she huffs.

"What do you mean? I'm great with people. Ask Xavier. He and I get along just fine."

"First of all, it took you a year to say more than three words to Xavier. Secondly, he enjoys idle conversation just as much as you do. So I wouldn't call you butt buddies."

"Who said anything about butt buddies? I said we get along." I shrug.

"Just be nice. It wouldn't kill ya."

"I'll see what I can do," I say with a grin.

Ethel sighs with a shake of her head as she walks away, "You're going to die alone, Wyatt."

"Hey, I'll have my dogs," I call after her.

A few minutes later I look out the office window to see who must be the new girl bending down petting Skye.

I roll my eyes. *Nice, Ethel.* That woman is ruthless in her pursuit to find me a woman—one that I've told her time and time again that I don't want.

Ethel pulled out all of the stops with this one, too. Just from what I can see she's not lacking in the looks department. She's average height, thin, with a taut, round ass. Her long blonde ponytail sways against her back. It appears she's laughing with Skye. *I can't say that I don't appreciate that.*

Unless her face is completely unfortunate—which I highly doubt—I'd say she's quite fine. Not that it matters. I'm not looking for a two-legged companion regardless of how gorgeous she is.

I shake my head. "What are we going to do with her?" I ask Cooper. "I told her that I have you and that's enough. But she won't listen, will she?"

Cooper cocks his head to the side. His left ear perks up as if he's taking in every word I say. "It doesn't matter, right boy? She's not going to last more than a day. Two tops. No one that pretty is going to be content shoveling dog shit for free."

Both of his ears rise, and he whines.

"You like her, do you? Well, that doesn't account for much. You like everyone."

I look down at my desk to see the line of Post-it Notes that Ethel has scribbled my messages on. They have a striped cat in the top corner, and next to the annoying creature it reads, "You're purr-fect."

Seriously, Ethel?

The office door opens, and I turn my attention to Ethel and the new volunteer standing at the entryway.

My brows knit tightly. "You've got to be fucking kidding me."

My face feels stone cold despite the rush of blood that's rising with my annoyance.

Georgia stands tall with a hard stare, evidently not happy to see me either.

I sneer, shaking my head. I never thought I'd see her face again. I hoped I wouldn't.

"Is it safe to say that you two know each other?" Ethel looks between the two of us in a way that makes her curiosity evident.

"No," I say, at the same time Georgia says, "Yes."

"No," I say again. "She doesn't know me."

Georgia places her hands on her hips in one quick motion, "Oh but you sure pretended to know me."

"I do know you."

Her hazel eyes lock with mine, pure disgust lines her features. "You don't know anything about me, Wyatt Gates. Not a damn thing."

"Why are you here? Is the little rich girl bored? Are you trying to prove something? Did you look me up?" I spout off questions in rapid succession.

She throws her head back in dramatic fashion, expelling a huff. "That's amusing." She turns her attention to Ethel and the hatred on her face softens. "I'm going to get back to work. Let me know when you're ready to give her that bath."

"I knew you'd only last a day. Feel free to leave early!" I call out to her as she exits the office.

Ethel closes the door once Georgia's out of the room and turns to me. "What was all of that about?"

"Nothing."

"It was something. That's more than you've ever spoken to a volunteer, though I can't say I particularly enjoyed the words coming from your mouth." She stares disapprovingly.

"I went to school with her. I don't like her."

"What does that matter? You don't like anybody, but you're never like that."

"She's not a good person, Ethel. I don't want her here. Make sure she knows not to come back tomorrow." I walk around the desk and fall into the chair.

"I most certainly will not." She crosses her arms in front of her hideous cat sweatshirt. "She has been nothing but pleasant all day. From where I stand, she's kind and sweet. I will not turn away perfectly good help because you want to throw a fit."

"It doesn't matter. She won't show tomorrow. I'm sure this is more work than she's done in her life."

Ethel drops her hands to her sides and opens the door to leave. "Well, I hope you're wrong," she says over her shoulder as she walks out of the room.

Cooper trots after her.

Traitor.

I stay holed up in my office for the rest of the day doing office shit—the stuff I never want to do—paperwork, calls, donation requests. I'd much prefer to be down in the kennels, helping with the dogs.

But I can't stomach seeing her. Just the sight of her makes me go into an internal rage. The visceral reaction I get when she's near, one of genuine anger, isn't a welcome one. Yet, I can't stop it. Georgia reminds me of a time in my life I'd like to forget.

Every day back then was a battle to survive. I was in such a dark place until I met her. I thought for the briefest of moments that she could be the light I craved. Then I discovered that she was the worst kind of shade. She baited and pulled me in without a fight. I dropped my walls—my protections—and let hope sink in.

In a world where I just wanted someone she made me trust. The blame lies on me, too. I knew better. I dropped my walls one by one letting her seep into my heart. We were young and my fascination with her was short lived, but the betrayal I experienced stays with me to this day, and it still hurts. I know that teenagers can be mean, but honestly, my heart wasn't strong enough to hold any more pain.

I still don't like people much. Ethel's the exception, but that's only because she won't go away. She doesn't give me the option to be without her.

Everyone else though? I could spend the rest of my life never interacting with humans again. For the most part, they're vile creatures—selfish, cruel, idiots. And yet no one has ever created such an immediate reaction in me as Georgia Wright does. Just the sight of her makes me sick, deep in my gut. She makes me feel out of control.

I've gotten really good at not allowing another person to affect me. In this business, you have to. I have my blinders on. I do what needs to be done and have no time for distractions. It's worked well for me for quite some time.

Yet, regardless of how much I want to be unaffected by Georgia, I'm not. And I think that's what infuriates me the most.

FOUR

*"Ironically, the person that hurt me the most
is also the catalyst for my strength."*
—Georgia Wright

Ugh. I hate him.
I hardly slept last night, unable to get his words out of my head. *Why do I care what he thinks?*

It drives me crazy that all these years later, his words still cut so deep. I'll never admit it to him or anyone else, but he broke my heart.

I was young, innocent, and opening up to the possibility of love and then…*BAM*…with a couple of sentences, he shattered my heart. Truthfully, he broke my spirit, and I've been fighting to get it back since.

The old phrase, "What doesn't kill you makes you stronger," applies here. Ironically, the person that hurt me the most is also the catalyst for my strength. He took all of the insecurities I had and threw them in my face, making me question everything. It's not easy when someone I love—or thought I loved—uses my deepest worries to cut me wide open.

All I've ever wanted to be is a good person, someone who is worthy of this life. I have no control over some aspects of my existence, but the quality of person I am—that's all on me, and I try to be a kind one.

It shouldn't matter what the asshole I knew briefly in high school thinks of me, and I hate that it does.

I have to go back.

I fall back on the bed, throwing my forearm over my face.

I don't want to.

The easy choice would be not to. There are endless causes that I could give my time to. But not returning to face him would seem like admitting that everything he thinks he knows about me is true. I can't let him live the rest of his life believing that he's right.

There's a knock at the door.

I drop my arm to my side to see Paige peek her head in.

"Hey, I just wanted to pop in to make sure you were up. You're usually up before me, wanted to check that your alarm didn't fail to go off before I leave for work."

"No, it went off. I didn't feel like running this morning," I say glumly.

"Are you okay?"

"Yeah, just dreading going into the shelter."

She nods knowingly. "It's rough. Yeah?"

"Yes, it is…but not because of the work."

This piques her interest. "I sense there's a story here."

"There is." I release a sigh.

"Let's get Chinese tonight and discuss everything." She smiles wide. "Sorry, I was unavailable last night."

"It's okay. You're in love." I shoot her a wink. She has a long-distance relationship going with one of Loïc's friends.

"Yeah," she says with a giggle. "I'll see ya tonight."

"Have a good day at work," I tell her.

"You too."

She leaves my room, and I roll out of bed and force myself into the shower.

I can't believe I'm putting myself through the wrath of Wyatt for an unpaid position. I guess one could say that pride is also a currency more important to me than money.

"Well, good morning, darling," Ethel says when I enter the kennel.

"Hi." I give her a sheepish smile. "Just couldn't stay away."

"Well, I for one am glad you're back. I'm sure the pups are, too."

"I am excited to walk the dogs again. You're right, they just love it."

She nods, "They do."

"I know someone who's not going to be thrilled to see me. Any chance he's rescuing a dog in Texas today and is driving there and back?" I quirk an eyebrow up causing Ethel to laugh.

"No, no Texan rescues, but you just let me worry about him. I won't let him bother you."

I follow her over to the new pregnant dog from yesterday.

"She looks better. Doesn't she?"

"She really does," I agree.

Ethel bends down to give the dog a treat. "She's still skinny of course. But a warm place to stay with food, water, and a nice bath can do wonders for the spirit. Isn't that so, pretty girl?" The last part she says to the dog who's shyly wagging her tail.

"Have you named her yet?"

Ethel stands and wipes her hands across her pants. "No, I thought you could do that."

"Me?"

"Yes. She was brought in on your first day. Thought it might be fitting for you to name her."

I shrug, "Okay, I'll think of a name today."

Ethel smiles and it lights up her whole face. "Sounds good. And Georgia, I don't know why you came here to volunteer or why you came back. But you have your reasons, and don't let anyone stand in your way of doing something that you need to do. We all have our paths to walk, and if you feel that Cooper's Place is meant to be on your journey then it is. Regardless of what one person may think. Are we clear?"

I nod. "You want to hear something funny?"

"What's that?"

"I thought I was given a sign, one that said I needed to be here," I say, amused. "Maybe it wasn't a sign after all."

"Or maybe it was." She purses her lips together.

The hairs on the back of my neck raise. I feel him. It's the same as it was years ago, this draw that my body has toward him. It's nothing I can explain, but it's there, and I don't know why.

"Ethel," he says gruffly, and she and I both turn toward him.

I hate how someone with such a cruel heart was given such a gorgeous body. I'd never admit that out loud, but I can't lie to myself. He's every bit as gorgeous as he was in high school, except now he's even more muscular, broader. His face and neck are wider, his jaw more defined. I detest how good the two-day-old scruff on his face looks.

He makes my skin crawl. I loathe him. I just wish his appearance didn't make my body feel all hot and weird. The sensations he causes have me all over the place, making me dizzy, ill.

After a few beats, when Ethel doesn't leave my side, he grumbles, "I have to talk to you."

Ethel nods, "Go ahead," making it clear that he can talk here.

He blows out a loud sigh, and I have to stop the smile that threatens to creep onto my face. He's visibly annoyed with my presence while trying to ignore me. It's comical really—it could get fun for me. I may actually enjoy my time around him.

It's when he opens his mouth and slashes me with his words that I hate him most. Uncomfortable Wyatt, I can do.

"I just got an email from someone across the tracks saying that they hear a couple of dogs underneath one of the buildings. I'm going to go check it out."

"Out by your old place?" Ethel asks, and if I'm not mistaken Wyatt flinches before giving her a small nod of his head. "More than one dog?"

"Yeah, two or three, they think."

"Okay, you should take someone. You're going to need backup with multiple dogs."

"I'll take Xavier."

"Can't. He's out walking."

"Okay, Dan."

"Also out walking the dogs."

"Benny."

"Called in sick."

"John."

"He's busy."

"Jesus, Ethel. Is everyone so busy that they can't drop what they're doing to help? I'll just go alone." He huffs before starting to storm off.

"Take Georgia," Ethel calls to him.

My eyes widen. "What? No," I whisper to her.

Wyatt doesn't even turn around. He continues off in the opposite direction and raises his hand above his head giving Ethel a wave. "I'm good."

"I said, take Georgia!" she yells.

He doesn't respond this time nor slow his pace.

"If I didn't love him so much, I'd beat him," Ethel grumbles. "Come on." She grabs my hand and leads me in the direction in which Wyatt just disappeared to.

"Uh…I don't think this is a good idea. Let me just stay here and work with the dogs. Please," I plead.

"He needs help. You're available to help. That's all there is to it. We're all here to do a job, and I'll be damned if I'm going to let his stubbornness get in the way of that. Not on my watch."

"I'll go outside and relieve Dan," I offer quietly as the two of us are now standing outside next to Wyatt's truck.

"Get in," Ethel instructs.

I do as she says. Opening the passenger door, I grab onto the handle above the seat and pull myself up. Wyatt's truck is tall and the engine grumbles loudly, a fact that I'm grateful for as it masks the argument between Wyatt and Ethel that's going on outside right now.

I look around. The truck seems on the newer side, it's clean. I don't know why that fact annoys me. I suppose I pictured Wyatt as a slob, anything to hate him more.

There are no personal items laying around, the cup holders in the middle arm console are filled with a large metal water bottle and his wallet. Pretty boring stuff. I don't know what I was expecting, long-lost letters of regret for the words he said to me? A diary or scrapbook?

After a minute the arguing stops. The truck jostles as Wyatt throws some things into the bed of the truck. Then he's opening the driver door and getting in.

I fasten my seatbelt.

"I have no idea why you came back," he growls as he pulls out of the parking lot. "Just do what you're told and don't talk. Are we clear?"

I opt to look out the window instead of answering him, he told me not to talk, after all.

FIVE

"If I didn't detest Georgia as much as I do, I might laugh at how adorable she is."
—Wyatt Gates

I'm not particularly thrilled to be heading to my old stomping grounds. I try to avoid this area at all costs, too many bad memories exist there. I'm even less enthused that I have to take Georgia with me.

Ethel.

I'm trying to remember what it is that I love about that woman. I'm finding it hard to recall at the moment. She's the sweetest person in the world, but she's also the most stubborn.

The inside of the cab is mostly quiet, except for the rumble of the engine. If Georgia's mere presence didn't bother me so much, I could almost forget she was even here. Almost.

Even when she's silent, I can't forget her. My body knows she's close. It warms at the thought of her. How is it possible to despise someone so much and be insanely attracted to them all at once? It makes no sense, and it's driving me crazy. I just want her gone.

I haven't figured out her motives for being here, and it really doesn't matter. There's no reason valid enough for me to want her to stay on working at the shelter.

We drive through Ann Arbor and into Ypsilanti. *Home sweet home.* This place stopped being my home the second I moved out the summer after senior year—also known as the summer my mom overdosed.

There are some nice parts of Ypsilanti, just not where I lived. I'm from across the tracks. The housing projects I called home were located literally on the other side of the train tracks. It's ironic how the tracks separated the two parts of the city. On one side was the not-too-shabby area, complete with hospitals, a college, restaurants, and nice subdivisions. Then there was my side full of Section 8 housing, drugs, gangs, and dog fighting.

I hated being here then, and I hate being here now. But if there's a dog that needs saving, I need to suck it up and get over it.

The truck bounces over the tracks, and I see the dingy brown apartment buildings where I spent my childhood. I pull into Building C's parking lot, turn the truck off, and get out.

"Wyatt?" Mr. Meaner stands before me with a brown bag in hand.

"Hi, Mr. Meaner." I can't believe this old man is still alive. He must have a liver of steel. He's Building C's resident alcoholic, or at least one of them. And contrary to his name, he's the happy drunk. I always liked him. I learned early on that most drunks aren't so happy.

"I got a call about some dogs stuck under a building?"

"I'm not sure about any dogs, but there is something going on over there by the corner of Willie's old place that's making a lot of racket." He swings his arm toward the apartment that he's speaking of, as if I could ever forget it.

Four hours on a smelly bus isn't good for much besides sleeping and homework, and I do both daily. I hate taking this bus to Ann Arbor every day for school. It's an epic waste of time. I can think of plenty that I'd rather be doing than wasting two hours every morning and night. I could be working more, for one.

Even with my two jobs and Mom's government check, we're barely making ends meet. I'm fucking sick of ramen noodles, like really sick of them. I also don't know how many more too old to serve burgers I can stomach. I'm not one to turn down food, but these fast food places aren't serving quality as is. That quality depletes rapidly when a sandwich has been sitting so long that it's deemed unsuitable for consumption and has to be thrown away or put in my pocket for dinner later.

But mom got me a scholarship to that snobby high school, promising me it will help my future. I don't understand how she can feign concern over my future when she has no desire to be present in it. Even if she's alive when I graduate, she won't be there. She'll be off in some drug induced stupor.

The bus finally reaches my stop, and I get off and make my way across the tracks toward our apartment building. This is the earliest I've been home from school in weeks as I normally work in the evenings. In place of the happiness I should be feeling at finally having an evening off, I can only feel dread. If I'm being honest, I'm always leery entering my apartment.

I reach out to open the handle of the door, but it opens before I can. In the entryway stands Willie, my mom's dealer.

He zips up his pants with a sick smirk in my direction. I step aside, allowing him to pass, which he does without a word.

I step inside and close the door, deadbolting it shut. I drop my backpack on the floor.

"Mom?" I call into the apartment that smells like rotten cheese for some reason. Guess I'll be cleaning tonight. "Mom, I'm home."

With each hesitant step I take toward her bedroom, I pray that she's okay. "Mom?" I crack the door to find her laying naked on her bare mattress. There's a needle lying next to her outstretched hand.

"Shit!" I race over to her and press my two fingers against her neck.

She grumbles and rolls over.

She's just sleeping.

I dispose of the drug paraphernalia and cover her up with a blanket. I place a pillow at her back, keeping her on her side in case she vomits while she's passed out.

I spend the next two hours scrubbing the apartment from top to bottom. I locate the smell, which is in fact cheese. Well, there's cheese on the trap next to the mouse that appears to have been dead for quite some time.

I shower and decide I'll go get a few groceries to make mom a nice meal for when she wakes. Pulling the coffee can labeled "groceries" out of the cupboard, I open it to find it empty.

My chin falls to my chest with a sigh.

I open the refrigerator to find it empty, save the carton of rotten milk, which I throw out. I grab my jacket and head for the door.

Hopefully they'll have some burgers to throw to the trash tonight.

"Stay here," I say to Georgia without looking in her direction. I decide to go assess the situation without her first. In fact, I plan on doing most of the rescue without her. Ethel made me bring her, but I'm only working with her if I absolutely have to.

I second-guess leaving Georgia with Mr. Meaner but decide he's too drunk to say anything too coherent anyway.

I can see the pups immediately. There are four sets of eyes staring back at me when I stick my head down to look through the hole underneath the building.

Upon further assessment these pups look like an older litter, maybe four or five months old. Not sure what happened to the mother, but I'm glad someone called in for these guys. They are bait dogs in waiting in this neighborhood.

"I'm going to help you, okay? Sit tight." I back away from the hole and head back to the truck for supplies.

After grabbing what I need I walk back toward the puppies.

"I don't need your help. You can go back," I address the keeper of the annoying footsteps behind me.

"I'm supposed to help you," she says pointedly.

"Okay, go help by sitting in the truck."

She doesn't reply, but she doesn't halt her pursuit, either.

"Why did you live here in high school if you went to school in Ann Arbor?" she inquires. Evidently, Mr. Meaner isn't too drunk to gossip.

I ignore her question.

I take out the rope and begin opening the cans of dog food. I situate the dog crate with the door open toward the gap beneath the brick.

"Are you going to lure them out with food? How many are there? What's the rope for?" She rattles off questions.

"Why won't you go away?" I hiss.

"Because I want to learn," she snaps back. "Stop being a dick and teach me."

I hold my palms up, "Why on earth do you want to learn this? Why my rescue?"

"I don't know for sure," she huffs. "But I do. Mark told me about it."

"Mark?"

"Mark and Stan? He said you help him."

"You know Mark and Stan?" I ask her, running my fingers through my hair in frustration.

"Sort of. We've met."

"And he told you to come work for me?" Nothing she's saying is making sense. Why would Mark suggest Georgia work at my shelter?

"Sort of."

I groan.

This could go on all day. For as much as I hate her, I have to admire the way she stands up to me. Besides Georgia, the only other person in my life to argue with me is Ethel. It's refreshing and annoying all at once.

"Whatever," I concede. "So we're dealing with older puppies. Chances are they haven't had much contact with people, so they'll still be pretty skittish. But puppies usually aren't aggressive. However, you must always be careful because a scared dog can bite. They're bound to be hungry, hence the cans of food."

I show her the leash. "If I can get this loop around a neck, I can pull it to tighten it and lead the puppy to this crate."

"And if you can't?" she asks.

"Then, I'm going to have to crawl in there and scare them out while you stand in front of the hole with the open crate. So, they'll run in."

"Like a trap," she nods.

"Yeah, I guess."

Her hazel eyes shine a brighter green than usual as she smiles wide. "Okay, I got it. Let's do this." Her voice excited, she claps her gloved hands together. If I didn't detest Georgia as much as I do, I might laugh at how adorable she is.

But I do. So I don't.

SIX

GEORGIA

"There was a brief moment when I thought that true love was possible, but Wyatt was there to show me that it's not."
—Georgia Wright

"Any exciting Friday night plans?" Ethel asks, handing me a bowl of food.

I bend down and place the bowl into Squirrely's cage, making sure that his gate is double latched before stepping to the next kennel. Squirrely didn't get his name for nothing. That boy can get out of almost anything.

"Actually, my sister London is flying in for the weekend to visit. So I'll probably go out with the girls," I tell Ethel as she hands me the next bowl of food.

She and I have a pretty good system going. She pulls around a wagon with the food and bowls, and I do the bending.

"How about you?" I ask.

She chuckles, "I'm too old to have Friday night plans."

"No, you are not." I chastise, "You need to stop saying that. You're only as old as you feel."

"Huh," she lets out a grunt. "I feel damn old. You just wait until you're my age. You'll understand. Plus, I work here on the weekends. The dogs still need to be cared for."

I take another bowl from her hand and look her in the eyes. "You need to take care of yourself, Ethel. Hire some weekend help. You need at least a day to rest, a day for you."

"I'll rest when I'm dead."

I let out an exaggerated sigh and place the bowl of food into the next dog's cage. I've successfully lasted two weeks here, and truthfully, I'm really proud of that. Wyatt hasn't made it easy.

I haven't gone on another rescue with him since we got Huey, Dewey, Louie, and Princess from under Wyatt's old apartment building. Ethel let me name them. Naming the rescues is one of my favorite parts of the job. Hope, the pregnant girl from my first day, should be having her puppies any minute. It would be cool if I could name them as well.

I'm not sure how long I'll stay on here, but I'm not ready to go yet. I truly feel that I'm meant to be here right now for some reason.

Despite the stress of dealing with Wyatt, I love it here. I love Ethel. She's quickly become one of my favorite people in the world. I adore the dogs, each and every one. My family never really had pets growing up, which was probably smart considering how much we moved. I never knew how wonderful, loving, and smart dogs are.

For all the stress that Wyatt causes, the dogs take it away tenfold. They have this ability to make me feel loved and important. Their faces light up every day when I get here. Their entire bodies shake with happiness at my presence. It's a cool feeling.

Most of them have been tortured, starved, and abused at the hands of humans, and yet they don't hold that against me.

They just want to love me. They just want to be loved. They're so loving and forgiving in a way that I could never be. Some days I cry all the way back to Paige's because it's all so overwhelming. I wish I could take them all home with me.

"You said your sister's name is London?"

I blink, my mind returning from my thoughts. It takes me a second to register her question. "Um, yeah. London."

"Do you have any other siblings?"

"Nope. Just the two of us. We're close. She's just a year older than me. She lives in the Tennessee mountains with her husband."

Ethel pulls the wagon behind her as we walk to the other side of the kennel.

"Both of your names are of places. That's neat."

I laugh. "Yeah, until you know why."

"Uh oh. Do I want to know?"

"It's where we were conceived. My parents actually made me in Atlanta, but they liked Georgia better. I mean, obviously my parents had to do it in order to make me. It's just weird to think about."

"Yeah, no one wants to think about their parents bumping uglies, but that's life."

"Ethel!" I say with a laugh, tapping her arm.

"What? Do people not say bumping uglies, anymore?"

I shake my head. "Oh Ethel," is all I can say.

"Cheers to us!" Paige says, holding up her glass. London and I clink ours together with hers saying, "Cheers!"

"These are good!" I tell Paige.

"Right? I've always wanted to learn how to make a good mojito. I think I've achieved it."

"You have. These are perfect," London agrees. "And seeing that I'm *not* pregnant, I can drink as many as I want!"

She says it with a smile, but I know she's bummed that she and Loïc still haven't conceived. I know this past year has been stressful for them. But even with the challenges they've faced, I've never seen my sister so happy. Loïc and London are the only couple I know that just may be truly in love, shattering my theory that soul mates don't exist.

"Before we leave for the club, we need to address the rhinoceros in the room," Paige says with a serious expression.

"You mean the elephant?" I question.

Paige's eyes go wide. "Uh, no the rhino."

"The expression is the elephant in the room," London backs me up, her lips turning up.

Paige waves her hands, "Whatever the animal, this is serious, and we need to talk about it."

London's eyes dart to mine, and we both look at Paige wondering what is going to come out of her mouth. One never can tell with her.

"What is up with your shirt, London?" Paige raises her eyebrows and puckers her lips causing us to laugh.

"What?" London says through giggles.

"Um, it's a turtleneck."

"Paired with a short skirt," London protests. "It's cute. Plus, I'm married. I don't need to look like a hooker. I'm not trying to attract anyone."

"You're married, not a nun. You're not wearing a turtleneck out clubbing. No way. I stomp my foot down on this." Paige makes a show of hitting her foot against the wood floor.

"The expression is *put* your foot down, and my outfit's fine. Right George?" She looks to me expectantly.

"I mean, you look gorgeous. But you are wearing a turtle-neck. If anything, you're going to get hot."

"See! It's a no go! Two against one." Paige grabs London's arm. "I have just the shirt for you. Come on." She pulls her out of the room.

London emerges from Paige's bedroom a minute later wearing a tight silver tank top with a very low V-neck.

"Nice!" I tell her. "Makes your cleavage look amazing."

London chuckles, "Because all anyone will be focusing on are my boobs in this shirt."

"Yes! Exactly," Paige nods. "You should text a pic to Loïc. He needs to see you in this outfit."

We down the rest of our drinks before I pull out my phone to request an Uber.

"Are you sure this isn't too revealing?" London asks me quietly.

"OMG, it's fine," Paige answers. "Come on, Old Maid. Our ride's here."

"You look amazing," I tell her as we exit the house.

"I need to sit down!" I yell over the music. "My feet are killing me!"

I hobble over to an open table followed by Paige and London. We give our drink orders to the server, and I take off my heels, rubbing my feet.

"Heels are the devil," I groan.

"They really are," London agrees.

"That's why I wore black flip flops," Paige says.

"How is it that you are the fashion police when it comes to my shirt, but you're wearing flip flops?"

"A—because you were wearing a freaking turtleneck, and B—because if you're dancing all night, you can't be wearing heels. It's common sense."

"I hate you," London tells Paige.

"I love you, too," Paige says as she blows London a kiss.

"Here comes another one," I say under my breath as a dude approaches our table.

"I got this." London stands.

"Hey, boobs. Why do you think they're all for you?" Paige asks her.

London meets the guy halfway and we watch as the two of them chat. London looks surprisingly content as she jokes with the guy.

"I don't trust her," Paige says. "Why is she so happy?"

"I don't know. It's weird," I agree.

London takes the guy's phone and starts typing away on the screen. As she gives it back to him, she says something that makes his eyes bulge. He nods, gives her a sly smile, and walks off.

She comes prancing back to our table.

"Did you give him your number?" I ask confused.

"I gave him *a* number," she smirks.

"What did you do?" Paige narrows her eyes.

"Same thing I've done with all of the guys who've asked me for my number tonight. Or should I say, asked my boobs for their number. Why is it so hard for a guy to look you in the eyes? Seriously." London takes a sip of her drink.

"You better spill the details," Paige says.

London shrugs, "I gave them your number, Paigey-Poo. I told this last one that there's bonus points in it for him if he sends me a picture of what's under his pants."

"You did not!" Paige shrieks.

"I did!" London is laughing so hard that tears are falling from her eyes.

"OMG," I laugh. "Dick pics are so gross!"

"Ew! Ew! Ew!" Paige cries. "I do not deserve that!" She laughs. "There is nothing wrong with showing some cleavage. Hey, at least I didn't make you wear that." She nods toward the dance floor.

We turn to see a girl dancing on the stage. Her outfit, and I use that term lightly because it's more like a piece of fabric, doesn't leave much to the imagination.

"I honestly don't know how that's not against dress code. You can almost see everything," I say.

"Her nipples are covered. I think that's all this place cares about. Plus, I don't think they have a dress code," Paige says.

"Well, society does, an implied one at least." I give an exaggerated shutter.

"I bet she would appreciate some dick pics. You should share them when they come, Paige," London jokes.

"You know there will be retribution if I open a message containing a penis. I'm just letting you know." She gives London a look that says she's serious.

London holds up her hands in surrender. "Hey, I'm a married woman. I had to give these guys something."

"I have to go pee," I whine.

"Then go to the bathroom," my sister tells me.

"That requires putting on my shoes," I say with a fake cry. "I can't do it. They hurt so bad." I nod toward my feet.

London nods in understanding. "Suck it up buttercup. You definitely don't want to be walking through the bathroom without shoes."

"Definitely not," I agree.

I stand, and holding one hand against the table for leverage, I lift my foot to put my heel on. I opt to leave them unfastened to give my feet more room to breathe. But when I complete the same motion for the other foot the unsecured heel wobbles beneath my feet, and I feel myself falling toward the floor.

I close my eyes and brace for impact, but the impact doesn't come. Two strong arms wrap around me pulling me into a tight chest.

I hope my knight in shining armor is cute because he feels and smells heavenly. My dream is crushed the second he speaks.

"Try laying off the booze," he says in a tight voice.

I push against him in order to steady myself on my heels. "It was my shoe," I snap back at him.

"And you're welcome," Wyatt says before turning to walk off.

I kick off my shoes and chase after him.

I grab his arm and he stops. "What are you doing here?"

"Last time I checked I don't need to tell you anything." He glares down to me.

"I'm not drunk. I lost balance because of my heels." I don't know why I feel the need to explain myself to him, but the explanation comes out anyway.

"I don't fucking care what you do, Peaches."

"Don't call me that!"

"No? You seemed to love when I called you that before."

I scowl, "You don't know anything."

I'm not sure what that response means, but it's what comes out. The truth is, I did love when he called me that. Hearing it now makes me think back to that time in my life when I was alive with hope for a new love. There was a brief moment when I thought that true love was possible, but Wyatt was there to show me that it's not.

I've met a lot of jerks in my life, but Wyatt's the only one that holds a permanent residence in my thoughts. He cut me so much deeper than the rest that it's never fully healed.

"I know enough. Now, are we done here?" He looks down to my hand that's still holding onto his arm.

He's right in that I am a little tipsy. Alcohol for me is like a truth serum. It makes me want to scream everything I'm feeling at him.

Why didn't you love me?

Why did you kiss me?

Why did you hurt me?

Why do you hate me?

Why did you make me hate you?

Yet I'm not so tipsy that I don't have self-control, so I don't say anything else. Instead, I loosen my grasp and let go of his arm. He rolls his eyes and disappears into the crowd on the dance floor.

I'm also sober enough to realize that I'm pining over a relationship that I lost when I was seventeen. Nothing's real at that age. Of course he was never meant to be the love of my life. I was a junior in high school. I couldn't be trusted to vote, let alone make sound decisions about love.

I never loved him and he never loved me. The kiss was just a kiss, not a declaration.

Why can't I let it go?

I'm met by curious stares from London and Paige when I get back to the table.

"Who was that?" Paige asks.

"Wyatt," I tell them, his name rolling off my tongue like a regret.

"Your jerky boss?" London questions.

"The very one."

"You didn't tell us he was so hot." Paige makes a spectacle of fanning herself.

"Well, when you subtract the asshole qualities from his looks, he's ugly."

"If you say so," Paige says. "Though, from where I was sitting, asshole or not, he was fine as hell."

"Oh my God, look!" London says to us as she motions toward the dance floor.

Wyatt is up on the dance floor stage talking to the woman wearing the piece of fabric that barely covers her nipples.

My mouth falls open as I watch him grab her hand. He lifts her off of the stage and then proceeds to leave with her in tow.

"Well, well, well…I guess hottie boss likes his ladies a little on the hooker side," Paige smirks. She and London begin chatting incessantly, but I can't hear what they're saying.

All I can focus on is the fact that Wyatt just took that woman home. There's an unease in the pit of my stomach that's registering somewhere between jealousy and sadness—neither of which make sense.

I can't possibly be jealous of that woman. I couldn't care less who Wyatt screws in his free time. I definitely can't be sad over Wyatt. *I hate him.* The despondent cloak of gloominess that's covering me can't have anything to do with him. *Why would it?*

These emotions don't line up with the way I feel toward Wyatt. It's all so confusing. Yet I'm feeling them just the same.

SEVEN

"Drugs have a way of robbing one of the things they love. It's a hell on earth that I wouldn't wish on anyone."
—Wyatt Gates

"French Fries," I say aloud. "Number one answer."

Cooper cracks open one eye from my lap as if to tell me to keep it down.

The woman playing for fast money on the gameshow *Family Feud* says, "Onion Rings."

"Idiot, the number one thing people eat with a hamburger is French Fries."

Cooper grumbles.

"She just lost her family twenty-thousand dollars, man," I tell him, though Cooper doesn't seem to be at all interested in marathoning *Family Feud* with me.

"I know, dude…but there's literally nothing else on."

As soon as Carrie wakes up, I can take her into rehab. I don't want to leave her here alone. I felt sick when I got the call from her last night as she was clearly fucked out of her mind.

Carrie grew up in an apartment down the hall from me. She was an amazing soccer player and got a full ride scholarship to

Eastern Michigan University because of it. The full ride was her ticket out of the poverty that had plagued her family for generations. Freshman year of college she injured her knee and was prescribed pain pills. Unfortunately, that led to an addiction that she's still fighting today.

She lost everything—her scholarship, her friends, her family. Drugs have a way of robbing one of the things they love. It's a hell on earth that I wouldn't wish on anyone.

I know from experience that an addict won't get clean unless they want it, and she does. Before last night she'd been sober for over six months. I'll never understand how someone can be clean for so long and then use again when they know what drugs will do to them. But I've never been an addict, so I've never felt the hold drugs can have on a person.

I've seen it too many times. Though, I wish I hadn't.

The host says, "Name a place you visit where you aren't allowed to touch anything."

"Museum," I say out loud. *Number one answer.*

"Hi." Carrie enters the living room. "Thanks for the shirt." Her voice is rough and scratchy.

"You're welcome. Thought it'd be more comfortable than what you had on. How are you feeling?" I pat the couch beside me.

She sits down.

"Tired, sad, embarrassed, antsy...you name it. All the usual suspects are up in there." She circles her finger around her head.

"How long?"

She sighs, "A couple of weeks."

"Why didn't you call me earlier?"

She smiles sadly. "It's not your job to save me, Wyatt. I can't keep pulling you down with me."

"In case you haven't noticed, I can take care of myself. You're not pulling me anywhere. If I can help you, I want to." I tap her knee.

"Why are you here? What about your work?"

"It's fine. Ethel opened up for me. I wanted to make sure you were okay."

"Tell her that I'm sorry."

I wave my hand in front of me. "Are you kidding? She loves going in early on a Saturday."

"Wyatt, I'm serious. I can't keep doing this to you. It's not fair." She pulls at the edges of the shirt she's wearing.

"Carrie, I'm here for you. I mean that. Okay?"

She nods.

"Someday, you won't need me anymore and I'll be cool with that, too. You're going to beat this."

"Yeah," she says very unconvincingly.

"Can I take you to rehab? I already called. They're expecting you."

She falls against the back of the couch. "I hate it," she says with a sigh. "I don't want to go back." Her voices shakes, her eyes shining with tears waiting to spill.

"I know, but you need help. You want to live? You want to fight? Right?"

A tear rolls down her cheek. "Yeah," she whispers.

"Then you know what you have to do. Let's swing by your place for your things, and then we'll get you checked in."

She bobs her head in agreement. "Okay," she says with more resolve. "I can do this."

"Hell yeah you can."

I feel like shit leaving Carrie at the rehabilitation facility, but I know it's the right thing for her. She needs more help than I can give her. That place always gives me the creeps. It's the faces more than anything. I've seen them all before—the hopeful, believing that this time they'll beat their demons. Then there's the haunted of the ones that are dying for their next hit. The broken, vacant eyes of the ones that have been there enough to know they'll never beat it. Those are the ones that get to me the most.

I barely remember a time when my mom didn't have a vacant quality to her expression. She gave up long before I understood the gravity of it all.

I didn't always live in the projects as a child. Once upon a time, I lived in a nice suburb. I had the American dream—happy parents, a loving home, and endless possibilities for my future. My dad was a doctor and my mom a nurse. I didn't have grandparents as they had all passed before I was born. Both of my parents were only children, so I also didn't have aunts or uncles. Yet I had the best parents in the world, and that is all I needed.

I don't recall a lot from before my dad's death, but I do remember happiness. I was six when he was shot and killed at a gas station by a junkie who wanted his watch. I was too young to notice the downward spiral of my mom at the time. But Ethel told me how it all happened. She and my mom had worked together as nurses.

According to Ethel, it started when my mom fell at work and broke her wrist shortly after my dad's passing. She liked the way the pain pills made her feel numb as she was still hurting and grieving for my dad. When she wasn't prescribed pain meds anymore, she'd steal them from the medicine cart at work. For a while, she was a functioning pill addict. Until her body became tolerant of the pills, and she needed to up her dosage.

She was eventually caught stealing and was fired. From there, she slowly used all of the money we had to feed her addiction.

I don't have many memories of my mom off of drugs. I really wish I did. Ethel said she was kind, smart, and funny. She was obsessed with game shows, and she and my dad would host big game parties at our house. She loved Halloween and Christmas and went all out for both. Ethel said that my mom would deck our house out with Christmas decorations on the first weekend of November because she wanted as much time as possible to enjoy the twinkling lights of the tree.

I have vague recollections of decorating Christmas sugar cookies and building a gingerbread house with my mom. I have a handful of hazy recollections with my parents. Yet I have hundreds of crystal-clear memories of my mom that I wish I didn't. Why can't my brain hold onto the good ones? Why are the ones that plague me always the most vibrant?

The passenger window of the truck is down, despite the frigid temperature outside. Cooper needs to feel the wind on his fur and let his tongue hang in the breeze while I drive. It's his favorite thing.

Every few minutes, he'll bring his head inside, shiver, and sneeze then put it back out. It's comical and I love how happy he is. He's always been so happy, even when he had no reason to be.

I stand outside in the parking lot watching as the paramedics roll a gurney covered with a white sheet toward the ambulance. Despite the cover, I see her anyway. I'll never stop seeing her lifeless body with a needle still in her arm. No sheet, coffin, or amount of time will erase my last vision of her from my mind—though I wish they would.

I don't even know what to feel. Truthfully, I just feel numb. I always knew that this reality was looming somewhere in my future, but despite knowing this would be my fate, one can never be prepared for finding their mom dead.

I've been mad at her my whole life. I've wanted her to get help for as long as I can remember, but she never would. I've never understood why I wasn't enough to make her want to be sober. I've spent so long being sad and angry that I'm just a void. I have nothing to give her death right now.

At least I'm eighteen and I graduated, so I don't have to deal with foster parents. I guess that's one gift she gave me— happy fucking graduation to me. I should be able to keep the apartment with my current jobs. Not much has changed. I'll just be coming home to an empty apartment instead of a junkie-filled one.

A movement off to the side of the building catches my eye.

"Goodbye, Mom," I say to the ambulance as it drives off.

I head over to the side of the building.

I cringe when I see him. He's young, probably just a year old. He has hundreds of maggots eating away at his wounds.

I hold my stomach, afraid I'm going to hurl.

"Oh my God." I swallow back the bile that rises in my throat.

I inch closer holding my hand to my nose because the smell is curdling. I can see the puncture wounds all over his body.

"Oh boy. Who did this to you?"

He looks up at me with the sweetest amber eyes begging me to help. I bend at my knees and extend my hand toward his muzzle. He licks it.

I shake my head.

People did this to him. People put him in a fighting ring and allowed him to be mauled to near death. Then they left him to suffer and die…and he licks me.

I run up to the apartment. I grab a sheet and the five hundred dollars that I've slowly been stashing away over the past two years for a car. I pick up the phone to call a taxi, but of course the line is dead. Mom used the phone money for drugs.

I dart down the hall and knock on the neighbor's door. My friend Carrie answers.

"Can you call a taxi for me, please. Our phone's dead."

"Sure," she says. "Is everything alright?"

"Yeah, I just need a taxi."

"Okay." She smiles and closes the door.

I head back out to the dog. He's exactly where I left him.

He doesn't protest as I wrap him in the sheet. I think he knows that I'm here to help him.

Thankfully, the cab driver lets us get in and he takes us to the nearest emergency vet office.

The dog has to stay the night at the vet.

I hate going back to the apartment without him. I spend the evening cleaning the apartment and throwing out everything of my mom's. There's nothing of value—sentimental or otherwise. All of her junk has a negative memory attached to it, so I get rid of it all. Finally, before crashing in bed I go out and buy the dog some food for when he comes back.

The next day I'm able to bring him home. I have fifty dollars left over from paying the vet bill, so I get takeout from a local steak place.

The dog's still weak but already looks so much better. He no longer has maggots. Some of the wounds needed some stiches, but most just need to heal on their own. The doctor gave me a bag of medicine for the dog and says once he's finished with his antibiotics he should be feeling great.

We sit in my empty apartment eating steak purchased with the last of my money. I decide to call him Cooper. He just looks like one.

"It's just me and you now, boy."

Cooper crawls over and lays in my lap. I gently hold him to me, careful not to touch his wounds. I bury my face in his neck…and I cry.

EIGHT

GEORGIA

"There's something in me that wants something in him. It's undeniable. But it's wrong. He's taken, and he's an asshole."
—Georgia Wright

*L*ondon left a couple of hours ago. I had a wonderful time with her. It's always great to spend time with my sister. Paige is currently in her room gabbing on the phone with Ethan. She was so busy with my sister and me this weekend that she hasn't spoken to him much, which means she'll be in there for hours.

I'm bored.

And restless.

I just feel off. I can't pinpoint why, but I've felt weird since my run-in with Wyatt on Friday night. I'm too old to let a bully from high school affect me. *I'm an adult, damn it.* I don't need Wyatt Gates's approval. I don't need him to like me. If he wants to go on believing that I'm the most self-centered bitch in America, then who am I to stop him? *His loss.*

I find myself driving without a destination in mind, though I know where I'm heading. *Maybe Ethel needs my help?* It's not fair for her to work seven days a week. I can lighten the load for her. That will make me feel better.

I'm greeted by Cooper's kisses the second I step foot into the building. "Hey, boy." I rub his big head.

"What are you doing here?" Wyatt asks, his voice deep and gravelly.

"I thought I would come help Ethel. She told me she'd be working all weekend."

"I sent Ethel home," he practically growls before walking away from me.

I follow him. "I can help you then."

"I don't need your help. Go home."

I ignore his request. "What are you doing?"

"Don't worry about it."

I continue to walk behind him. "Look, I'm not leaving. I came here to help...someone. Since Ethel's not here, I'll help you."

He stops abruptly and whips around to face me. "Are you the dumbest woman in the world? Why don't you understand simple requests? Go. Home."

"Are you stupid? I said, no."

He pulls his hands through his hair. "You drive me insane."

"Ditto."

"Why do you want to be here?" he shouts, his face turning red.

"I don't know! Okay? I just do," I yell back holding my ground.

He throws his head back, and I can see his nostrils flaring as he takes in a deep inhale. "Fine," he says, defeated.

"Good." My voice is too chipper for its own good. "So what are you doing?"

"Hope's in labor," he grunts out.

"Hope's having her babies and you were going to make me go home!" I glare at him.

He just shrugs with a look of disinterest.

"You're kind of a jerk, Wyatt," I grumble.

"If you want to stay, I'd shut up if I were you. Or I'll pick your ass up and throw you out."

I cross my arms over my chest. "Fine, I'll shut up."

"Good."

Wyatt directs Cooper to lay down on the dog bed by the office. He grabs his laptop and a stool and sits outside of Hope's kennel.

"So what do we do?" I ask and giddiness takes over me.

"What do you mean?" He shoots me a quick glance.

"With Hope? What do we do to help her?"

"We just wait. Nature kicks in. She'll do everything on her own."

I walk over to Hope and sit down beside her, petting her head. "I'm so excited. I've never seen anything born before."

Wyatt doesn't answer.

I sit in Hope's kennel and watch her pace. She's restless, panting, and walking back and forth. Wyatt has put some more blankets in there for her, and she keeps scratching at them with her paws, trying to fluff them up.

"I feel like she needs help," I tell him.

"She doesn't."

"She's restless."

"She's in labor," he states the obvious.

"So she's acting normal?"

He nods.

Ugh. This is making me antsy.

"Is she your girlfriend?"

Wyatt ignores me as he types away on his laptop. He's always working.

"The girl in the club. Is she your girlfriend?" I ask again.

He sighs and lifts his eyes from the screen. "What part of shut up don't you understand?"

I shrug, "I'm just making conversation. We might be here a while."

"No one's making you stay. In fact I wish you wouldn't."

I stand and walk closer to the stool he's sitting on. "Why did you kiss me if you hated me?"

He shuts the laptop and places it on the work bench beside him.

"We were seventeen. That was a lifetime ago. Why does it matter?" His stare is cold, his face rigid—but I see a warmth in his eyes. It's not obvious, but it's there.

"I want to know. Just tell me."

"I didn't hate you when I kissed you."

My heart is beating uncontrollably in my chest. I can't believe he's actually talking to me. "What changed your mind?"

"The truth."

"According to who?"

What truth is he talking about?

He doesn't answer; instead, he hops off of the stool and walks over toward Hope's kennel.

"Is it time?" My voice comes out high pitched and excited.

He points toward Hope. A puppy inside a little mucous-looking sac is coming out of her.

I cover my mouth with my hands, watching. It's disgusting and miraculous all at once. The puppy falls onto the bedding, and Hope starts cleaning the baby and eating the placenta.

"Oh my God!" I cover my mouth for a different reason this time. "She's eating it." My stomach feels nauseous.

Wyatt chuckles and it's a beautiful sight. "Yeah, they eat it."

"Why?" I whine, swallowing hard.

"It replenishes her nutrients. It's just what animals do."

I shake my head, and my body shivers thinking about chewing on placenta.

Yuck.

Hope licks and cleans the new puppy for a long time until finally another starts to come out. She repeats the process six times over. It takes more time than I thought it would, usually thirty to sixty minutes between puppies.

I lean my head against the back of her cage, my eyes heavy.

"You can go home," Wyatt says, but this time it isn't cruel.

"No," I yawn. "I'm committed, now."

"It's not as thrilling anymore?" he asks, quirking up an eyebrow, his gorgeous blues smile though his mouth doesn't.

I stand, stretching my arms up over my head and yawning again, this time with a big, loud groan.

"No, it is. It's amazing. I'm just tired. I didn't realize how long it takes."

"There should just be one more."

"How do you know?"

"We did an ultrasound on her when she first came to make sure all the puppies were still alive in there. She was pretty malnourished."

"Yeah, I remember." Though it was only a couple of weeks ago, it feels like so much longer. "That was my first day."

"Yeah, I remember," Wyatt says, his voice low.

My stare shoots toward him, finding his intense eyes on me. There's a space in time, not even a moment—more like a heartbeat between a breath—that I see something in his gaze. It's there and then it's gone. It was so fleeting, and yet my chest hurts at its absence.

Wyatt's now standing over Hope leaving me to focus on the past, the previous seconds where I felt something real.

"Here comes the last one," he says, his voice bringing me back to the present.

I blink and turn my head toward Hope. I watch as the puppy falls from her and she licks at it, as she's done with all of the others.

"Crap," Wyatt says. "Hand me that towel." He extends his arm out toward me.

I grab the towel off the bench and give it to him.

"What is it?"

"It's not breathing." He picks up the puppy and places it in his hand over the towel.

"It's dead?" My voice is panicked.

"It happens," Wyatt says, rubbing the puppy in between his hands in the towel.

Tears fill my eyes and a lump forms in my throat. "Save it! Oh my gosh. What do we do?" I cover my mouth with my hands watching Wyatt.

His big hands hold the small baby between them. Then he swings it in a quick downward motion before whipping it back up again.

I shriek, "Stop! What are you doing?"

He ignores me and repeats the movement.

"Wyatt!"

"I'm trying to get it to breathe, Peaches. Chill out." He starts to rub the little pup between his palms again.

A shrill cry comes from its tiny mouth, and it starts to squirm.

"Oh my gosh! It's alive!" My body bounces with energy and relief. "You did it!"

He uses the towel to clean the remaining wetness from birth off the puppy that's now squirming in the palm of his hand.

Tears cascade down my cheeks—relief, exhaustion, and happiness are just a few of the many emotions that pour out with them.

"Grab another towel," he tells me.

I do as he says.

"Put it over your hand."

I drape the towel across my hand, and Wyatt places the small puppy in my palm.

"Cover it up with the fabric and rub it gently to warm him up."

"It's a boy?" I ask Wyatt, blinking back tears.

He peers at me and almost looks sad. I feel a powerful pull toward him. My body craves his. My chest aches as I fight this innate draw. There's something in me that wants something in him. It's undeniable. But it's wrong. He's taken, and he's an asshole.

All the puppies and emotions of the night have me confused. Exhaustion is playing tricks on my mind.

Wyatt closes his eyes before opening them again. He rubs the back of his neck. "I'm not sure. I haven't checked yet."

"Can you check?"

He takes a step toward me and reaches for my hands. I freeze.

He removes the towel from the baby and lifts its legs before covering it back up. "It's a girl."

"Aww." I hold the pile of fabric to my chest. "A girl." I smile.

Wyatt clears his throat. "Alright, well now you want to put her up next to her momma so she can nurse."

I nod, "Okay." Kneeling, I uncover the baby girl and place her next to her siblings who are already contently nursing.

I stand and Wyatt and I watch Hope with her new babies.

"She's not doing anything."

"Yeah," Wyatt says with a sigh. He kneels down and places the little girl closer to Hope. The other puppies squirm, pushing her to the side.

After a minute, he picks her up and stands.

"We're going to have to bottle feed her, unfortunately. She's a runt. She's not fighting to eat, and the other puppies will just plow over her." He holds the baby to his chest and walks away.

I follow him.

"I'll feed her," I tell him.

He hands me the puppy and gets her bottle ready.

I sit in the recliner in the break room with the puppy in the crook of my arm. A bottle in the other hand, I watch as she sucks the milk down, at least most of it. Some of it is dripping down her furry chin.

"Keep it in your mouth, sister," I giggle.

When she's finished she falls asleep and I just hold her. I feel my eyelids getting heavy. Wyatt comes in.

"She finish it all?"

"Yeah," I nod, holding up the empty bottle.

"Good. We have to give her a bottle every two hours."

"Every two hours?" I'm exhausted just thinking about it.

"Yep. Do you want me to take her so you can head home?"

"No, I'm fine. I could use a blankie though."

"A blankie?" A smirk finds his lips.

"Yes, please. I'm just going to take a little nap here." I wiggle back into the chair, pushing the button on the side that extends the footrest.

Wyatt turns to leave.

"Hey, Wyatt. Can you make sure the blankie is free of pee or vomit or anything else equally gross?"

He lets out a chuckle, "I'm not going to let you cover up with a blanket that smells like shit. I'm not a total asshole, Peaches."

I yawn, "I don't know anymore, Wyatt."

He squints and opens his mouth to say something before shutting it and walking out. I cup my hand around the slumbering fur ball on my chest and close my eyes.

In the back of my mind, I'm mildly aware of a warm blanket covering me up, but I'm already gone—halfway between sleep and reality.

In my dreams, I see him as he was when I was young and hopeful—before the kiss and the harsh words. I had just spent an entire evening with Hope as she brought adorable bundles of life into the world. And despite my better judgement, hope blooms within me, filling me with ideas of more.

More of what? I'm not sure.

NINE

"Cooper saved me in more ways than one."
—*Wyatt Gates*

"Come on, E!" I shake my head with a laugh.

Ethel shrugs, a smirk plastered across her face. She feigns a sudden understanding as she peers down at her shirt. "Don't you love it?"

"It's the most ludicrous thing I've ever seen." I roll my eyes.

Ethel sports a sweatshirt of the galaxy. Atop the colorful Milky Way is a giant cat head with two paws, one holding a taco and the other a piece of pepperoni pizza. The cat's tongue is out as it licks the pizza.

She ignores my comment. "I know, it's great. You know this exquisite thing just popped up in my Facebook feed with the link and everything. It's like my phone knew I needed a new cat shirt."

"Because you don't have enough," I scoff.

"I was just talking about my cat shirts with Georgia, and the next day I had these links on my Facebook. Sometimes I think my phone is listening in on me. It's creepy, but at the same time it saved me the effort of searching. You know?"

"I know that you look ridiculous."

"Thank you. I love it, too."

I just shake my head and walk over to the desk to read my messages.

"All of the care packages are ready?" I ask without lifting my eyes from the desk.

"They sure are. Georgia and I finished them last night. You should take her with you. She'd love that."

"No."

"Wyatt?" She sounds disappointed, but I don't care.

"I said, no."

"Well, I said, yes." Ethel's voice is stern, a complete one-eighty from the way she usually sounds.

I snap my head up to find her glaring at me.

"Geez, E. Okay. Didn't know it was that important to you. Fine." I throw my hands up.

"I just don't understand why you have such disdain for her. She works her butt off here, going above and beyond what any other volunteer has ever done for us. She lives to help others, and you're an idiot if you don't see that. She's not here to bother you. She's here for her. It would fill her soul to go with you today. She deserves that."

"It's not my job to fill her fucking soul," I huff.

"Language," she frowns at me. "And it is your job to be a decent human being. I don't care what she has or hasn't done in the past. I only know the girl here now, and she's pretty fantastic, if you ask me."

"Well, I'm not asking you," I grumble.

"You need to forgive her. Whatever she did...you need to forgive her."

"I don't want to."

"You know the thing about forgiveness?" she asks.

I play along. "No, E. What's the thing?"

"Only the strong can forgive, and it won't change the past. But it can drastically change the future."

"My future's just fine," I tell her as she starts to leave the office.

She turns to me right before she exits. "Not from what I see," she throws in her little Ethel jab and then walks out.

I groan loudly.

I hate when she does that.

She's always attempting to enlighten me with her wisdom, but I rarely want to hear it. Sometimes I want to tell her that she's not my mother. But I would never be that cruel. I'm a dick, but I'm not heartless...especially where Ethel is concerned. As much as she annoys me, she is the closest person I have to family, and I love her.

I grab my jacket and head toward the kennels. Georgia is with Hope and her puppies. It's been a week since Hope delivered the puppies, and Georgia has pretty much lived here since, much to my annoyance. Though with Georgia's help, the runt is strong enough to carry her own when she's in with the rest of the puppies, and Hope is no longer rejecting her.

"Grab your coat, Peaches."

She kisses the little brown runt on the forehead and sets her down with the rest of the puppies.

"Where are we going?" She hops up.

"Out. Help me load the bags up." I thread my arm through the handles of the duffle bags lined up against the wall. Georgia puts on her coat and does the same.

We put the bags in the back of my truck.

"Did you see that Mila's eyes are open? She's the first one to open her eyes. Isn't that awesome?" She hops into the truck and shuts the door.

"Who in the hell is Mila?" I ask her as I push the button to start the engine.

"The puppy you saved, the runt. I named her Milagros, which means miracle in Spanish. I call her Mila for short." I look over as she snaps her seatbelt and smiles. "She's a little miracle, isn't she?"

"You speak Spanish, now? Is there anything you can't do?" I sneer, pulling out into traffic.

"Befriend you for one, but that's more to do with you than me. And yes, I speak enough to get by. We lived in Spain for a little bit when I was younger."

"You moved around a lot."

"Yeah, we did. It's why I'm so charming. I've learned to get along with pretty much anyone. Well, except for you," she chuckles. "You kind of learn to fit in anywhere when you're constantly moving."

"Where'd you go after you left Ann Arbor junior year?" I ask a question I've been wondering for years. One day I was calling her a stuck-up bitch and the next she was gone. I'd always wondered where she went.

"Hillsborough. It's in California in the San Francisco Bay area."

"Why'd you move so suddenly?"

She shrugs. "That was our life. Dad bought a company, we moved. Then we'd move again when he sold that one to buy another. He went where the money went, and we followed."

"Didn't that get old?" I can't stop the questions from escaping my mouth like vomit.

"Sometimes, but I was used to it. It was hard when I got close to people. Though, leaving Ann Arbor wasn't hard at all." She throws in the last part as a jab toward me.

"Yeah, I imagine it would've been pretty easy."

Driving through Ann Arbor, I have to slam on my brakes several times to avoid hitting college students. They just walk into the road, headphones on, faces looking at their phones without so much as a glance into the street. Pedestrians are like gods here in this college town. They step into the street and the cars part, allowing for the students with their over-priced rich kid clothes and abnormally large heads to cross without so much as a glance.

I hate this place. I don't know why I stayed. I could've gone anywhere. I have nothing tying me here, no family or friends to speak of—only horrible memories. And yet I stay.

I park in the structure on the corner of Fourth Street.

"So are you going to tell me what we're doing?" Georgia asks, wrapping her coat tightly around her to block out the bitter wind.

It's the end of February in Michigan when we're all extremely ready for the sun and warmth of spring to arrive, but in actuality we have another six weeks of winter.

"We're delivering the bags you and Ethel packaged up yesterday." I reach into the back of the truck and grab one.

Each duffel bag holds nonperishable food for both dogs and people, thick socks, a warm blanket, a hat, gloves, a dog jacket, flea medicine, and gift certificates to local eateries that are dog and homeless person friendly.

I'd managed to work out some deals with local restaurants to help get warm food in the bellies of the homeless population in Ann Arbor. I have to admit, there are some cool people in this city that are very willing to help.

Bag in tow, I walk toward the exit of the parking garage. "I think you know our first delivery."

"Mark and Stan?" Georgia asks eagerly.

"Yep."

"Awesome!" She almost skips beside me.

"Well, if it isn't two of my favorite people?" Mark says as he sees us approach. He's leaning against the brick wall of the bank, his usual spot.

"Hey, man. How are you?" I ask him.

"Good. Real good." He nods and pats Stan on the head. "Good to see you again, beautiful." He smiles to Georgia who's kneeling beside Stan and petting his back.

"You too. Are you staying warm?" she asks him.

He grins, "Can't complain."

I give Mark the bag of goodies. "Usual stuff. Is there anything specific you need?"

Mark shakes his head, "Nah, bro. I'm good."

"Alright. Well, you know where to find me if you need anything. You still have my number?"

Mark nods.

We chat for a few minutes, and by we I mean Mark and Georgia. She really can talk to anyone. I watch as she interacts with both Mark and Stan. I look for the judgment and wait for hidden condescending remarks but they never come.

Truthfully, I watch her more than I should waiting for the spoiled snob in her to show, and I haven't seen it yet. I suppose that should make me happy, but oddly enough, it makes me feel worse. The Georgia I thought I knew and the woman I see before me holding Mark's hand pretending to read his palm are two very different people.

"See this line here?" She points to a spot on his palm. "This is your life line. It says that you're going to have a long life."

"Ah, shit. Well, I better figure out what to do with my life then, huh?" He shoots her a semi-toothless grin.

"You and Stan could come help at the shelter. One of our girls, Hope, just had the cutest litter of puppies. You'd love holding them. It's my daily therapy."

"What do you need therapy for?" Mark laughs. "You're damn near perfect."

Georgia smiles warmly. "I'm definitely not perfect, and we all have some darkness in us that we wish we didn't. Right? I think more people in this world could benefit from some puppy therapy."

Mark nods with a look of complete adoration toward Georgia. "Yeah, I bet they could."

I clear my throat. "I hate to break up the party, but we have some more deliveries to make."

Georgia says goodbye to Stan and Mark and springs to her feet.

"We'll see you soon," I say to him before Georgia and I turn to head back to the truck.

"It's really nice that you help the homeless in the community," she tells me when we get back to the truck. "You don't seem to judge them. That's really cool."

I don't judge them? What is she talking about?

"Why would I judge them?" I ask gruffly.

"It's nothing against you. Just society in general tends to look down on them, especially ones with dogs. I've known quite a few people in my life that do."

I scoff with a roll of my eyes. "I bet you have."

Georgia hops up into the cab of the truck and slams the door. She turns her body toward me. "Stop! Just stop!" she yells.

Her sudden change in tone catches me off guard.

"I'm sick of you treating me like I'm a horrible, stuck-up bitch. News flash—I'm not! I don't know why you thought I was back in high school, and I definitely don't understand why you think I am now. I've done nothing to give you ammunition for your made-up narrative. You don't have a clue who I am because you're too goddamn stubborn to open your eyes and actually get to know me."

She closes her eyes and pulls in a deep breath. When she opens them again, they're shiny—wet with tears that she's too strong to allow to fall. It's a gut punch, and I find myself feeling guilty for treating her so harshly.

She takes another breath and continues, "You know when I saw that it was you who owned the shelter, my immediate reaction was one of dread. I'll admit that all of the hate I felt for you for saying what you did in high school came to the surface. Maybe I was a little rude in the beginning, but I've tried to move past my feelings and to be kind to you whether I felt you deserved it or not because that's what adults do. Yet you're dead set on acting like a teenage boy with your rude attitude and harsh remarks thrown in whenever you can. I don't deserve it. I work harder than anyone else that you actually pay."

She throws her hands up in the air, her palms face me. "You know what? If you want to fire me, then fire me. But do not treat me like shit. You will treat me with respect from now on. Are we clear?" She glares at me, and damn if she's ever looked more beautiful.

Shit.

I break from her stare and start the truck up. As I'm backing up, she says, "Well?"

"Well what?"

"Are you firing me?" Her words are drowning in attitude, and it takes major self-control to keep my mouth from turning up into a smile.

"No, I'm not."

How could I justify firing her? She's right. She works harder than anyone else. She doesn't ask for anything, including a paycheck. I am being an immature dick.

I hate that she's right.

Maybe I had my reasons to hate her when we were young, but who doesn't do or say stupid shit when they're a teenager?

"Good." She crosses her arms against her chest and sits back in the seat.

I steal a glance at her profile, and she's so incredibly stunning without even trying. Her blonde hair is in a loose braid over one shoulder. She doesn't appear to be wearing any makeup, yet her long lashes are dark and frame her hazel eyes in the most indescribable way. The way she's pouting now, with her lips out a little further, makes her normally irresistible lips even more so.

She deserves an olive branch, and so I throw her one. "My mom died when I was eighteen, right after high school graduation. The day she died, I found Cooper. He was in bad shape, real bad shape. I spent all of the money I had been saving for years to fix him. I continued to work hard after that, but there was always something unexpected to pay for, and eventually I couldn't keep up and was evicted. I had a backpack full of my things and Cooper. That was it. He and I were homeless for the better part of a year."

I swallow hard. No one knows this part of my life but Ethel. I don't dare look at her for fear of seeing pity in her eyes.

"It was hard living on the streets. People look at you different, if they look at you at all. To most, it's as if you don't exist. It's as if they actually see right through you. It was impossible to find work, and the few odd jobs I found paid just enough to feed me and Cooper. I hung out with some others that lived on the streets. Some of them were into drugs. I'd been around drugs my whole life, so it wasn't new to me."

I stop, hesitant to continue, but for some reason I do. "I'm not going to lie, I was tempted. The idea of escaping my reality was a strong pull. Yet I'd seen what drugs did to my mom. She wasn't a good mom, to be honest. I looked to Cooper, and I couldn't risk anything happening to him. I knew if I was high, then I wouldn't be able to take care of him the way I should. He'd been through so much. I couldn't stomach the thought of him being taken when I was stoned and someone hurting him. He was my only family. He was my everything. Cooper saved me in more ways than one."

I pull in behind the hardware store where a homeless friend Nancy and her pit mix LuLu stay and put the truck into park.

"A lot of people think it's selfish for homeless people to have a dog. But I don't think the dogs are unhappy. They're loved, and that's all any animal wants. In most cases, they're fed better than their humans. These dogs are everything to their owners. And sometimes the love and responsibility these people feel for their dog is all that's keeping them alive. I try to get them off the street. I offer them jobs. Some of them take me up on my offer, some don't. Xavier is one who's been able to get off the streets and turn his life around. But not everyone wants off of the street for various reasons. Who am I to judge them or their journey in life? So I help them and make sure their dogs are healthy because I can."

I turn off the truck's ignition and step out, shutting the door behind me. The pressure and stress that's ever present, constantly pressing down on my chest, feels a little lighter. Georgia officially knows more about my life than any other person. I'm not sure how opening up to her makes up for the way I've treated her, but it feels like it does, in a way.

Georgia meets me at the back of the truck as I pull out another duffel bag. "How did you get off of the streets?" she asks.

I can't help but smile. "Ethel found me."

TEN

"I hate that I feel this pull toward him,
but more than that I can't stand the fact that he hates
me and I don't even know why."
—Georgia Wright

*T*he wine bottle and grape décor really needs to be updated, the tables are too close, and the food really isn't anything like the pasta found in Italy. But there's no denying the softness of this breadstick.

The waiter rushes past our table and takes a step back when he notices our breadsticks and salad bowl are empty.

"Refill?" he asks.

"Yes, please," I say with my hand in front of my mouth, as not to spray him with partially chewed goodness.

Ethel sits across from me and laughs. "How are you going to have any room for your meal?"

I shake my head. "I won't. Don't you see? That's the beauty. I fill up on this delicious salad and yummy breadsticks, then I get to eat my pasta tomorrow. Pasta's always better as leftovers anyway. The sauce absorbs into the noodles making it way more yummy." I shove the last bit of the breadstick into my mouth and lick my fingers. "I will try to save room for dessert."

Ethel chuckles, "Well, this is so sweet, Georgia. Really. I don't remember the last time I've been taken out to dinner."

"Everyone deserves a nice birthday dinner. Though, I would've splurged for some place a little fancier than Olive Garden."

"No, I haven't been here in over twenty years. This place brings back fond memories. It was my late husband Earl's favorite restaurant. Whenever we went out to eat, which wasn't often, he'd want to come here. Funny thing is that he always ordered the sirloin, never a pasta dish. It never made any sense to me."

She stares off past my shoulder, a dreamy smile on her face.

"Well, I wish I would've been able to meet him. He had to be wonderful if he was married to you."

"Oh he was," she nods. "He was a great man."

"I'm really sorry that Wyatt didn't show. I thought he would." I peer toward the hostess stand again to make sure he isn't standing there waiting, but of course he isn't.

"It's not a problem. He's always so busy."

"Yeah, well…" my voice trails off. Speaking ill of Wyatt on Ethel's birthday wouldn't be very kind.

"You two seem to be getting along better lately."

"We had a heart-to-heart the other day." I shrug.

At this Ethel really laughs. "Wyatt doesn't do heart-to-hearts. Spill the juicy details," she says as she dabs the side of her eye with the cloth napkin.

"I basically yelled at him and told him to stop treating me like crap. I think he felt sort of bad because he opened up some after that. Like he told me a little about his mom and the drugs and about you finding him on the street."

Ethel's eyes go wide. "He did?"

"Yeah," I nod casually. I'm being intentionally vague because that's literally all he told me, but I want Ethel to tell me more.

"I'm surprised. He doesn't talk about his mom or anything, really, at least not to others."

"It was during our duffel bag drop-offs. So I know you found him and Cooper and got them off the street, but how did it all play out?" I take a bite of the whole pepperoncini from the salad that was just delivered; the tartness makes my face scrunch up.

"Normally I wouldn't say anything because Wyatt is a private person. But it sounds like he's already told you the major bullet points. So he must trust you."

I nod, urging her to continue.

"I think I told you how I used to work with his mother, Natalie? We were nurses together? Well, Wyatt's dad was murdered when he was six—shot by someone he didn't know at a gas station. Natalie didn't handle her husband's death well. Shortly after the funeral, she fell and broke her wrist and became addicted to the pain pills she was prescribed. I think they helped her numb the pain that was so unbearable for her. You know, I saw her changing right before my eyes. She and her husband and little Wyatt were our family. Earl and I couldn't have kids, and Natalie and I grew close and so did our families."

I tilt my lips into a grin. I try to imagine what a toddler-aged Wyatt looked like. "I bet Wyatt was so cute when he was little."

"He was. He's always been simply adorable, even now—despite his rough demeanor, he's such a handsome man." Her expression saddens. "So, anyway I saw her changing, but I thought she was just working through her grief. Eventually, I guess she started stealing pills from our medical cart. She was caught and was fired. She and Wyatt continued to live in their nice home for a while, but Natalie's addiction grew, and after she burned through their savings, she started selling off their possessions until eventually they lost everything."

"That's so sad," I say.

"It is. They moved to these horrible, cheap apartments in Ypsilanti. I knew it wasn't a good area, but Natalie was a grown woman. I couldn't tell her what to do. I hadn't realized at the time that her addiction had moved beyond pills. I still thought she was in control. She pushed us away. I tried to stay in her and Wyatt's life, but she made it clear she didn't want Earl or me around. We saw them less and less, until we didn't see them at all."

A tear falls down Ethel's cheek.

"I feel horrible because I didn't know how bad it was for him. I was clueless. I never thought she'd let it get that bad. He had a really hard childhood, one that no little boy should have to go through. I blame myself. I should've forced myself into their life. I should've realized her behavior was due to the drugs. I should've gotten her help. I didn't know."

"Ethel. Of course you didn't. It's not your fault."

"Wyatt tells me the same, but I don't believe it. I should've helped him. I was all he had, and I didn't know. I failed him." She holds the napkin to her eyes.

Shame for wanting to pry into Wyatt's past takes hold. I wanted to know details, but I didn't want to make Ethel cry at her birthday dinner.

"I'm so sorry," I tell her.

She takes a deep breath, "When I got news of his mother's passing, I went to find him. But his apartment was empty. He was gone. I'd naively hoped he was off at college or on another adventure. I didn't know at the time how bad things had been, so I assumed he was off living the life an eighteen-year-old should.

"Then the following spring, I was walking through Ann Arbor window shopping. I remember the day so clearly because it was the first day we'd had sunshine in over a month. It had been a long and brutal winter. I passed a homeless man and his brindle dog on the street. I stopped to give him some money, and when I looked into his eyes, I gasped. His eyes are so distinct, so blue...they gave him away. I knew it was him. I dropped to my knees, and I hugged him as I cried. I told him how very sorry I was that I didn't find him sooner. I took him and Cooper home with me that very second, and I haven't let him out of my sight since."

"He still lives with you?"

"No, he's gotten his own place since, but we practically live together as much as we're at the shelter." A smile returns to her face and I'm glad. I much prefer her laughter to her tears.

I'm a horrible person for prying.

I pull the gift from beside me and hand it to her. "I know it's not the end of dinner yet, but do you want to open your present now?" I ask her, a wide smile across my face.

"Wow, Georgia. You didn't have to get me anything. That's so sweet."

I clasp my hands together in front of my chest so eager for her to see her present. She pulls the shirt out of the bag and starts laughing, the wonderful sound that erupts from her deep down and lights up a room.

"Do you love it?" I clap.

"Oh darling. I love it."

She holds the pink shirt out in front of her. The front has a tabby cat wearing a wizard's hat riding a dog through a forest where all of the trees are lush with glittery hot pink leaves. The cat is lifting one paw in which it holds a cup of coffee. The image makes no sense whatsoever, and that's why it's completely brilliant.

"What in the hell is that?" Wyatt's gruff voices asks from behind me.

"Isn't it great?" I grin.

He shakes his head with a roll of his eyes and sits in one of the empty chairs at the table.

"You're late," I tell him.

"I was busy."

"Well, I'm just glad you're here." Ethel taps the top of his hand with hers.

Our pasta dishes arrive, and the waiter sets them in front of us. "Would you like to order anything, sir?" he asks Wyatt.

"No, and actually, can we get these wrapped up and get the check, please?" Wyatt asks.

The server looks momentarily confused but nods and leaves us.

"What the heck, Wyatt? This is Ethel's birthday dinner. We're not leaving until we're ready." I glare at him.

"I'm sorry, E. There was an emergency rescue, and I actually came here because I need your help. Do you mind?" He looks to Ethel.

"Yes, she minds!" I scoff. "There're always emergencies at the rescue. You can't deal with it for an hour without her so she can have a nice meal?"

"It's okay, Georgia. Honestly, the salad and bread did fill me up. I don't mind taking my meal for later. As you said, it will be better tomorrow."

"I know." I look to her. "But that's not the point. You don't have to leave just because he beckons you. You deserve a break."

The server stands beside us with two to-go boxes atop a stand. He takes Ethel's dish and begins emptying it into the container. We're all silent as he repeats the steps with my meal. I'm so angry, I don't even know what to say or do.

How dare Wyatt?

The waiter gives the bill to Wyatt. I snatch it out of his hand. "I don't think so. You may be ruining her birthday dinner, but you're not paying for it," I huff out and hand the server my credit card.

"It's really okay, Georgia. I had a wonderful dinner. It was really special," Ethel tells me with a warm smile.

I give her a weak grin in response.

As we walk out of the restaurant, our dinner in hand, Wyatt says, "You know there's a lot of work to be done dealing with the emergency. We could also use your help back at the shelter."

I scowl, "You've got a lot of nerve."

He shrugs and opens his passenger door before helping Ethel up. "Alright, fine. We'll manage without you."

"I'll be there," I grumble before turning to head to my car, but not before I swear I see Wyatt crack a smile.

I follow Wyatt's truck the few miles to Cooper's Place. When we pull up, I'm shocked that the entire parking lot is full of cars. *What kind of emergency is this?*

There are more vehicles than I've ever seen here. I follow Wyatt and Ethel indoors, and we're practically blown away with an enormously loud, "Surprise!"

The place is decked out in everything pink and cats. There are probably fifty helium cat head balloons accompanied by a hundred pink ones floating around the space. There's a cotton candy machine. Fair food carts are stationed around the open space, all with a feline-related sign. The elephant ears sign is covered up with glittery magenta letters that read, *Cinnamon and Sugar Kitten Paws.*

I walk around taking it all in. Most of the dogs are out of their kennels, and they're all wearing a pink boa around their neck. They look so cute and happy. Their tongues hang out as they get loved on by the guests. There's a huge cake with pink frosting that's adorned with a large cat picture.

The snacks at the food table all have fun names. The party mix is labeled, *Cat Food.* The bowl of chocolates is labeled, *Kitty Litter.* All of the presents at the gift table are packaged in some sort of cat-themed paper or bag.

This is honestly the most detailed, coolest surprise party I've ever seen. I can't believe Wyatt was behind it. I watch as Ethel continues to make her way around the room, hugging all of her guests. Her face is wet with tears, but she looks so happy.

I feel my eyes fill with tears just watching her, my heart full of happiness. There's a whimper at my feet. I look down to find Mila with a pink bow around her neck. She looks adorable.

I pick her up and hold her to me. "Hey, Mila. You are so cute." I kiss her head.

"I was just looking for her." Wyatt's beside me now. "I told the guys to let the dogs out, but I didn't mean the puppies. I'm afraid they'll get stepped on. Plus, this has to be overwhelming for them."

"Yeah," I agree. "You did all this?"

"I guess. I mean, I hired a party planner. She did most of it."

"Who are all of these people?"

"Some of them are old friends of hers from her nursing days. Some are people that've adopted our dogs that we've stayed close with, past employees, and volunteers."

I shake my head in awe. "This is really something special, Wyatt. So nice."

"You've changed your tune since the restaurant, I see," he smirks.

"Well, I didn't know. You didn't tell me."

"Did you think that I'd let Ethel's seventieth birthday pass without celebrating it?"

"Honestly, I don't know with you. You're so hard to figure out. I wish you would've told me. I wouldn't have been such a jerk at the restaurant."

"Nah. You taking E out to dinner worked great. It gave us time to set up. And your reaction made it so she didn't suspect anything."

Wyatt has a smile on his face as he watches Ethel. It's so rare to see him smile, and I'd be lying if I said that he's not absolutely gorgeous when he does.

"You should smile more. It's a good look for you," I tell him.

The grin drops from his face. "I'm not a smiling type of person."

"Exactly what type of a person are you? I mean you walk around here all grumpy and mean. You act like you don't like anyone. Yet you save helpless animals for a living. You hand out supplies to the homeless. And you throw the coolest surprise party I've ever seen for one of your employees. It doesn't add up."

"Ethel isn't just an employee," is his response.

"I know." I think back to the way she spoke of him at dinner. "She really loves you."

"Yeah, well. I'm a hard one to love. Just another reason she deserves a party." His gaze darts to mine. "Just put the puppy away when you're done holding her," he tells me before walking off.

As he strolls away I find myself wanting to follow him. Why do I want to chase after someone who's made it clear they don't like me? I hate that I feel this pull toward him, but more than that I can't stand the fact that he hates me and I don't even know why.

ELEVEN

SEVENTEEN YEARS OLD

*"Georgia's beauty is more than skin deep, and I think
that's what I love about her the most."*
—Wyatt Gates

Her lips are everything I dreamed they'd be—soft, full, and irresistible. She threads her fingers through my hair, pulling me closer to her, and it takes everything I have not to back her into that wall and explore every inch of her.

Georgia Wright is the epitome of perfection. She's the most beautiful girl I've ever seen. I can't believe that I found her here, in this horrible place. She doesn't belong within these walls with the stuck-up assholes. She's kind and sweet. Georgia's beauty is more than skin deep, and I think that's what I love about her the most.

She doesn't see me as the poor kid from Ypsilanti. She sees me for me. She might be the only one here that does. I expect the stuck-up rich kids to treat me differently, but even the teachers look at me with an air of…pity, maybe shame? I'm the charity case with the drug addict mother.

Georgia moans softly into my mouth as her tongue dances with mine.

Holy shit.

It takes all the willpower I have, but I pull my lips from hers. Leaning my forehead against hers, we both catch our breath.

I hate that I have to leave Georgia to go to work. I'm walking away from her gorgeous lips to go flip greasy burgers. Sometimes, life's really not fair. "I have to go," I say, remorse weighs heavy on me.

God, I want to stay here and kiss her. Better yet, I want to take her somewhere private and kiss her more.

"Okay," she whispers.

I step back, tucking a piece of her blonde hair behind her ear. "Can I see you this weekend?"

Her eyes light up at my question. "I'd love that. Yes."

"Do you know where Gallop Park is?"

She nods.

"I can meet you there at six. At the bench beneath the overpass by the river at the far entrance. Do you know where that is?"

"I do," she answers.

"Okay, then I'll see you tomorrow." I smile, still unable to believe that I finally kissed Georgia.

"Six o'clock," she says.

"Six o'clock." I squeeze her hand before opening the study room door and walking out.

My smile is short lived. Halfway across the library I'm met by two of the biggest douches in school. "You realize that the study rooms are surrounded by windows? What? Didn't feel like taking her home to the ghetto to make out?" Kevin says. His loyal follower Dwight laughs.

I don't have time to deal with them. I walk out of the library and turn down the hall. Their annoying footsteps follow me.

Just go away.

"You got it on video, right?" Kevin says to Dwight.

"Sure did," Dwight's squeaky voice replies. *I wonder if he's ever going to hit puberty?*

"Good because Beckett owes Georgia a hundred bucks. He's never going to believe it without the video."

The hopeful excitement that danced around in my belly just moments ago is replaced with bile threatening to come up.

I stop and jerk around. "What are you talking about?"

Kevin's eyes go wide in mock concern. "Did Georgia not tell you about the bet?" He holds up his hands. "Wait, please tell me you didn't think she actually liked you, did you?"

He's an asshole, and my better judgment tells me to ignore him and just walk away. But I don't. "What bet?" I ask through clenched teeth, my head starting to spin.

"Last weekend at Beck's, Georgia said that she could get you to do anything for her." He looks to Dwight. "Didn't she say something about having Wyatt wrapped around her finger?"

Dwight nods, "Something like that."

Kevin shrugs, "Yeah, so anyway. Beck said that he didn't believe her, and she bet him a Benjamin that she could get you to kiss her this week. I know you've probably never seen one…I should clarify…a Benjamin is another name for a hundred dollars because the president Benjamin Franklin is on the hundred-dollar bill."

"Fuck off. Like I'd believe anything you say." I turn to leave.

I think of Georgia, a popular girl from a very rich family, and realize that I'm everything she's not. I don't care about any of that stuff. I'd want her regardless of her status, but I'm smart enough to know that to many—it does matter, all that shit matters. I just didn't think it was important to her.

"Whatever. Believe what you want. I don't like you, man, but I also don't want to see Georgia make a complete fool of you either. I mean…think about it," Kevin says.

I glare toward the two of them.

"Why did she tell us to hang out at the library and have our phones ready to record? Do you normally see us in the library? No, it's not our scene, man." Kevin looks to Dwight and then back to me. "You can't honestly think a girl like Georgia would be into white trash like you, can you? You know how rich she is, right? Her daddy, for one, would never let that fly." Kevin laughs, and I have an overwhelming desire to punch that cocky grin off his pampered face.

I stand, scowling at the two of them. My thoughts are all over the place.

Kevin shrugs, "Whatever, believe what you want. Can't fix stupid." He playfully punches Dwight's shoulder, and the two of them turn to leave.

"Let me see the video," I say.

Kevin lifts an eyebrow and grabs his phone from his back pocket. He holds the phone out to me, and I see Georgia and I kissing through the glass of the study room door.

"But, you know, Dwight and I always randomly hang in the library with our phones on record, right?" The sarcasm drips from his words.

"Delete it," I warn.

"But Georgia needs it to get her—"

I cut him off, "I said fucking delete it." I step toward him, pulling my shoulders back.

He holds his hands up in surrender. "Fine. Whatever. I'll just tell her I was too late to catch the kiss." He shrugs and deletes the video. "It's not like she needs another hundred anyway, but you really should be careful of who you trust. I get that you're not the brightest, but come on Gates?"

"Walk away before I punch you both the fuck out," I advise through clenched teeth.

Kevin and Dwight laugh.

"Nah, you wouldn't do that," Kevin grins smugly. "You'd lose your scholarship and be forced to go to the poor-ass school in your neighborhood. I mean, you'd be trash either way, but at least here you're trash with a somewhat decent education. Maybe it will count for something?"

Dwight laughs, and he sounds like a girl.

They're not worth it.

No one in this fucking place is worth it.

Especially her.

And now, I'm late for work.

TWELVE

"Georgia makes it impossible to hate her.
She's incredibly annoying in that way."
—Wyatt Gates

"I don't think so, buddy," I say to Cooper as he buries himself back under the comforter. He's so spoiled, always insisting that he sleeps under the covers. "Bedtime is over. We're going for a run."

I pull the blanket back off of him. Cooper grumbles and shoves his face under the corner of the comforter. "Come on, Coops." He remains still. "Right, you're completely invisible now. I can't see you at all."

I laugh at my big guy. He looks so pathetic, laying on the bed with just his snout and eyes covered up. I think it's hilarious how he thinks he's hidden just because he can't see me.

"Let's go, boy. I can see you by the way. You're not fooling anyone."

I leave him to go brush my teeth real quick. Waking up early to go for a run isn't my idea of a good Sunday morning, either. But I need to burn some energy off. I've been sleeping like shit lately. I'm so restless.

I've been dreaming a lot about the seventeen-year-old Georgia that I thought I might've loved before I knew the kind of person she was. Yeah, so she doesn't seem to be like that anymore, but it doesn't matter. She and I have nothing in common. We come from two very different worlds.

Thinking about that time in my life isn't pleasant even if I remove Georgia. I hated everything about my high school years—the school, the people, lack of money, my mom, her drugs. The list is endless—I don't like reliving any of it, and because of Georgia, I am.

I need to clear my head.

I rinse off my toothbrush and wipe my mouth on the towel. Looking down, I find Cooper at my feet. He sighs and falls to the bathroom rug in dramatic fashion.

"Look who's back. You disappeared there for a while." I bend and hold his big head between my hands. I kiss him on the softest part of his forehead, right between his eyes.

"I know you don't want to go for a run, but you're not getting any younger. We need to keep you in shape so you'll live a long time. You're almost fifty-six in dog years, man. You could be an AARP member; a morning jog will do you some good."

I head out of the bathroom, and Cooper follows. "And maybe we'll stop and get you a sausage, egg, and biscuit sandwich. Okay?"

Cooper wags his tail as I put on my running shoes. "Yes, I know a sandwich like that defeats the whole purpose of running, but they're your favorite, and I spoil you way more than I should." I rub his head, and he follows me out of the house.

Brisk morning runs aren't everything they're made out to be. I don't have much time to think because I'm too focused on the burning sensation in my lungs. Breathing in cold air isn't pleasant.

Once we hit the three-mile mark, I stop, and we walk. Cooper pants heavily. "We're out of shape, aren't we, boy? You ready for your sandwich?"

We walk to our favorite breakfast place in town. It's a glorified fast food joint, but they let me bring Cooper in, and their food is good. I order eight breakfast sandwiches, enough for me, Cooper, Mark, and Stan to each have two. I can't be this close to where Mark and Stan hang out and not bring them food.

After Cooper and I eat ours we head toward Fourth Street. I can see Mark sitting there as he usually is with Stan at his side, but this morning there's someone else there too.

I let out a sigh when we're close enough to see who it is. Cooper notices her, as well. His body starts shaking with excitement. "You're such a traitor."

"Hey, Wyatt! Hey, boy!" Mark greets us.

"We brought you and Stan some breakfast." I hand him the bag.

"Well, isn't today my lucky day. My Georgia Peach brought us some breakfast, too." He smiles toward Georgia who is sitting across from him. They have a small, travel-sized chess board between them. Mark notices me looking at the board. "I'm trying to teach her to play."

"I'm not very good," she laughs.

"Do you two play often?" I ask.

"No, this is only our second time playing. But Georgia always stops by to say hi after she runs."

Georgia's dressed in running gear. Her hair is pulled back in a ponytail and she has a sports headband on. Her cheeks are rosy and her eyes are bright.

"Cooper and I went running, too."

"I didn't know you ran," she says.

"We don't as much as we should." I leave it vague, omitting the fact that this was our first run in months.

"I'm glad you're taking him out," she nods toward Cooper. "It will keep his heart healthy."

"Yeah."

I want to tell her that she doesn't need to worry about Cooper or his heart. He's mine, and I'll take care of him. Yet I know she was only being kind, and if I were to comment, I would only be acting like an asshole—which I'm trying hard not to do—so I don't say anything.

Cooper starts whining and pulling his leash.

"What is it, boy?"

I allow him to pull me where he wants me to go, and we end up about a half of a block down from Mark. Cooper looks to me and then looks down an alleyway behind some restaurants.

"What is it? Did you see something?" I ask him.

"What is it?" Georgia whispers behind me, startling me. I hadn't realized she followed.

"I don't know. Hold Cooper." I hand her his leash.

I hesitantly make my way down the alley. I look behind the trash cans and in all of the crevices between the buildings. I don't see anything. I start walking toward the street when I hear something scratch against metal beside me.

To my right there is a large green dumpster. I open the thick plastic lid, and my heart sinks. It doesn't matter how many rescues I do, it always breaks my heart.

"It's okay, baby. I'm here to help you."

I motion Georgia down and pull my cell out of my pocket.

I call Ethel. "Hey, are you in the office? Okay. Can you bring the van down to Fourth Street to the alley entrance right next to the parking structure? Yeah. Make sure there's a crate in the back. Thanks."

"What is it?" Georgia asks.

I nod toward the dumpster, and she looks inside bringing one of her hands up to her mouth with a gasp.

Tears fill her eyes. "What is wrong with people?"

"I ask myself that every day. Can you run and ask Mark if he has a pocketknife in his backpack? I don't have anything on me to cut that off of her mouth."

"Sure."

"You can just leave Cooper here."

She drops his leash and runs out of the alleyway.

I turn an old metal garbage can upside down and place it outside of the dumpster. I jump on top of it and crawl in. The large bin is empty besides the dog. At least the dumbass who did this threw her away after the garbage came and not before.

She cowers in the corner, her eyes full of fear.

"I know you're scared. Humans haven't been good to you, have they? You don't have to be scared anymore."

She's an all-black pit bull. Her body is covered in puncture wounds. Her ears have been hacked off with a dull blade. She has duct tape wrapped so tightly around her snout that it's cutting into her skin. The edges of the tape are red with blood.

"Here." Georgia reaches over and hands me a small knife.

I take it and slowly inch toward the frightened animal with my palm out. "Shhh. You're okay. I'm going to help you."

I pet her head and notice a small twitch of her tail. I smile. "Yeah, that's it. Good girl." I pet her a little more making sure she knows that I'm not going to hurt her. Then I work at cutting the tape from her muzzle.

"I'm sorry. I know. I'm almost done." Her entire body shakes with fear.

I'm so relieved when the final piece of tape comes loose.

"There, now you can breathe."

I look up to Georgia. "I need you to stand on the silver garbage can. I'm going to hand her to you. Then I'll jump out and take her."

"Okay," she nods and steps up.

I pick up the little girl gently, reassuring her the entire time, and hand her to Georgia. Then I climb out of the dumpster and extend my arms so that I can get the dog back. I hold her close to my chest and exit the alleyway to find Ethel and the van waiting.

I place the dog in a crate in the back of the van and motion for Cooper to jump in. He does. I pull the knife out of my pocket and hand it to Georgia. "Can you tell Mark thanks for me?"

"Sure." She takes the knife from my grasp. "But can I come back with you?"

"Yeah."

"Okay, be right back." She smiles and runs off to return the knife to Mark.

I climb into the passenger seat.

"Same shit, different day," I tell E.

She sighs, "Poor baby."

"She's so sweet, too."

Georgia slides in, closes the door, and Ethel drives off.

"I can't believe she let you cut that off of her mouth and pick her up. She didn't even snarl or anything," Georgia says from the back seat.

"It's often like that. They're so trusting of humans despite being so abused by them. It's the pit bull spirit. They just love people. They're the best dogs. That poor girl doesn't have a mean bone in her body, and she was so abused by people. Still she wags her tail when I pet her." I shake my head, still so angry at the piece of shit who did this to her.

"Will she be okay?" Georgia asks.

I nod, "Yeah. She'll be a great dog. She needs some antibiotics and TLC, but she'll be fine. She's going to make some family really happy. She'll love them unconditionally."

We get back to the shelter and get Luna situated. Georgia named her Luna because as she says, "She's as black as night, but her spirit shines as bright as the moon, and Luna means moon." Georgia really invests in the dogs' names. I pretend to find it annoying, but it's kind of endearing.

After Luna is bathed, fed, and medicated, I check on all of the other dogs. Everyone showed for work today, which is rare, and they all did their jobs well, which is also rare. The dogs all look good and happy.

"E, go home," I say to Ethel.

"It's fine. I have some reading to do. I'll stay."

"For the love of God, go home. Spend time with your cats. I'll see you tomorrow." I kiss her on the cheek, grab her by the shoulders, and push her out of the office.

She laughs, "Fine, but I need my purse and my coat." She points into the office.

"Okay, but then you leave. Enjoy your Sunday."

"What about you?" She looks concerned.

"I'm fine. I have Cooper, a couch, and a TV." I motion toward the new setup that I have going in the office. I splurged and bought some essentials since I'm here so often. "We'll order a pizza, watch some basketball. It will be awesome. I'll give Luna her second round of meds later and make sure all the dogs get walked again tonight. We're good. I promise."

Ethel leaves, and Cooper and I get situated on the sofa. I aimlessly flip through the channels. There're no good games on. I catch the *Jurassic World* movie.

"You in the mood for dinosaurs?" I ask Coops.

He lets out a loud snore, like a congested pig. "I'll take that as a yes."

A way into the movie, I hit pause, deciding to go check on Luna. Cooper hops off the couch and follows me. "Do you want to see if she wants to come hang with us in here?" I ask Cooper. I always worry about the new dogs when they first come. I know being in a kennel must be scary for them.

When Cooper and I hang out in the office, I'll often bring a couple other dogs up to relax. I wish they could all fit on the couch with us. Every dog deserves to know what that feels like.

I close in on Luna's cage. I'm startled when Georgia's bright hazel eyes greet me.

"What are you doing here? I thought everyone left."

"I was just going to go home to read, so I figured I might as well do it here and sit with her. I didn't want her to be scared."

Georgia was sitting on the concrete floor, her back leaning against the side of the kennel. Luna's head with all the evidence of her past abuse rests on Georgia's lap.

"You don't have a book."

She holds up her phone. "Kindle app. I always have a book with me."

"Well I was just coming to see if Luna wanted to come sit up on the couch with me and Cooper." I look to Georgia, waiting for all of my pent-up anger toward her to surface, but it doesn't come. Georgia makes it impossible to hate her. She's incredibly annoying in that way. "We're watching a movie and going to order pizza. You can come up if you want."

Georgia laughs, "Was that last part hard for you to say? Your face was all scrunched up, and you appeared to be in pain as you said it."

I shrug, "It wasn't easy."

"Well, even though I know you're not super thrilled about me joining you, I accept. My ass is going numb sitting on this floor, and I'm kind of hungry." She looks down to Luna and gently pets her back. "And I do want to hang out with her a little longer so she's not alone. You know?"

I nod because I do.

"Come on, Luna baby," Georgia says sweetly, encouraging our new resident to follow her to the office. Luna's hesitant at first but then slowly follows behind Georgia.

It's actually pretty impressive that she's gained Luna's trust so quickly. I'd never tell Georgia, but she's a natural with these rescues. They all trust her.

"So what are you watching?" Georgia asks, the four of us situated on the sofa. I sit at one end with Cooper's head on my lap. She sits on the other with Luna's head in hers.

"*Jurassic World.*"

"You mean *Jurassic Park*?" she asks.

"No, *World.*"

She appears confused.

"You know, the one with Chris Pratt," I tell her.

"Remind me who he is again."

"Are you serious?" I narrow my eyes in question. "Star-Lord from *Guardians of the Galaxy*?"

"I haven't seen that one. I haven't been in the States much since I graduated from college. I'm behind on movies."

"Where've you been?"

"South America, Africa, and China. Mainly."

"Doing what?"

"Trying to help people."

"Why?" I question.

She presses her lips together, the corners turning up into a grin. "I don't know. I guess because they need the help. Why do you help dogs?"

"Because they need it."

She nods, "Exactly. Maybe you and I aren't so different."

I shake my head, "No, we definitely are. Completely different."

"You keep telling yourself that, Wyatt. Whatever helps you sleep at night."

I opt to change the subject. "So tell me the last *Jurassic* movie you saw. We can't start with this one if you haven't seen the prior ones."

Georgia's eyes light up. "Ooh, are we going to do a marathon? Like hang out and stuff? This is a big step. We're like basically friends now." She smiles wide and quirks her eyebrows up.

"Don't get all crazy. Just tell me which one. Or should we just start from the beginning?"

She leans her head against the back of the sofa, her expression soft, her grin kind. "I think starting from the beginning is always good."

Maybe.

Sometimes.

But not always.

THIRTEEN

GEORGIA

"Wyatt Gates is my weakness. The harder I try to let him go, the more fiercely my heart holds on."
—Georgia Wright

Wyatt Gates is kissing me, and it's everything I had hoped it would be.

His tongue gently requests entry as it runs along my lips, and I open my mouth inviting it in. God, yes. Wyatt deepens the kiss. His fingers are gripping the nape of my neck, threading into my hair, pulling my mouth into his. I wrap my arms around his neck and hold him close to me.

"Hey, Peaches." His fingers grasp my arm, shaking lightly.

My mind is foggy, but I try to ignore his words. I want his lips back. I close my eyes tighter waiting for the kiss.

"Georgia. Wake up."

"Ugh," I groan. "Go away."

I'm bitter. The Wyatt of today stole me away from the Wyatt of my dreams.

I don't want the real Wyatt, the one that hates me, the one that will never see me as anything but a nuisance. I want the one that for a small moment in time kissed me in that study room like I was the only woman he wanted to kiss for the rest of his life.

I want those lips, that Wyatt, and that moment back.

Why am I still aching for something that happened so long ago?

I open my eyes to find his beautiful blues staring back at me, curious. His gaze makes me ache because I want him. Fresh from my perfect dream, all of my emotions hover at the surface. Every bit of me wants every bit of him. I want his lips. I want his hands. I want his eyes to continue to look at me with anything but hate.

In this space, fresh from a memory and vulnerable, I can't lie to myself.

I still want him.

He's been cruel and vile…and I shouldn't. I wish I didn't. But I do.

I want him so badly, and part of me doesn't even care that he doesn't like me. If he'd have me, I'd take him anyway—just to feel those lips one more time.

My thoughts betray me, and I'm disappointed in myself. This isn't me. I'm not weak. I don't need a man's touch to make me feel whole. I don't need anyone.

I've kissed my share of guys, and no one has made me feel the way that Wyatt did. But it wasn't real. I was young. I've built that kiss up in my head for so long. Of course no kiss has come close since. Reality is never more satisfying than a dream.

I sit up. Resting my elbows on my knees I hold my face in my hands.

"I've finished walking and feeding the dogs. I'm going to... Why are you crying?" Wyatt asks concerned.

Dragging my fingers across my cheek, they pick up wetness along the way.

I am crying.

I stand and wipe my tears from my face.

"What is it?" he asks, his hands on either side of my arms, holding me close.

"Careful," I warn him. "One might think you care." I put a hand on his side and gently push him away from me.

I'm just exhausted and emotional. I need to get out of here. I take a few steps away from him as I swipe the tears with the backs of my hands.

"Georgia, stop," Wyatt demands and for some reason I comply. "I don't understand," he says from behind me.

I turn to face him. "I'm just tired, Wyatt."

My hands drop to my sides, mirroring the defeat I feel in my heart. "I'm exhausted. I'm tired of pretending that the hatred you feel toward me doesn't bother me, when it does. I'm tired of working my ass off here just to feel emptier when I leave." Tears stream down my cheeks, and I no longer try to stop them.

"I'm tired of going through life trying to fill a void that a stupid boy caused with the words he said when I was just seventeen. And most of all I'm tired of dreaming of that boy and desperately wanting him, only to wake and discover that he's gone, and the reality is that he never existed in the first place."

Wyatt just stares at me, his expression unreadable.

I throw my hands up in defeat. "I thought I was supposed to be here. I thought fate led me here for a reason. But I don't know if I believe that anymore," I tell him, my voice shaking.

"I've spent my adult life chasing happiness only to see you staring back at me when I close my eyes, reminding me that the only person I've ever loved didn't even see me. I'm a good person, Wyatt. I know I am. I don't need you to agree to make it true. I don't need you to love me back to make me whole."

Why am I talking about love? It's only real in fairytales, right?

I hold my hand to my chest and press in to relieve the pressure. "And I hate that after everything, though I don't need it, I *want* it. What's wrong with me?" I ask, my voice soft and defeated. I shake my head and drop my chin to my chest.

"I need to go," I sigh. Scanning the room, I take everything in, except Wyatt. Looking for what, I'm not sure. Maybe a goodbye.

I'm not certain what tomorrow will bring, but in my heart I feel it's time to move on and find another organization to help. There are countless ones that need it.

I bounce from place to place helping others because it makes me feel good inside. This—here—doesn't feel good. It hurts. I can't stay.

I leave the office without a backward glance. I don't need to see him or his judgmental stare. I know what he thinks of me, and nothing I could say will change it. Some people are too stubborn to believe anything that doesn't fit into the narrative they've created inside their head. Rather than seeking the truth, he chooses to ignore the facts right in front of him. I'm done.

Maybe.

I don't know.

I'll decide tomorrow after a good night's sleep.

Walking away from Wyatt is something I've done before, and I'm thinking in the near future, I'll be doing it again.

But these dogs…

Out of habit, I grab a treat bag and walk by each kennel. I give treats and pet heads. I say goodbye to each perfect face. Reaching Luna's area, I bend, handing her a treat. She's still so sick and weak, but she wags her tail anyway.

"I love you," I tell her. "You're going to find such a great home with people that will adore you. I promise. You won't have to hurt again."

Tears roll down my face. I hate saying goodbye to the dogs. I'm not ready to leave. This place is magical and truly saves lives. The people that work here—Ethel, Xavier, and the rest of the guys—are wonderful people with some of the kindest spirits I've come across. They feel like family and walking away from here means walking away from them, and the dogs.

How can such an incredible place make me so sad? But it's not the place. I know that. It's the person. I wish I didn't still harbor feelings toward him. If my heart didn't crave him, it wouldn't matter how he felt about me. If he were a nobody, it wouldn't bother me. Yet he left this imprint on my soul years ago, and I haven't been able to shake it since. I want more than anything to be able to detest him the way he does me. If that were the case, I could stay. But feeling my heart break a little more every day isn't something that I'm equipped for.

I've always thought that I was strong, maybe even stronger than most. I've seen the worst that mankind has to give, and I've been able to stand tall through it, even extending a helping to hand to those that needed support to get up.

Wyatt Gates is my weakness. The harder I try to let him go, the more fiercely my heart holds on.

I can't get over him, and because of that, I can't stay here.

I open Hope's cage, walk in, and shut it behind me. Leaning against the wall of her enclosure, I slide down until I'm seated on the ground. The chubby puppies start jumping on me. Some lick at the tears on my face, and I can't help but smile. Puppies really are amazingly therapeutic.

"You're all getting so big." I smile through the tears. "And look who's the biggest?" I wrap my fingers around Mila and hold her up to my face, giggling as she licks my nose.

"I wish I could take you with me." I hold her to me, and she nuzzles into my neck.

Maybe I could come back for her when she's ready to be weaned from Hope and her siblings. I need to figure out what my next step is. As much as I love her, I don't tend to stay in one place for too long, and that's not a good life for a dog.

"I'd take you if I could, but I'm a mess. I'm just…"

Lost.

I pet her soft fur.

"Alright, babies. I have to go." I kiss them all on the top of their heads and pet Hope before stepping out.

Tears continue to fall as the puppies all jump up on the gate, wanting out. Soon enough, they'll all have homes. I pray that their new owners are good people. I know that Wyatt does background and home checks on the adoption applicants. But still, I worry. Humans can be so cruel. With one final look at the first puppies I was able to see born, I turn to leave.

I jump, startled to see Wyatt standing a couple of feet away watching me in that way he does. His eyes narrow as they study me. His hands rest in the pockets of his track pants.

My morning run seems so long ago. I've spent the entire day with Wyatt. We chatted with Mark. We saved Luna. We took care of the rest of the dogs in the shelter. We ate pizza and watched at least part of a movie together before I fell asleep. Then I dreamt of him—again—and everything changed.

It's so surreal how I can start my day as one person and end it as a completely different one.

Wyatt lifts his hand from his pocket and rubs the back of his neck. "I don't understand what's happening." His voice is different than it usually is. It beckons me closer. I take a step in his direction. "I just...I..." I breathe deeply. "I don't think I can volunteer here anymore."

"What's changed? I couldn't get you to leave when I was horrible to you, and now that I'm trying to be decent, you want to go?"

"I know." I force out a chuckle because he's right. "It's just not working for me."

I hate that when I look at him, I still feel like the seventeen-year-old girl that thought he was the most incredible boy in the world.

"Do you know why I have to leave? It's because when I look at you, I still see the high school boy that stole my heart right before he broke it. After all this time, I didn't think you still had any hold over me. But being here with you, I realize that you do."

He pushes his fingers onto his temples. "You don't even know me, Georgia. You don't know what you felt. We were kids." His words come out short, frustration lines his voice.

"I know you. I did then and I do now. It's you who can't see me, Wyatt. I get that you've been through more heartache than most. The world hasn't been kind to you, but none of that is my fault. Maybe you need someone to blame? I just don't understand why it's me?" I sigh, a sad smile lines my face.

"Goodbye," I say before turning and walking away.

"Wait."

I stop.

Wyatt closes the distance between us. I feel his presence behind me. My body hums when he's near, regardless of whether I want it to or not. He's always elicited this reaction in me. It's visceral, unstoppable. I hold my breath in anticipation.

I don't turn around. Instead, Wyatt circles around me until we're face to face.

His blue eyes study me in a manner that I haven't seen since high school. His features are softer. His eyes appear almost sad. He raises his hands up to my face, taking my cheeks beneath his palms.

My chest burns from lack of air, and I pull in a ragged breath to relieve the pressure. His gaze continues to sear me with its intensity as it travels from my eyes to my lips. He leans in, pulling my head toward his.

Wyatt's lips press against mine, and a whimper escapes my mouth only to be caught by his. The beats of my heart echo loudly in my ears, and my knees feel weak. I hold onto Wyatt's waist so I don't fall over. When my hands touch his sides, he groans, and the kiss intensifies.

He moves his hands up my face and threads his fingers into my hair. Our kiss is desperate now. It's been so long, but my lips remember his like it was yesterday.

They need his.

Want his.

Crave his.

I kiss Wyatt like I may never kiss him again.

Not one kiss that I've experienced has come close to the way I feel when Wyatt kisses me. Knowing this now, I commit this moment to memory. If I never kiss Wyatt again, I want to remember it all, every little detail.

His hands tug at my hair. My scalp burns just enough at the pressure to drive me crazy with lust. His lips caress mine. His teeth pull my lip between them. His tongue dances with mine. His moans are quiet, desperate, and insanely hot.

The pressure builds within my core. I press my body to his, needing to feel him. I want him more than I've wanted anyone.

And then he stops and steps back.

I gasp at his absence.

"What?" I breathe heavily. "Why?" My mind is a jumbled mess of emotions.

He shoves his hands through his hair. "Just come back tomorrow. Okay?"

"Why did you kiss me?" I demand.

Wyatt's head falls back, and he groans toward the ceiling before catching me with his glare. "I don't know," he sighs. "Because I fucking needed to feel your lips."

He takes a few powerful steps away from me as if he needs to distance himself. He glowers in my direction. "I hate the fact that you're here. I hate that I want you so fucking much it's painful. You're right. Just go." He waves his hand toward the door.

"Why?" I yell. "What did I do?"

His shoulders fall. "You were the one bright light I had. My life was shit. That school and everyone in it was shit. But it was all worth it to walk into class to see you every day. I thought you were different than them. I wanted to believe it though I knew better. Sure you seem different now, maybe. But a tiger doesn't change its stripes, Georgia. Is this a game to you? Why are you insisting on bringing everything up?" His voice shakes with anger, but underneath it all I hear the vulnerability.

"Did something happen? Did someone in school hurt you?"

"You did!" he roars. "You ruined me."

"How?" I step toward him, but he backs away.

"The video. The bet. You know how. Just stop playing stupid. I know everyone there saw me as trash. I thought you were different. But you were the worst."

I feel the color draining from my face. *The video? The bet?* "What are you talking about, Wyatt? What video?"

"The video that you told Kevin and Dwight to take of our kiss so you could show Beck. You remember the bet you made with Beck? For a hundred bucks?" He glares at me, but in his eyes there's only sadness.

I shake my head. "I don't even remember a Kevin or a Dwight. I vaguely remember a guy named Beck, but I know I didn't make a bet with him."

"So you conveniently don't remember?" he snarls.

"Do you know how many schools I went to? How many people I met? I was in Ann Arbor for three months at the beginning of junior year. All I remember from that time is you! But I'm a hundred percent certain that I never made a bet with anyone about kissing you! Never! You know the people at that school were jerks. It hasn't crossed your mind that they made up this bet thing just to be assholes? You didn't think to ask me if it were true?"

"Why would I question it? They were pretty convincing. You were one of them. I wasn't."

I shake my head, "I wasn't one of them. Just because my dad has money, you assumed I was an ass? You're the ass, Wyatt. I had no idea that you were poor back then. I didn't know you were a scholarship student that bussed in every day. All I knew of you I based off of our interactions—which I lived for. I was infatuated with you. I thought you were the most beautiful boy I'd ever seen. You're the one that was judgmental."

I take a step toward Wyatt, and this time he doesn't move away. I look him in the eye. "Did you know that you were my first kiss?"

"No."

"Well, you were. You were my first kiss, my first real crush. I thought you were everything. Not only did you break my heart with your words, but you broke my spirit over something I didn't even do." I press my lips in a line and breathe in through my nose willing my tears to stay at bay. "You were cruel, and I didn't deserve it."

I lift my finger up and press it against his chest. "I'm sorry that life has dealt you a shitty hand. I really am. No one deserves to go through the things that you have. But that doesn't give you the right to hurt someone who's done nothing to deserve it. Jerks exist in all groups of people. What those boys did to you is just as bad as the words you said to me. Think about that."

Disappointment washes over me as I walk toward the exit. I turn the handle of the door, but before I leave, I turn and say, "Thank you for telling me the truth, though. I've let your words hurt me for too long. I shouldn't have, but I did. Now knowing the reason behind them, I can let it all go. I hope you can learn to let some things go, too. You can't hold so much anger toward your past because you can't change it. It will only make you miserable. Today is what matters."

My lips press together, the corners raise forming a grin. "Goodbye, Wyatt. The universe brought us together twice. Who knows? Maybe I'll see you again."

I walk to my car, proud. I'm not going to pretend that I didn't wish things turned out differently. As handsome as Wyatt is, and as much as my lips crave his, he's not right for me. Strength is wanting him and walking away, anyway.

I chuckle, thinking of the sitcom *Friends* and the million times I watched episodes with my sister growing up. To quote Rachel, "And that, my friend, is what they call closure."

Closure feels great.

FOURTEEN

"There's no such thing as true love. If there were—
Georgia wouldn't be mine."
—Wyatt Gates

"Who forgot the goddamn clip on this kennel?" I yell, looking around at the wide eyes of the guys as they clean out other kennels.

No one takes responsibility.

"Who cleaned this kennel? If you forget to clip the door shut, the dogs can jump up and knock the door open. Then we have a loose dog that can run out and get lost. Is that what we want? There are reasons procedures are in place!"

"It was me, boss," Xavier says, taking the piece of metal from my hand and clipping the door shut.

"No, it wasn't." I narrow my stare. Xavier isn't cleaning kennels today. He literally just got back from a rescue run with me.

He raises a hand as if swearing an oath. "Nope. Definitely me." If I weren't so pissed, I'd laugh.

"Shut up, already. It wasn't you." I roll my eyes. "But you know who it was. Don't you?"

He doesn't answer.

"Boss, how about you go do your office stuff. I'll check all the kennels," he tells me.

"It was the new guy, wasn't it?"

"If you don't want him to be *that new guy that quit*, let me talk to him. It's his first day on his own. Cut him some slack," Xavier tells me.

"New or not, he has to follow procedure or dogs will get hurt," I say, more than annoyed.

He places his hand to my chest. "I get it, but you need to chill. You've been stomping around here like a toddler who was told he can't have dessert until he eats his vegetables. You don't pay these guys millions to clean up shit. So don't expect them to stick around with your attitude."

"They knew what to expect when they were hired. I've never pretended to be nice. I'm not Ethel."

"Yeah, well, let's just say you've been a larger asshole than usual lately. Where is Ethel anyway? We prefer working with her."

"She's at a doctor's appointment. She'll be back later."

"Well, we anxiously await her arrival. Until then, how about you go to the office and find a dog to rescue or make some appointments with adopters. We'll handle everything down here."

"Fine," I frown. "But you tell the new guy to remember the fucking clips."

"Aye, aye, sir." Xavier brings his hand to his head in a salute.

"Can you stop being an idiot?" The corner of my lip turns up.

"I don't know. Can you stop being a dick?"

"Probably not," I answer truthfully.

"Then I can't stop being an idiot either." He shrugs.

I let out a sigh. "Get back to work."

"Sir! Yes, sir!" he chants, saluting me once more. This time I do laugh. Before I've gone too far Xavier says, "Oh, Wyatt?"

"Yeah?"

"You know you can call her. She'd come back."

I stare at him, unsure how to respond.

Moments pass and I don't say anything and walk away.

"Hey, how'd it go?" I ask Ethel when she gets back from her appointment.

"Good. You know, just getting all that yearly girly stuff done."

"Um, I don't know, and I don't want to know about any of those procedures."

She hangs her coat on the hook on the wall. "So the guys tell me that you've been quite the jerk today."

I scoff, "Hardly. I'm not going to coddle my employees like you do. It doesn't mean I'm a jerk. They need to grow the fuck up."

"You know, I had dinner with her last night."

I rip my focus from the papers on my desk and whip my head up, narrowing my eyes. "Why?"

"Because I love her and miss her."

"You love everyone, but you're not out on dinner dates every night. Why do you have to go out with her?"

"Just because you ran her out doesn't mean that I'm going to end my relationship with her. She's a good girl. She called and wanted to get together. She misses the dogs, you know. She wanted updates. I'm pretty sure she misses everything about this place…and everyone." Ethel's pointed stare in my direction doesn't go unnoticed, though I pretend it does.

"For the record, I didn't run her out. She chose to leave. There's a big difference. I am who I am, E. I can't be someone I'm not just to make her stay."

"You are who you are, but few see that side. Most see who you pretend to be." She stands beside the desk now. Her arms cross over her shirt that has a plaid cat flying a hang glider.

"Cats can't be plaid, for the record," I gripe with a glower at her shirt.

"They also can't hang glide. What's your point?"

I push my chair back and stand. "What do you mean who I pretend to be?"

Ethel presses her pointer finger against her lips several times in thought. "I think you push people away before they can get close to you because you're afraid to lose them."

"Seriously, don't you own any non-cat shirts?" I glare, irritated by her dumb attire.

"She told me about that kiss." Ethel raises her eyebrows.

Yep, not going there.

"And you know what, the new guy forgot the clip. I have a right to be a jerk about that. They have to learn that's not acceptable."

"She also told me about what you said to her in high school. That really hurt her, you know. She's very self-conscious about coming from money and wanting to be a good person despite of it."

I tap the desk. "I think Xavier is talking back too much. I get that we're friends. But I'm still his boss."

"She said you're the best kiss she's ever had." Ethel puckers her lips and opens her eyes obnoxiously big.

I throw the papers on my desk into the top drawer. At the same time, Cooper decides to wake from his slumber on the couch and peer toward Ethel and me with one ear cocked up as if he's listening.

"Have you checked on Luna today? Do you think that cut on her neck is healing okay? It's looking kind of puffy to me, like it might be infected." I step over to the cabinet we keep the medicine in to check if we have antibiotics left.

"One of her friends contacted her about going to Africa with a church group to help build wells and schools. She's thinking about going."

I pick up a box of antibiotics. "We should probably just start her on another round. It can't hurt. Then if she is getting an infection, it can clear it up."

"I don't know that she'd be back if she goes. Her family doesn't live here. She just happens to be staying with a friend. That's the only reason she's in Michigan."

Cooper hops off the sofa and stretches.

"Remember we have that donation drive on Saturday. You're still free to come with me, right?"

"She said that she doesn't believe in true love. That made me feel sad. I know that the love I had for Earl was real. He was the only man I ever loved." Ethel walks around petting all of the cats who lounge lazily in their cat trees.

"Can you set up another adoption event for these damn cats? I'm sick of them being here." On cue an obese orange one rubs his body against my leg, purring. "Read the body language, man. I'm not the one you want. Go to her." I point toward E.

"I don't think I believe her though." Ethel scratches a tabby cat's butt as he sticks it up in the air for her.

Cats are so weird.

"I mean, surely this fat thing," I nudge the orange cat with my foot, "would be happier in a home. What cat wants to live in an office?"

"Nope, I definitely don't believe her," Ethel shakes her head. "I know she loves you."

I freeze as the air leaves my lungs.

"What?" I ask in disbelief.

"I don't know why, really," she continues. "Surely it's not your charm. But sometimes love is like that. It's a connection thing. You can't explain why it's there. It just is."

"She said she loves me?"

"Not in those exact words, but in many other words she did. You just have to listen to hear it."

I groan, "Let me guess. She said, 'I need a new jacket' and you translated that into 'I'm in love with Wyatt.'"

Ethel laughs, "No, not like that."

"Like what then?"

"I can see it. I know she does." She picks up a black cat that's trying to crawl over to her. She holds the cat in her arms, stroking his dark fur. "And I know you love her, too."

"Alright, now you're just being crazy." I grab the medicine log book to record the pill I'm about to give Luna.

"I love you, Wyatt, like my own. You know that. But I have to be honest, you're about as hard headed as they come. That girl is good for you. For some crazy reason, she loves you. Don't take too long deciding what to do about that because she's going to be gone, and you're going to be alone." She sets the black cat down and starts toward the office door.

"I like being alone," I say to her back as she walks away.

"No one likes being alone," she calls over her shoulder.

"I do," I argue. "And you do realize that there's a plaid cat's ass on the back of your shirt?" The cat on the front of her shirt is also on the back, as if one is looking at him coasting away. There's a big cat butt and the underside of the glider as it soars away.

Where in hell does she find this crap?

After she's gone, I turn to Cooper. "I'm not alone anyway. Right boy? I have you." I ruffle the fur on his head.

I think about Georgia moving away and I admit that it doesn't sit well with me, but it is what it is. Ethel's wrong, though. There's no way that Georgia could possibly love me.

And Georgia's right. There's no such thing as true love. If there were—Georgia wouldn't be mine.

FIFTEEN

GEORGIA

"I don't need to be tamed—I love being free.
I simply want to be seen."
—Georgia Wright

"Africa, really?" London's face is displayed on the screen of my cell phone as we chat.

"I don't know," I say with a sigh. "It sounds good. There's definitely a need. Do you know that some women carry giant pitchers of water on their head for miles? It's literally miles to the closest clean water source for some of these people. Can you imagine?"

"But you promised Mom and Dad that you'd stay in the States."

"And I have."

"It's been like three months, George," London laughs.

"Well, I'm bored and sad. I miss the dogs."

"Then go back."

"I can't."

"You can. You're just too stubborn."

She's right. I could return to Cooper's Place. I know they'd take me back. They can use the help. But it's weird now.

"Go volunteer at another shelter," she suggests. "That place isn't the only one that needs help. In fact, I'm sure there are rescues down here that would love your help. Come stay with us."

"I don't want to go to another one. It wouldn't be the same. Plus, I'm not staying with you and Loïc. You need your space."

"We have plenty of space."

"You know what I mean."

Newlyweds that are trying to conceive don't need a permanent house guest.

"You don't have money to travel to Africa anyway."

"I do. Dad's been giving me an allowance from the trust fund to pay for my expenses here. I've been getting way more than I need. I have plenty for a plane ticket and living expenses over there. I don't need much."

"How do we come from the same family?" London sighs with a grin. "You could look for a real job, one that uses your degree and pays you a salary. That might be fulfilling?"

"I don't want to. I'm not like you. I don't need fancy things or a big house. I like being free. Helping others makes me happy. I hate that I have a huge trust fund in my name. It makes me feel guilty. I'm at least going to take advantage of my resources and put my time to good use."

London knows all of this, so does my entire family. Yet I seem to have to explain my choices to them every couple of months. They love me, but they don't understand me.

"Someday, you'll meet someone that'll tame your wild spirit. Then you'll settle down. Until then, it's fine to travel around. I envy you in that way. I just worry about you. I want you to be safe."

"I know you do. I don't need to be tamed—I love being free. I simply want to be seen."

"I see you." There's concern in her voice. "I know you, George, and you're right—you're perfect the way you are. I just want you to be happy."

"I am, or I will be." I glance outside at the dreariness. "Maybe I just need some sun."

"Oh my gosh, yes! I always feel blue that last month of winter when it's almost like sunshine and warmth will never come again. That's one bad thing about Michigan."

"Definitely. Anyway, enough about me. Let's talk about you."

"You sure you want to open that can of worms? I'm a bit of a hot mess at the moment."

I smile. "Yes, please. I need your mess to distract me. Spill it."

London tells me of her fertility woes and stresses of life and marriage. I welcome all of the details. I'm sad for my sister and wish she didn't have to go through this. Though, the distraction of someone else's life problems is a nice change. I spend too much time wallowing in my own stuff.

I don't need Wyatt or his rescue. I literally have an entire world of people I can help. Starting with my sister. I doubt I'll have any harrowing words of advice. Yet sometimes one feels better by having someone hear them. I can do that. I can listen.

My arms wrap around my knees as I hold them close to my chest. When one can't find the answers in life, there's always a Netflix binge. I'm currently engrossed in a new-to-me show, and it's intense.

I'm glad my sister's not here. I've bitten off the tips of all of my nails. I know it's a disgusting habit. I only do it when I'm really anxious, and this show is making me nervous. It's so good.

I jump with a yelp when there's a knock.

Chill, Georgia.

It's just someone at the door. Pressing pause, I throw off the blanket and make my way to the front door.

My jaw drops when I open it and see who is on the other side. I quickly recover and close my gaping mouth.

Wyatt stands on the front porch. Cooper stands at his side, his tail wagging and tongue hanging out of his mouth. In Wyatt's arms is Mila, my miracle puppy.

I'm so excited to see her that the shock that Wyatt is also here is momentarily forgotten. I immediately take her from Wyatt's grasp and hold her to me, kissing her soft fur.

"It hasn't been that long, and she's so much bigger already," I say.

"Yeah, they're going to be ready for adoption in a couple of weeks. I thought you might want to have her. I know she's one of your favorites."

I step back from the doorway and invite Wyatt and Cooper to come in out of the cold. With Mila still in my arms, I kneel down and pet Cooper who returns the affection with some doggie kisses to my face.

I head into the living room. Cooper and Wyatt follow. I sit on the couch with Mila. She becomes extra squirmy, so I let her down to explore.

"You know, she's probably going to find a place to pee," Wyatt warns me. He takes a seat in the oversized chair across from me.

I shrug. "Good thing we have wood floors." Then I look to him. "What are you doing here?" He looks down as if there's something fascinating on his shoe before lifting his head and locking his eyes with mine. "I don't know, honestly."

"I can't adopt Mila," I respond to his comment from moments ago. "I'm moving soon. I can't take her with me, unfortunately. I wish I could. I don't have a stable enough life for a pet right now."

"Where are you going?"

"Africa, I think."

He bobs his head in acknowledgment.

"Okay, well, good." He drops his palms to his thighs and stands. "Sorry to bother you. We have to go." His tone is firm and his words short.

I follow him into the kitchen as he looks for Mila.

"Wait," I say on an exhale.

He turns to face me.

The room is silent, save for our breaths. In the background, there's some rustling in another room. I'm sure it's Mila ripping apart something, as that's what puppies do. But I don't care to investigate. I'm frozen, locked in Wyatt's stare.

I can't believe he's here, and if I'm truthful with myself, I don't want him to leave.

"Why did you come here?" I ask him again, taking a step in his direction.

He shakes his head and takes a step forward, lessening the distance between us even more. "I don't know."

"Tell me," I breathe out. My heart beats wildly in my chest. It hasn't been that long since I've been in Wyatt's presence, and yet my emotions are running rampant. I'm terrified that he'll leave, and I'm equally afraid that he won't.

His eyelids close. I can almost feel the internal torment radiating from him.

When he opens them, his eyes lock with mine. "I don't know what to say, Georgia."

I swallow my nerves and breathe in some courage. "How about the truth?"

He forces out a chuckle. "I don't know what that is."

"You do. It may be hard to find, but it's in you somewhere. You merely have to have the strength to say it."

His head falls back with a groan. "I hate this."

His fists squeeze at his side, and I can see his chest expand with labored breaths. I'm not sure what's going on inside of him but he's feeling something, and I have to know what it is. I have to.

"All right, listen. I'm going to ask you a yes or no question. Say the first answer that pops into you head. Don't overthink it. Just answer immediately."

His eyes narrow and his lips press into a line.

"Just do it," I tell him, my voice pleading.

"Okay," he agrees reluctantly.

My questions fall from my mouth in rapid succession. "Yes or no. Do you want me to come back to work?"

"Yes."

"Do you miss me?"

"Yes."

"Do you have feelings for me?"

"I don't know."

"Do you want to kiss me?"

"Yes."

My chest tightens, and I bite my lip. "Kiss me."

There's hesitation in Wyatt's eyes. His gaze darts to my lips and back up again. His lids close and he pulls in an audible breath. When he opens his eyes, they're darker, sure, and full of need. He takes one more step and circles his arms around my waist, pulling me into him.

His body is so strong against mine. It feels warm and I melt into it. The way I want him makes me feel weak. But I can't stop the attraction I have. He's like sunshine heating me despite the vast cold that surrounds me. I can survive without him in the cloudy, frigid winter. But it's so much better in the light.

His lips move hesitantly at first—seeking permission, wanting more. Raising my arms, my fingers thread into the soft hair at the nape of his neck. A mix between a sigh and a moan leaves my mouth. It's a sound of relief and that's all the encouragement Wyatt needs.

He kisses me hard now. His fingers dig into my skin and the desperation I feel makes me frantic with need. Our hands explore one another over our clothes—kneading, pulling, grasping. The countertop presses against the small of my back as Wyatt leans into me. Our lips haven't separated as each of our tongues worships the other.

Wyatt's desire is evident as the firmness of it presses into my belly making my knees weak.

His lips leave mine and they work their way down my neck. I push my pelvis into his, needing relief.

"Yes or no. Do you want me?" I pant, hoping Wyatt tells me what I know to be true.

"Yes," he sighs against the skin of my neck. Goosebumps erupt over my entire body. "Yes."

Grabbing the hem of his T-shirt, I pull it over his head and drop it to the floor. He mirrors my action and does the same to me. His stare burns my skin as he slides down the straps of my bra and gently kisses my shoulders.

I splay my hands against his abdomen. The ridges against my palms make my heart beat faster with lust. Pushing him back, I undo the button of his jeans. His chest rises and falls as I pull down his zipper.

He makes quick work of removing my bra. When his mouth covers my nipple, my head falls back with a moan. It's almost a pained sound because the pleasure is so intense, it's approaching unbearable. I need Wyatt more than I've needed anything in my life.

He sucks and pulls as my hips push into him. My hands grab at the skin of his waist, drawing him into me. Dragging his teeth along my nipple he tugs, stretching it out until he releases it. I whimper.

Dropping to his knees, he pulls down my yoga pants and thong. I step out of the fabric leaving me naked and completely bare to him. He slides his hands up my body, searing me with his touch before he drags them back down my skin. He drops his head back and captures me with his gaze. My chin to my chest, I can't take my eyes away from him.

Wyatt isn't one for many words, but I see him just the same. I always have. My eyes water as I stare into his because there's so many unspoken words that I feel down into my soul. Without a sound he requests access and I nod, desperate for him to touch me.

He lifts one of my legs and drapes it over his shoulder. I close my eyes, dropping my head back as he begins to explore, first with his fingers and then with his tongue. My head explodes with pleasure, and it's all I can do not to crumble. Wyatt fills me with his fingers as his tongue drags against the perfect spot. It's a slow worship, at first. My hips involuntarily rock into his mouth, needing to be closer.

His tongue picks up speed, and the surge of pleasure starts building, more intense now. I'm out of my mind. Heated sobs exit as I cry into the lust-filled space. The explosion starts in my toes then shoots upward until my entire being is bursting with bliss. Wyatt pushes me over the edge and I fall.

I succumb completely to the experience, taking in as much as my body will allow. I want it all. My knees buckle and I feel myself going down, but Wyatt holds me up. He lifts me into his arms as my body hums with the aftershock of gratification.

I don't have the strength to open my eyes as he carries me out of the kitchen.

"Is this yours?" he asks, his voice hoarse.

I crack an eye open to see my bedroom.

"Yes," I whisper.

Wyatt lays me down on the bed and removes his jeans.

"Do you have condoms?" he asks.

I point toward the top drawer on my night table. I open my eyes to see Wyatt covering his length with a condom and I'm immediately on fire once more. I've never seen anything more beautiful than Wyatt's naked body.

Holy hell.

He's atop me now, his arms against the bed on either side of me. The tip of his length is against my opening, his stare burning into me.

"Are you sure?" he asks.

"Yes. Please," I plead.

Wyatt enters me in one quick movement and we both groan.

"Fuuuck," Wyatt cries out as he thrusts into me.

He pushes my legs back. Grabbing my ankles, he holds my legs on either side of my head. I'm completely open now, exposed to him, and when he pushes into me, I feel him so deep it aches. I cry out as he picks up the pace, hitting me harder and harder within.

I grasp at the sheets as my body desperately chases its release.

Wyatt growls my name, and the carnality in his voice sends me over the edge. He slams into me once more and holds me to him as our bodies quake in pleasure. His back is slick with sweat as my hands cling to it.

After we've come down from our orgasms he rolls off me. We both lay on my bed, faces toward the ceiling—our breaths still coming out hard.

Suddenly, I'm very aware that I'm lying naked next to Wyatt, my first crush turned asshole.

Crap. I just had sex with Wyatt.

I pull the sheet that's scrunched in a ball at the bottom of the bed up and cover us. So many emotions race through my mind. I feel like crying and smiling all at once. What does any of this even mean?

"Wyatt?" I say hesitantly.

"Yeah?"

"Will you kiss me?" The question comes out before I can stop it. For some reason, I need the connection of his kiss. I need to know our actions of a moment ago weren't a mistake.

He doesn't answer. Instead, he rolls over on his side. He reaches out then pulls me toward him. Then, slowly, he presses his lips against mine.

A tear rolls down my cheek and I don't even know why.

Wyatt's kiss is soft and sweet. It's over quickly. He doesn't move away, our faces are a breath apart.

He studies me and I him—searching for answers.

"You regret it. Don't you?" he asks.

"That depends."

"On?"

"On what happens next."

"What do you want to happen next?"

"Wyatt, I can't give you the answers. You're the one who is always pushing me away. I need you to figure that out for yourself."

Despite my best efforts to detest him, I feel something real for Wyatt. If I'm being honest, I always have. I shouldn't—I know this. I've seen how toxic we are together, but I can't stop wanting him. More importantly, I can't stop hoping that he'll want me.

His blue-eyed gaze is gentle as it roams over me, taking me in—his eyes examine my face making my breath falter. He's looking at me like he used to back when we were both so young. I've dreamt of this stare—deep, beautiful, and all Wyatt.

He doesn't have his guard up or his jerky persona. Right now, I'm staring at the boy who stole my heart years ago. At this moment, I have the Wyatt I've always held a vacancy for in my heart regardless of how many times I tried to fill it.

He swallows hard. "I think about you all of the time." He sighs, "I fucking dream about you almost every night. Even when I thought I hated you, you consumed my thoughts."

"Thought? As in past tense?"

He shakes his head, "I don't hate you. God, probably the opposite. I don't know. You have to realize that people have let me down my entire life. So when those assholes told me all of that shit about you, I believed them. I was wrong to, I know. But the fact that a beautiful, kind, popular girl liked me didn't fit into the narrative of my life. What those jerks said about you did. The fact that I liked you so much and was so hurt jaded me—against people, against you. I've held so much anger toward you for so long, and it's been hard to admit that I was wrong." He lets out a dry chuckle. "I'm kind of stubborn."

"Yeah, I see that. You know, what you said to me hurt, too. I've resented you for a long time."

"I'm sorry," he tells me, and I know that he is.

"But when I see you and how kind you are to others when you think no one's looking, the things you do for so many, the way you help those who can't help themselves—I know that you're the same person you were. Actually, no—you're better."

He kisses me lightly on the forehead before laying back down. "I'm not good at this stuff. I don't let people in." His voice is full of defeat. "I have a really hard time trusting people, and because of that I'll probably always be alone."

"No, you won't. You're too good of a person. You're impossible not to love. Maybe you don't see it, but I do. Ethel does. Others too."

I scoot up next to him and wrap my arm around his middle, leaning my head on his chest. "No one can promise forever. Stuff happens. But don't you think there's something between us worth exploring?"

He doesn't answer, so I continue, "I feel this pull toward you. Even when you were a total grump, I wanted to be by you. Do you feel it too, this connection? Or is it just me?"

He scoffs, and if I were looking at his face, I know he'd be wearing a smile. "It's not just you."

"So then what?" I ask.

"Will you come back to work?"

"Depends."

"On what?"

"On what else?"

"What do you want me to say? Do you want to like hang out and stuff?"

I laugh and sit up, pulling the sheet up around me. "You're really bad at this aren't you?"

"I told you I was."

"Will we be exclusively hanging out?"

He nods, "Yeah."

"Okay, I can do that." A cheesy grin spreads across my face followed by one from Wyatt. His smile gets me every time.

Realization dawns on me as an image of the blonde, scantily dressed woman flashes in my brain.

Oh crap!

"Wait. Don't you have a girlfriend?"

Wyatt looks confused. "No."

"What about that blonde chick from the club?"

His lips purse as he thinks for a second before realization dawns. "She's just a friend."

"With benefits?"

"No, Peaches. Just a friend."

"So you just pick up your drunk, barely dressed female friends from the club often?"

"If they need me to."

"To what? Take them home to play *Scrabble*?"

"Not usually. We're more into *Monopoly*," he smirks.

I hit his arm. "Wyatt, I'm serious."

"She's one of my childhood friends. She needed help and I helped her. That's all. I'm many things, but a liar isn't one of them. You can trust me to be honest with you."

"Okay."

He grins, "But I'm kind of liking this jealousy thing. It's kind of hot." He grabs my waist and pulls me onto him.

I shake my head. "It is not."

"With you, it is. Though, you're pretty gorgeous regardless."

"You're pretty gorgeous, too. I've always thought so."

Wyatt's eyes darken and I feel the familiar pull deep within my gut. I toss the bed sheet to the side and throw my leg over his pelvis to straddle him. Leaning down, I kiss...my boyfriend? My Wyatt? It doesn't matter what I call him, he's mine. This kiss is different than any other we've shared. There's no underlying insecurity. I'm utterly certain that this is where I'm meant to be, with my lips on his.

Wyatt kisses my neck and I release a sigh of pleasure.

"Full disclosure," he says between kisses. "That puppy is probably shitting all over the house."

I giggle, "I don't care. I'll clean it up."

His lips kiss across my collarbone. "She's also probably chewing a hole in the couch and destroying your phone charger."

"All replaceable." I moan as his mouth covers my nipple.

When I slide down onto Wyatt's shaft we both vocalize our pleasure.

"Fuck, Peaches. You're perfection. Where have you been all of my life?" Wyatt's voice is all gruff and husky as he grabs my hips to control the pace.

I know his question is rhetorical, but I answer anyway.

"Trying to make my way back to you."

SIXTEEN

WYATT

*"If God wants to make up for all the shit I've
been forced to live through, Georgia would be
a fucking amazing apology."*
—Wyatt Gates

"*D*on't forget that Daisy, LuLu, and Santa Baby
need their meds before you leave. The log is on
the filing cabinet," I tell Xavier as I fuss with a
lock on one of the kennels that's been sticking.

"Seriously, dude. Go," he huffs out.

"I know," I snap. "I'm just making sure that—"

Xavier cuts me off. "You're not telling me anything I don't
already know. I've been here a long time. I know how this all
goes. You're just being your control freak self. Give it a rest for
one night. You have a pretty girl waiting to take you on a date.
Go. Stop being a pansy ass."

"Hey, I said I was taking the night off. I never said anything
about a date." My need to keep my private life private is strong.
I've never shared much of anything with anyone, except for
Ethel, but that's only because she's too nosy for her own good…
and I love her.

Georgia's been back at the rescue a week now and I thought we'd been discreet with our relationship. Whatever is going on between Georgia and me is still new to us. I'm not ready to have the opinions of all the guys here regarding it.

It's been good, though. It's different for me, being in a relationship. I'm still hesitant, afraid that the ball is going to drop any day. Georgia reassures me that it won't. She's turned down her friend's offer to go dig wells in Africa. She says she's content right here with me and the rescue.

"I'm not blind, man. Seriously, it's like you think you're all suave like James Bond. You're not James Bond."

"Who said anything about James Bond?" I ask with a glare. "I'm just going out. That's all."

"Fine. Whatever." Xavier shrugs and places the clip on the kennel I was just fussing with.

I walk toward the exit before turning back. "Make sure everyone knows to remember the clips."

"Go away already!" he yells back.

"This floor could use another mopping, too," I suggest.

He pretends to ignore my instruction. A sly smile crosses his face. "Remember, no glove no love," Xavier orders.

"Stop."

"Sock that wang before you bang."

"What is wrong with you?" I stare.

"Cover your stump before you hump." His voice is sing-songy and he wears an obnoxious grin.

"I'm leaving." I turn the knob.

Right before the door closes behind me, I hear, "You can't go wrong if you shield your dong."

"Asshole," I mutter to myself, my lips turning up.

"Hey, that's quite the greeting." Georgia stands in front of me on the small cement patio at the entrance of the shelter.

She places a hand on either side of my shoulders and stands on her tiptoes, planting a peck on my lips. It's still uncomfortable to kiss her like this. Not that I don't enjoy her lips on mine—of course, I do. I just have to remind myself that this is real. I'm dating—I guess one would call it—Georgia Wright. I recognize that she was never the person that those boys made her out to be back in high school. She's never deserved all the hatred I've thrown her way. Yet it's still odd, and I have to constantly remind myself of the current situation.

"Sorry, that was directed toward Xavier," I tell her. "So what do you have planned for this secret date?"

"I just want to take you out to have some fun. You're always so serious."

"I am serious. It's kind of a personality trait," I say truthfully.

"I know. You're all work and no fun, but everyone needs some fun sometimes. Right?"

Images of the entertainment we participated in the other night flash through my mind. I would definitely enjoy myself if we were to have that sort of fun again. I feel myself getting hard beneath my jeans and I have to quickly think about something else. I clearly don't date much, but that doesn't mean I have to behave like a pubescent boy.

"All right. Well, let's get in the truck, and you tell me where to go."

Georgia directs me to drive into downtown Ann Arbor and park in one of the structures. She threads her fingers through mine as we start walking toward University Avenue.

"We're here!" she says excitedly as we walk through the door of Pinball Pete's. "Have you ever been?"

"Can't say that I have."

Surveying the space, Pinball Pete's seems to be an old-school arcade. There are standing game machines everywhere. I spot *Pac-Man*, *Donkey Kong*, *Tetris*, *Frogger*, and *Rampage*. There are pinball machines lining the aisle and rows of ball games along the back wall. The place is full of beeps, dings, and bells.

It even smells old, reminding me of the scent of a vintage bowling alley. I remember attending a classmate's birthday party at a bowling alley right before my dad was shot, and it smelled just like this. It's the only time I've ever been bowling, and I can still remember it so clearly.

"Isn't this great?" Georgia asks, her voice full of enthusiasm.

"Yeah, it's cool."

"I was reading up on it. There're very few retro arcades left. I thought you'd love it."

We stand in front of the quarter machine, insert money, and each get a bucket full.

"Which game is your favorite?" I ask her.

She looks around. "I haven't really played any of them before. London and I weren't really into video games. Which one is your favorite?"

My lips turn up. "Honestly? I don't know if I've ever played any of these."

"Are you serious? You've never played *Pac-Man* or..." she scans the names of the games, "...whatever other popular games are in here?"

"No. After my dad died and my mom...well, you know...we didn't have much money. I never played any of these or had any of the old gaming stations, either. I didn't have money until I was older and by then I had other things to spend my money on. I guess I missed the whole gaming buzz."

Georgia's shoulders slump. "I took you on the worst date ever." She pouts out her bottom lip.

"No, it's very thoughtful. I love it. Just because I didn't play when I was a kid doesn't mean I can't learn now, right? Come on." I grab her hand. "Which one should we start with?"

"I feel like *Pac-Man* is the most popular. At least that's the one I've heard about the most," she says.

"Well, we are the blind leading the blind here, aren't we?" I let out a chuckle.

"Look! There's a girl *Pac-Man*."

"You try it first," I tell Georgia as we approach *Ms. Pac-Man*. She sits down on the stool and inserts two of the quarters into the slot.

The game starts. "Okay, so there are balls," she says.

"Move the joy stick. I think she eats them."

Georgia moves the stick and the yellow creature with the big mouth starts chomping on the balls.

"There are colored ghosts," she exclaims. "Do you think they are friends or foes?"

"I'm guessing they're the enemy."

"But what if they give me more power or something. Like a super charge."

"A super charge for what?"

"For eating more balls."

I let out a loud laugh. "I don't know, Peaches."

"I think they're…" she drives Ms. Pac-Man into the blue ghost and she dies, "…crap, they're foes."

I tell her to try again, and she puts more money in. This round she's careful to run away from the ghosts and not toward them.

"There's a bunch of cherries!" She steers clear of the fruit. "Do you think they're bombs or something?"

"Maybe, but I kind of feel like cherries are good for you."

"I think they're going to kill me, just like the ghosts." She jerks her hand against the controller to move quickly away from a group of ghosts in pursuit. "Shoot, the only way to get past the ghosts is to go through the cherry."

"Well, try it."

She steers Ms. Pac-Man through the cherries and points pop up.

"Oh! It gave me more points! Yay! What do I do with the points? Shit!" She sighs as she dies in the game. "Stupid ghosts."

"Maybe we should Google the rules to the games before playing?" I suggest.

"No way, that's cheating. We need to find out just like we would've had we played these games in the '80s."

"We weren't alive in the '80s," I remind her.

"That's true, but I'm sure there were still arcades around in the '90s, too. Weren't there?"

"I could Google it?" I arch an eyebrow.

"We're so lame," she giggles. "All right, your turn."

We make our way through the arcade playing any of the games that look fun. We make up rules that probably have nothing to do with how the game is actually played.

"Look, there's a princess and a giant monkey. I think you need to rescue her," Georgia tells me as my little man climbs a ladder. "Watch out for the suitcases he's throwing at you. I'm pretty sure those will kill you."

"Why would he throw suitcases at me? I think they're oxygen tanks. They look like the ones you use scuba diving."

"Why would he throw oxygen tanks at you?" she asks.

"Maybe they blow up?"

"They're barrels," a guy next to us says dryly.

Georgia and I both look toward him, but he doesn't take his eyes off of the screen of the game he's playing.

I shrug and turn back to the game. "What do you think those things are in between the ladders? A fire extinguisher?"

"Or a light switch that he needs to turn on? I bet the monkey hates light," Georgia suggests. "Oh, or a bomb. Maybe you should avoid those too to be safe."

"It's a hammer, and you want it," the dude next to us mumbles causing us both to laugh.

We're clearly not *Donkey Kong* experts. Heck, there's not a game in here that Georgia and I know how to play. Yet, oddly enough, I'm having fun. I find myself laughing more than I ever remember doing.

I don't know when exactly I turned into such a moody asshole. I don't recall always being this way. I was different when I was younger, when hope still existed in my heart. But, somewhere along the line, I changed. Perhaps it was gradual or maybe it wasn't. All I know is that I don't have any memories of feeling this light—this happy. Being with Georgia stirs up all of these emotions that I thought I was incapable of experiencing.

Life has a way of jading a person. Then, a door is opened, and a breath of fresh air enters, filling my lungs for the first time.

When she walked into my office a couple of months ago for the first time, I thought I would choke on the stubborn resentment that I held toward her. I was beside myself with rage wondering why this girl who had caused me so much grief was coming back into my life.

She was even more attractive than she had been in high school—the quintessential girl next door with her rocking body, long, wavy blonde hair, and hazel doe eyes that are always greener than they are brown. She was too gorgeous for her own good. I hated her for being beautiful. I hated her for hurting me. I hated her for coming back.

It's pretty pathetic that my own obstinate rage blinded me to what was standing right in front of me the entire time. She's always been kind. Georgia's always been exactly what I needed her to be, but I couldn't see her because I was blinded by self-loathing and sadness.

I realize now that Georgia's my air. She gives me oxygen—allowing me to breathe in deep for the first time. I didn't even know I was suffocating in the first place, but I was.

This relationship thing between us is new, and unfamiliar, so I force myself to play it cool. But deep down, she's always been the girl that held my heart whether my pride allowed me to admit it or not.

And now she's here. I've held her and touched her. I've been inside her. I've cherished every part of her body and she is mine. It's surreal really, so very mind blowing, but that's life.

"Grab the light switch." I shoot a look to the guy beside us and correct myself before he can. "I mean the hammer," I say to Georgia right as a barrel falls on the little dude's head on the screen and she dies.

"Stupid monkey. He's an ass. Isn't he?" She turns and wraps her arms around my neck.

"Definitely," I agree.

I kiss her softly, pulling her bottom lip out as I lean I away from her.

"I saw some type of bowling game over there that looked fun," she tells me.

"Lead the way."

We grab our small buckets of quarters and close in on the "bowling" game, which is actually called skee ball. This place is fun, but it makes me realize how different both of our childhoods were from others. I was working side jobs in an attempt to make money to feed myself and take care of my drug addicted mother while other kids were playing video games and going to birthday parties. Georgia was sipping lattes in Rome or getting manicures at a spa instead of going to bowling alleys or bouncy houses with friends. Our histories, vastly different, though unusually sad at the same time.

Georgia jumps up and down with excitement when her ball lands in the small hole at the end of the aisle labeled one hundred. "I got it in the hundred." She claps with excitement as a string of tickets shoots out of the machine. "I got tickets!" She snatches them up. "What do you think you do with these?"

"I saw a counter with prizes and stuff. I think you cash them in for something."

"Oh my gosh. This is amazing. We need to get more tickets!"

My lips turn up in a grin and I shake my head as I watch her bite her lip in concentration trying to get the ball in the big numbered holes. Every time one of her balls lands in anything she cheers. I insert quarters into the skee ball machine beside her and work on earning some more tickets for her. The two of us spend the rest of our change playing this game.

With empty quarter buckets and a handful of tickets, we head over to the prize counter and are instructed to insert our tickets into the ticket counter.

"A ticket counter. That's fun," Georgia says wide eyed. She then excitedly places the tickets into the counting machine. When all of our tickets are entered, the machine prints out a receipt that says 237 tickets.

"Two hundred and thirty-seven. That's a lot. Let's go see what we can get!" She pulls me over to the prize counter, and the arcade employee shows us our options.

"Are you freaking kidding me?" Georgia says with huff. "We literally put at least thirty dollars of quarters into that game, and all we won are two small packages of fruit snacks?" She holds the small square packages in front of me, her lips turned down.

I can't help but laugh. It turns out that 237 tickets is in fact a very low number here at Pinball Pete's. Our options were fruit snacks or a pencil.

"We could've bought thirty, twelve-count boxes of fruit snacks for thirty bucks. Seriously, what a rip-off. If we wanted a tiny bag of chewy sugar we could've had…let's see, thirty times twelve is…" she works on the math out loud, her eyes looking up to the ceiling. "Well, thirty times ten is three hundred, then thirty times two is, what? Sixty? So three hundred plus sixty is three hundred and sixty." She takes a breath. "We could've taken our money and purchased three hundred and sixty packages of fruit snacks!"

She holds the two small packages in front of my face, emphasizing our lack of prizes. I snatch one from her. "Eat your fruit snacks. You worked hard for them," I chuckle, tossing a red gummy candy into my mouth.

We walk out of the arcade and cross the street. "So what's next?" I ask her, actually excited to see what else she has planned. She was adamant about planning a fun date for me. I was resistant at first because it knocked my man-pride down a few notches, but an arcade was something I would've never planned, and it was a blast.

"There's this place that everyone around here raves about. It's called Bubble Tea. Have you ever been?"

"Can't say I have."

"Well, you pick out the flavor of tea you want and I think there are juices you can choose, too. Then you pick out what gummy you want. It's right here." Georgia leads us into the building.

Her description is pretty accurate. We literally pick out flavors of both the liquid that go in our cups and the gummies, which are in the shape of round little balls or stars. The concoction is mixed together and put into a cup with a wide straw, the circumference broad enough to suck up the gummies at the bottom of the cup.

"Another first?" she asks me with a giggle as we hold our bubble tea in hand.

"Yep. You?"

She nods and places her lips around the straw. I do the same, and we both taste our tea. It's weird because the sweet liquid hits my tongue first and then the lumpy gummies enter my mouth. I slide the gummies to my cheek so I can swallow the tea and then I chew them up. It's super sweet and sugary. The different flavors of the juice and candies conflict with one other.

I finish my first gulp and wait for Georgia to finish hers. She's sliding her tongue around her teeth, evidently trying to remove the gooey gummies that have gotten stuck there.

I press my lips together in a line, trying not to laugh as she struggles to rid her mouth of remnants of the gummy candies. "So what do you think?"

She tilts her head in thought. "Um, it's interesting."

"What do you think?"

"Honestly?"

She nods.

"It's vile."

"Oh my God, right?" The volume of her voice raises and it's almost shrill. "It's so bad. I'm feeling nauseous."

"It's way too sweet and weird," I admit.

"What's the big deal with these globs of gummy crap in the bottom? Honestly, it's like sucking up boogers. It literally makes me want to vomit."

I laugh so hard that my side hurts. Georgia wipes the tears of laughter from her eyes and scrunches up her face as she throws her bubble tea into the trash. My cup of crap follows. We look to the long line of customers waiting for their bubble teas and shake our heads.

"I don't get it," I say, grabbing Georgia's hand as we walk out.

"I don't get it either and all they serve is that tea. Look at that line. I read that this place was popular, but I truly don't understand why. Who could drink that?"

"I have no idea," I grin. "Not us, apparently."

"I'm so sorry," Georgia says, her voice low.

"For what?" I ask as we walk hand and hand down the busy Ann Arbor sidewalk.

Georgia stops walking and turns to me. "I guess I suck at planning dates. I wanted to do something super fun that you'd love. I take you to an arcade when you've never played arcade games and then I try to kill you with that cup of sugary mucus."

"Are you kidding? I can't remember the last time I've had so much fun. I don't think I've laughed that hard in my life, Peaches. In fact, I feel like a bit of a fraud because the fun we've had today isn't me. You're going to start liking this version of me and be sorely disappointed tomorrow when I'm a grumpy ass again."

Her lips tilt up and her hazels shine with joy. She shakes her head. "I adore all of the versions of you. Even when you're grumpy. I actually find your serious side kind of sexy." She bites her lip, her gaze drops to my mouth before returning back to my eyes.

"Oh yeah?"

She tilts her head down in a nod.

Raising my arms, I hold onto either side of her face and kiss her hard because I can't kiss her any other way in this moment. I'm so crazy for this girl, it's insane. She's kind, beautiful, fun, sweet, and holy shit do I want her—all of her.

Loads of people pass us as we stand kissing in the center of the sidewalk, yet I don't even notice them. I only see her, my Georgia.

Is she mine? I'm terrified to ask. If God wants to make up for all the shit I've been forced to live through, Georgia would be a fucking amazing apology.

When my lips pull away from hers, she keeps her eyes closed for a fraction of a second longer and simply smiles. She looks tipsy when her eyes find mine. I know how she feels. I find her intoxicating, as well.

"I planned dinner, too," she says with a dreamy sigh.

"Do tell."

"Well, everyone seems to rave about this local pizza place called the Pizza House. But I don't know if I trust the locals' opinions anymore after the drink of death."

I run my thumb over her cheek before dropping my hands from her face. "I've actually been to the Pizza House, and the hype is legit. It's good."

"Finally." She sounds relieved.

Hand in hand we walk to dinner and I try to play it cool. Yet the reality is that I can't believe this day with this girl is happening. It's been wonderful, and perfection isn't part of my reality. I simply need to calm that inner voice that's saying it won't last. Everyone's bound to find the good, even in me. Shit knows, I've had enough of the bad to last a lifetime.

SEVENTEEN

GEORGIA

"I see Wyatt—the beautiful and the broken—
and I love all of him."
—Georgia Wright

I'm not sure when the smell of bleach, wet dog fur, and the faint aroma of urine started to feel like home, but somehow it now does. Over my travels, I've lived and worked amongst all sorts of smells, some worse than the others. Some scents carry such vivid and scary memories with them that when I catch a whiff of anything similar, it takes me back to the time and place where the memories originate. I can close my eyes and imagine being there.

No matter where life takes me, bleach, wet fur, and dog urine will always bring me back here, and I hope when I think about Cooper's Place—I'll smile. Goodness knows the grin I'm wearing now is evidence of the pure happiness I'm feeling here.

"I want to go alone," I repeat, and Wyatt looks to me uncertain.

"Are you sure?" He cocks an eyebrow. Sitting across from me, he holds five playing cards in his hands.

"Yes, I can do it," I nod, not completely confident in my new *Euchre* skills but kind of sure. Maybe.

Oh no.

"She said she wants to go alone. Put down your cards, boss man," Xavier tells Wyatt.

Wyatt puts his hand of cards face down on the table. "Let's see what you've got, Peaches." He shoots me a wink causing my cheeks to flush.

Wyatt and I are teammates against Xavier and his girlfriend Luciana. The work day is over and the rest of the employees have gone home. Luciana brought tacos from her parents' restaurant and the three of them are trying to teach me how to play *Euchre* as we sit around a card table in Wyatt's office.

When I told them that I'd never heard of *Euchre*, they insisted on teaching me, claiming it's the best card game there is. Apparently, it's really popular in some of the Midwestern states, especially in Michigan. Xavier seriously gasped when I told him that I'd never heard of it.

"What's it going to be?" Xavier asks.

"Hearts," I tell him.

He chuckles and looks to Luciana. "Hearts it is."

"Hey, no table talk." Wyatt narrows his eyes toward our opponents.

Xavier raises a hand in surrender. "Dude. I didn't say a thing," he replies, his lips turning up in a smile.

Wyatt purses his lips together and keeps his eyes narrowed on Xavier causing Luciana to giggle.

"Okay, babe. Your turn," Wyatt tells me. I pull an ace of spades from my hand and lie it down on the table.

Xavier is next and sets down a ten of hearts, taking my ace. "Oops, sorry," he says sarcastically and takes the cards. He then lays down the jack of hearts, which forces me to lay one of the two hearts I have.

Another three cards are laid on the table, and Xavier and Luciana take them all. Since I called the hearts and didn't win, they get extra points.

Wyatt throws his head back and the most beautiful laugh comes from his lips. He's laughing more than I've ever heard him before. It makes me so happy.

"Peaches, why on earth did you go alone and call hearts when you only had two crappy ones?" he questions.

I bite my lip. "Well, I had a couple of aces in other suits, so I thought I was good."

"You had a shitty hand," he tells me. "An ace won't do you a bit of good if douchebag over here," his thumb cocks toward Xavier, "has a hand of trump, which you named hearts even though you didn't have either of the jacks. Remember the jack of hearts and diamonds would've been crucial to have if going alone." He smiles warmly at me and I know he's just trying to get me to understand this game, which I find very confusing.

"Yep, horrible hand," Xavier says.

Luciana nods in agreement, though she's too sweet to say it out loud.

"I suck," I admit with a sigh.

"You'll get it." Wyatt rubs my thigh. "Just don't go alone for the time being." He winks.

"Deal," I agree.

Luciana shuffles the deck, and I pick up one of the puppies that sleeps in my lap and kiss him. He yawns and breathes his puppy breath onto my face. Puppy breath…another scent that will always connect me to Michigan.

The sting of my epic suckage at all things *Euchre* is softened by the fact that I get to snuggle with sleeping puppies while playing. Dating a guy that owns a shelter has it perks.

We play for a couple more hours and because of me, Wyatt and I lose every time. It doesn't seem to bother him that I'm not picking it up easily. In fact, he's smiled more than his normal grumpy self. I love when he smiles. He's incredibly handsome always, but that smile of his—gets me every time. Xavier and Luciana say their goodbyes and head home for the night.

I put the puppies back with their mother and plop down on the office couch, lying across it. Cooper licks my hands as they dangle off the edge. Wyatt sits down at the end of the sofa and places my feet in his lap. He removes my tennis shoes and rubs my feet over my socks. I groan in pleasure.

"That feels amazing," I tell him with a sigh. My eyes closed, I relax. I'm startled when a fur ball jumps onto my chest, purring loudly as he nuzzles into me. "Geez," I say to the feline that so rudely interrupted my quiet time.

"This one's new," I say to Wyatt. "Actually, we have a few new office kitties, don't we?"

"They're Ethel's," he says. "We're cat sitting them while she visits family."

"Oh yeah, I forgot to ask where she was today. Where's her family?"

"I have no idea. I didn't know she had much family. I think she has some cousins in Florida?"

"She went to Florida? How long is she going to be gone?" I'm glad she's taking time off, but I feel bad that I didn't wish her safe travels. "She didn't tell me she was going anywhere. I would've said goodbye."

"I'm not certain she went to Florida. She's been weird lately. I try not to ask too many questions."

I reach down and pat his arm. "You should ask questions. Show her you care."

"She knows I care."

"I know she does but still. Sometimes we have to go out of the way to show the ones we love that we love them."

"I promise you. She knows I love her."

"Okay, just saying." I stretch my arms out over my head with a purr as Wyatt moves his adoration over to my other foot. The orange fluffy cat snuggles against my side. "This one's sweet," I say of the cat.

"Yeah, so I'm told. Ethel calls him Pumpkin."

Wyatt finishes massaging my feet and stands. He holds out his hand for me and I grab it. He pulls me up off of the sofa. "Come on, let's go home," he says.

My breath hitches at his request, particularly the word, *home.* I don't know why, it's stupid. I know he's not implying anything by it, but my heart rate quickens just the same.

Wyatt must notice my reaction because he clarifies, "My home. Do you want to stay over at my place?"

I smile wide, reassuring him that he didn't say anything wrong. "Absolutely, let's go."

I jolt awake, my entire body stands on edge. I blink, adjusting to the darkness around me. My heart still races from the nightmare I just escaped from. It takes me a moment to remember where I am.

"Wyatt's," I whisper to myself, exhaling a relieved breath. I sit up and lean against the wooden headboard. My fingers grasp onto the soft linens beneath me and release as my raged breaths calm.

I hate dreams like the one I just woke from, the kinds that are so real and so scary that I'm terrified they'll pull me under so far I won't be able to wake up.

You're good. I tell myself. *You're good.*

The moonlight shines in through the window falling onto Wyatt's bare back. I study him as he sleeps, so peacefully, his ridges of back muscles showcased in the soft glow. He breathes softly and I can't get over how incredibly beautiful he is. It's a regular thought of mine. I'm always catching myself admiring him, stealing glances while he works, studying the way he cares for others, now—apparently watching him sleep.

Sometimes I feel like the seventeen-year-old girl that could barely breathe in his presence while feeling giddy that the cute boy is talking to me.

We're doing so much more than talking now.

My stare lingers over the thin sheet covering his ass, and I know very well what it's hiding. Memories of earlier flash through my mind and I shiver. We're so compatible, Wyatt and I. Our bodies fit together so incredibly that I want him all of the time. I've never experienced this type of connection with anyone else in my life. I crave Wyatt when he's not near.

We're nothing alike, truthfully, but I think that's why we work so well. Separate, we're good—but together we're great. We fit together like two imperfect puzzle pieces clicking together to make the most stunning picture.

He's quiet, where I'm loud. He's reserved, and I'm forward. He loves softly and I love out loud. He internalizes his fears and pain, where I have to release them—crying more often than I should.

As much as we're different, we're the same—cut from the same cloth. We're both sensitive and caring to the point of heartbreak. We look at the world as something we can make better. We see a problem and attempt to fix it. We give everything to those we love. We have opposing deliveries, but the intent is the same.

I watch him as an overwhelming feeling of love fills me. I think I love him. We've only been dating a couple of weeks, but I think I loved him before all of this—if that's possible? I thought I've been in love before, but I know now that I haven't. I've adored traits of my boyfriends of the past, whether it be their love of travel, human rights efforts, or the adventure they brought me. But I didn't love any of them completely, as an entire package. I chose what to see in them that I liked and I ignored the rest.

That's not the case now. I see Wyatt—the beautiful and the broken—and I love all of him.

I cherish him.

I want him.

Every piece of him. So desperately, it terrifies me.

"Hey," Wyatt's voice heavy with sleep breaks my thoughts. His hand reaches out for mine.

"Hi."

"Are you okay?"

I nod. "Yeah, just a bad dream."

"Come here," he beckons softly, opening the sheet in front of him.

I slide down, turn toward the window, and scoot my body back into his. He adjusts until his body melds with mine perfectly. His skin is warm and smooth against mine. I push back into him a little more. He covers us with the blanket and wraps his strong arm around me, holding me tightly to him.

I sigh as he gently kisses my bare shoulder before laying his head back down. He holds me so close. I feel so protected, cherished, and warm. Lying in Wyatt's arms is like heaven—completely perfect. My eyes close, and my lips turn up. I absorb his breaths as his chest rises and falls against my back. Sleeping here with Wyatt brings me such a sense of comfort and security. I drift off to sleep thinking of his kind heart, beautiful blues, and strong hold. Right before slumber pulls me under, another sensation surfaces. It's brief and gone before I can truly decide if I felt it at all. In the space between heartbeats the unsettling feeling of being trapped emerged, but then the next beat of my heart came and it was gone.

EIGHTEEN

*"The way everything has played out makes me
think that there's another power at play—as much as
I don't believe in it, fate keeps coming to mind."*
—*Wyatt Gates*

*G*eorgia's arms drape around my neck. "I'm going to go get the room ready for the adoption interviews."

"Okay."

We're alone in the office, well, besides a snoring Cooper and too many slumbering cats. I'm still not a fan of public displays of affection, especially here. So we've tried to keep our new relationship on the downlow. Though, we're not very good at it. I should say, Georgia isn't very good at it. She's such a loving person by nature. I, on the other hand, have practiced keeping others away for my entire life. She's one person I'm no longer capable of keeping at arm's length.

"You sure you want me to do this on my own? You wouldn't be more comfortable if you or Ethel sat in with me?"

I shake my head, "Nope. You're ready. It's a perfect job for you. You're way more of a people person than I am. Plus, Ethel's running late. You're now here full-time and all of a sudden she becomes lazy."

"Hey, she's not lazy," Georgia chastises.

"I know. I'm just kidding."

"She deserves a few hours off here and there. She works so hard, and truthfully, she should be retired. She's only here because she wants to help you."

"She won't retire. She's too stubborn."

"Well, there's a lot of that going around." She stands on her tiptoes and kisses me.

It's just a quick peck at first, then it deepens, as it always does. Georgia's lips are irresistible. If I didn't have a rescue to run, I'd be kissing them all of the time.

She pulls away. "I have to go get ready. They're going to..." I capture her mouth with my own. My tongue delves deeper wanting to savor her. She steps back with a sigh, "I really have to." She points toward the door.

"Fine," I grumble.

"Later," she promises.

"Later."

Cooper wakes, lifting his head from the sofa to check everything out. "Do you want to help, Coopie?" she asks Cooper in a high-pitched voice, the kind that people tend to use when speaking to dogs for some reason. He jumps off the couch and prances out of the office behind her.

What a traitor.

I smile.

"I do love that sight." Ethel startles me, jolting me away from my Georgia daydreams. "Wyatt Gates is smiling."

"Whatever." I turn toward the desk.

"It's about time. I'm so giddy I can hardly contain myself."

"Well, please try," I say dryly. "By the way, nice of you to show up."

"I told you I'd be late. This lady needed some time to herself."

"That's fine. Take as much time as you need." I look to her and notice that she looks more tired than usual. "Everything okay?"

"Everything's perfect," she smiles.

Ethel has been over the moon since Georgia came back to work, even more so now that we're a couple. It's been a little over three weeks since I showed up on Georgia's front porch with Mila and Cooper hoping to fill a void that I couldn't explain. I didn't know what I had hoped to accomplish when I showed up at her house unannounced. But I knew I needed something. Deep down, I knew I needed her.

As much as I tried to convince myself that Georgia was no one important since high school, she's never vacated my mind. It's seems so silly that a girl I flirted with, copied off of in biology class, and shared one kiss with could have such a staying power in my mind. But she has. The way everything has played out makes me think that there's another power at play—as much as I don't believe in it, fate keeps coming to mind.

Our relationship is just shy of a month, and I'd be lying if I said I still don't have insecurities. The demons of my past continue to rear their ugly heads and make me doubt everything. Then one look from Georgia brings me back from the darkness.

Despite what she says, I'm not an easy person to love. Yet she's always here patiently loving me.

"Sit." Jasper, one of our Bully mixes, complies with the command immediately. "Good boy," I tell him as I give him a treat.

I work with the adult dogs to make sure they're all trained in basic commands and manners before they're adopted out. Pit bull-type breeds are loveable and sweet, but they're also very strong. An untrained dog is often like a bull in a china shop. They already have a bad stereotype. I don't want to risk one jumping up on their owner because they're excited and accidentally knocking them down. I can't prevent all mishaps from happening, but if I can stop someone from getting hurt by their excited pet, that's one less negative story about this breed out there.

I'm setting him up for the "stay" command when Georgia enters.

"Hey, how did it go?" I ask. She's been interviewing potential adopters all day.

"Good. Really good. Pending the home checks, three adults and four from Hope's litter have found homes."

She tells me a little about the dogs that were chosen and what their new owners are like. Her face lights up as she speaks of the kids that are going to be able to grow up with their new four-legged family member.

"Isn't it great when the families have kids? I would've loved to have a dog growing up," I tell her.

Her mouth falls into a frown, and her bottom lip begins to tremble. Her eyes fill with tears. "What is it?" I rush toward her and pull her into my arms.

She shakes her head and continues to cry into my chest. Putting my hands on her arms, I hold her back so that I can see her face.

"Please tell me. What is it?"

"Well," she sniffs. "The last couple that I met with chose," she sucks in air between broken sobs, "Mila."

There's so much sadness in her eyes. I know how she feels. It's impossible not to love all of these dogs. It's very difficult when one you've built a special bond with leaves. I've gotten better at letting them go over the years, but I remember how much my heart hurt in the beginning.

"I'm sorry. I know how hard this is."

She hugs me tight, pressing her cheek against my chest. "I love her so much. I can't imagine not seeing her every day. She's our miracle puppy."

"I know. It's tough to let the ones you love go. You have to think about how you played a part in finding her a forever home. You loved and cared for her while she was here. You helped save her. Now she's going to go to a good home with a family that will adore her. That's the best thing we can do for our dogs."

Georgia nods, "I get it, but she's mine. From the moment she was born, she's been mine. I was so stupid. I should've adopted her while I had the chance. Now, it's too late. I don't know what I'm going to do without her." My arms wrap around her back as it heaves with sobs.

I hold her as she cries. I'm not sure there is a solution to a broken heart, other than time. Jasper catches my attention in my peripheral as he sits just as I left him.

Wow. What a great dog.

When Georgia's tears cease and her breathing steadies, I kiss her on the forehead and release my hold on her.

"Feel better?" I ask.

"No," she huffs. "It sucks, but I'm hungry."

I chuckle, "Well, we can't have that. We definitely need to get you some food."

"Yes, please," she says softly.

"Let's put Jasper away." I grab a handful of treats. "Do you know that he sat perfectly that whole time? He's awesome. We should look into possibly putting him into some sort of therapy dog training program."

"That would be perfect. I can do that," she says.

"Okay." I turn my attention to Jasper and give him his treats while rubbing his head. "Good job, boy. Good job," I tell him many times.

Holding my hand at my side, I say, "Come." He follows on command.

"What are we doing after dinner?" she questions.

"I'm not sure. Why?"

"Can I stay the night at your place tonight?"

"I was hoping you would," I admit.

"Okay. I was thinking that maybe I could bring Mila, too. We can hang out all night, and snuggle, as a goodbye."

"You don't think that will make it harder on you?"

"Probably." Sorrow lines her voice. "But I still want to."

"It's your call."

She slides her fingers through mine as she walks beside me. Normally, I wouldn't allow us to hold hands in front of the guys. The display of affection feels out of place here at work. But I don't mind now. Georgia's sad, our connection provides her some peace. It's surreal that I have the ability to give someone comfort. I'm not a bad person, I know that, but I'm never in this position. I've never felt this way for someone and had those same feelings reciprocated.

I just feel good. For the first time in a long time, I'm completely happy. Each morning when I wake up next to Georgia is like the first time. I simply stare—convincing myself that she's real, that we're real.

I'm not the praying type, and yet I find myself constantly beseeching a higher power to make her stay, to make us work, to make what we have truly real.

One thing that's always rang true for me in life is that if it feels too good to be true, it's because it is. I just pray that this is the first time where that saying doesn't apply. I don't ask for much in life, but I'm asking for Georgia.

Selfish as the request may be, I need her to be mine.

NINETEEN

GEORGIA

*"There's never been a time in my life where every aspect
of it was perfect, but at this very second—I know what
it's like to exist amongst perfection."*
—Georgia Wright

blow my nose loudly into the tissue and grab another one to dry my eyes. I'm bawling uncontrollably over a TV show. My favorite character in my
new guilty pleasure is currently being murdered by the love of
his life.

Like, what the hell, writers?

"Life's not fair that's for sure," I say as I watch, my vision
blurred with tears, as he takes his last breath.

Since I've been with Wyatt, I haven't had time to continue
my TV marathon and today's a perfect day for it. Paige is out
of state visiting her boyfriend, and Wyatt's at the rescue working, like always. I'm usually there with him. I love being at the
shelter. But I needed to take today off.

Mila's adopters are picking her up, and I just can't be there
for it. The last thing the young couple that's adopting their first
dog needs is a blubbering mess tainting their experience.

My heart aches and I don't know if the pain will ever diminish. I blame myself. She could've been mine from the start if I could've committed.

But adopting her would've held implications I wasn't ready for. It would've bound me to a grown-up lifestyle, one where I wouldn't take off for another country on a whim.

"I'm an idiot," I say aloud to no one.

I let Mila go to another family when I know that no one will love her more than I do all because I'm afraid to settle down.

Why am I so afraid?

My passport sits on the end table beside my bed. It's a constant reminder of my ability to leave. Oddly enough, it gives me comfort. But why? I don't want to be anywhere else other than where I am. Yet I leave out items, such as my passport, that let me know that I could leave if I wanted to.

There's a knock at the door and then Wyatt's voice sounds from the foyer. "Hey, Peaches?"

"In the living room," I call back. I hastily pick up the barrage of snotty Kleenex that lie about and throw them in the trash in the kitchen.

I turn to find Wyatt standing under the archway of the room's entrance. He's holding a massive bouquet of flowers made up of different types in varying shades of pink. It's absolutely stunning.

"I brought you a present." He grins at me in the beautifully infectious way he does. I can't help but to smile back.

My entire face lights up. "They're so pretty. Thank you so much. This is so sweet of you." I take a couple of steps toward him, and he swings his arm to the side with the assortment of blooms in hand leaving his other arm in full view.

I gasp and bring my hands to my mouth.

My eyes fill with tears, but this time they are tears of utter joy. I look from Wyatt to the lump of cuteness in his hand. My Mila.

"How did you? What does this?" My thoughts are jumbled as I jog forward and grab her from him. Holding her to my chest, I rock and kiss her soft fur. She licks my face and I giggle.

"She's yours," he says.

My attention jolts up to Wyatt. "What do you mean?"

"She's yours. You've officially adopted her. You can keep her."

"I don't understand. What about the adopters? You didn't break their hearts did you?" I don't know why I care so much about the couple that wanted her. I should just be happy that she's mine. But I know it'd be wrong to take a puppy from them just because I want her.

"Well, I called them that night after you interviewed them. I told them the situation and let them know that it was completely their decision. They talked it over, and when they called back they told me that it was actually a relief that I had called because they left the rescue torn. They were having second thoughts about Mila because they also really loved her brother, Bo. They were going back and forth on whether or not they picked the right one. So they told me that you wanting her so badly was a sign, and they adopted Bo instead. They left today with huge smiles on their faces and Bo in their arms. They definitely aren't heartbroken."

I squeeze Mila tight, fresh tears fall to her fur. "That is like the most perfect story in the history of stories."

"Oh yeah?" he chuckles.

"Definitely. Thank you so much for doing this for me."

"Anytime." He winks.

Mila in my arms, I stare at Wyatt. I can't believe how much I love him. Even before we were together there was a part of me that knew I loved him, but if there were ever any shadow of a doubt, there's not anymore.

He's kind, giving, beautiful, and so good. He's one of the best people I've ever met.

I kiss Mila on the head and let her down. Wyatt hands me the bouquet, and I lower my face to the arrangement and breathe in. The scent makes me feel so many things, but mainly—happiness. There's never been a time in my life where every aspect of it was perfect, but at this very second—I know what it's like to exist amongst perfection. Obviously it's fleeting because a flawless reality isn't sustainable. But it's here now and I'm going to enjoy the heck out of it.

I drape my arms around Wyatt's neck. "I love you," I say aloud for the first time.

His blues stare back at me, revealing so much. No response leaves his lips, but he kisses me. His mouth against mine, the connection is firm and sweet, then slow and heated all at once. He can't tell me how he feels with words, but this kiss utters it all. Every emotion that I'm feeling, Wyatt is feeling it, too. He doesn't have to tell me because I already know.

This is new territory for the both of us. We're scared, yet excited. We're enveloped in adoration for one another while burying our fears. Because, let's face it—there are worries. Neither of us has been in a legitimate long-term relationship that held any promise. We've both been hurt. We've both hurt others. We've both built a life designed to protect us against the insecurities of our past.

We're imperfect, that's for sure. Though, just maybe our flaws are what make us work.

Wyatt's lips continue to caress mine. They cherish me with every movement. They want me as they pull out my bottom lip. They need me as his tongue enters my mouth. They desire me as we walk to my bedroom, our lips never separating.

As Wyatt enters me, I feel it—his love for me. It's unspoken, but it's there. It's present in the way he looks out for and cares for me every day. It's there in the shy glances and hopeful smiles at work. He loves me quietly, and that's okay. If I'm being honest, I'm not quite sure if I'm ready to be loved out loud.

TWENTY

*"Money can buy pretty much anything, but they're
wrong when they say it can buy happiness."*
—*Georgia Wright*

I lie on my side in a bed at Paige's house. Let's be real.
This isn't my bed, my room, or my home. Have I
really ever had any of those things? A place that's
really mine? I've lived in more places than I can remember. I've
slept in twin beds, double beds, queen beds, king-sized beds,
cots, hammocks, and on the floor. None of those spaces were
mine. I was merely borrowing them until I had to leave again.

Even when I moved around as a child, not only did I get a
new house each time but I got a new bedroom set. Moving
furniture was an inconvenience to my parents. So they sold
each of their homes furnished and had new furniture set up in
our new home before we got there.

I've never really had anything that was truly mine. I was never
somewhere long enough to build friendships that would stand
the test of time and distance. Material things weren't important
because we just bought new. Money can buy pretty much anything, but they're wrong when they say it can buy happiness.

I wasn't anywhere long enough to secure roots into the ground. Without roots, a flower will blow away in the wind. And without the nutrients from the soil, a flower will die. I've been drifting my entire life, desperate to grow roots strong enough that they'll hold steady and keep me grounded. Sometimes, I think the only thing keeping me alive is the movement, is the wind carrying me, not letting me fall.

Yet I feel like I'm closer to finding a home than I've ever been, one where I could actually settle into and stay. So why do I want to leave?

Holding my passport in hand, I flip through the pages. This is mine. This passport and these experiences that make up my history—this is me.

I look at the stamps from all of the different countries in which I've resided. I've been all over the world. Each stamp reminds me of a time spent in a country where I did something good. Each experience fed my soul just enough to get me to the next.

I'm happy. I love it here. But I'm also terrified. I don't know how to do this. I don't know how to feel complete when I'm standing still. How is it possible to wear a big, authentic smile every day, be surrounded by love, and still feel alone?

Mila wakes from where she was napping at the foot of the bed. She crawls up to me and licks the tears from my face before snuggling in front of me, pushing her back against my front.

I kiss the back of her neck and wrap my arms around her middle. "Why am I always the big spoon. Huh?" I tease with a sad chuckle as I bury my tear-soaked face into the rolls at her neck. I know when she's a big girl she'll have grown into all of this extra skin, which makes me a little sad. I love her rolls so much.

I love her so much.

How can I think about leaving her?

"It wouldn't be forever. I'd be back," I say out loud, though I know she's no longer listening because her puppy snores fill the space.

Parents have to travel for work all of the time, leaving their kids for a little while. It'd be like that. I'd go just for a small span of time. She could stay with Paige or Ethel. Then I'd come back for her.

I justify the decision in my head because the truth is, I've already decided. I have to do this—for me. If Wyatt loves me then he will understand. If I can save one little girl or boy from a horrible life then it's worth it.

Mila will understand.

Wyatt will understand.

Everyone will.

They have to.

"Please tell me you're kidding!" Wyatt shoves each of his legs into his jeans and pulls them up with a jerk. Intense irritation lines his features—no, more than irritation—fury, and I hate it.

I want to go back to moments ago when he was worshiping my body with his, when his lips paraded over my sensitive skin making me squirm. I want to go back to the kisses, the moans, and the sensations that only he can bring me.

My body, still bare and heated from our lovemaking, misses his, and I pull the bed sheet up around me. The second I told him of my plans he bolted from bed, from our embrace…from me. I recognize that I waited until after we made love to tell him. His reaction isn't a shock.

"I'll be back. This is just something I have to do," I plead for his understanding.

"So you're leaving Mila? Just like that? You've only had her for a month! You're leaving me?" He grabs a T-shirt and pulls it over his bare chest. I mourn the loss of his exposed skin. He's gorgeous, and a piece of me wonders if I'll see him again without clothes. Will he be able to forgive me?

"I'll be back for Mila, for you. Kylie said they need me, try to understand."

"Who the fuck is Kylie? If her needs are so important to you, why is this the first time I'm hearing her name?"

"She's a friend. We met in China." I kick my legs over the side of the bed and grab my panties off of the floor and pull them up. "Colima has the highest human trafficking rates in Mexico, Wyatt. It's so sad. These young girls are taken and are abused, exploited, used…who knows what else. But their families never see them again. Can you imagine?" My words get caught in my throat. The sadness I feel for these girls makes my eyes water.

"And this Kylie person works for the government or some other organization with any sort of authority?"

"No, she's a human rights activist. She travels all over trying to help those in need."

He drops his chin in an abrupt nod. "Right. She sounds completely qualified." Sarcasm lines his voice. "Do you realize what kind of people work in sex trafficking? I'll give you a clue, not good ones."

He grabs his phone and starts frantically typing on the screen. "Here we go." He reads from his phone, "Colima, Mexico has the highest per capita murder rate out of the entire country. That's a fun fact. Look! It's been mainly taken over by drug cartels, producing a majority of the methamphetamines in the country." He taps his lips with his finger as he continues to scroll across his phone with his other hand. "We have more here about murders, kidnappings, drugs, cartels."

His face jolts up from his phone, his blues wide with anger, "Sounds like an amazing place for you to go hang out."

Fully dressed now, I stand and take a few steps toward him, attempting to close the gap between us. But every time I move closer, he moves away.

I throw up my hands in defeat. "You're not telling me anything I don't already know. Of course, it's a dangerous place. It's number one in human trafficking. It's only to be expected that there would be some other issues there. I'm not a stranger to dangerous situations, Wyatt. I've been to many questionable places. I'll be fine."

"You don't know that," he shakes his head, his eyes narrowed. "Please help me understand why you feel like you have to do this? I really want to get it, but I don't. To me, this is reckless and fucking stupid."

"I just feel like I have to. There's a need, and I can do something to help."

"What can you do? Get yourself killed? You're not the goddamned special forces, Georgia. You're just a girl."

I hate how my name sounds like a curse as it rolls off of his lips. I miss the jovial way he says his nickname for me. I can't stand this angry version of Wyatt I see before me. Sure, he's upset. But why can't he understand that this is important to me. This is who I was before I came here to stay with Paige. I'm not just going to change who I am.

"This is who I am. Why can't you understand that?" I plead.

"You're what? A person who puts herself in dangerous situations? Someone who leaves as soon as they start getting comfortable? Someone who's constantly running away?"

"I'm not running away!" I protest, my voice shakes with frustration. "I'm helping people. Someone has to help them."

He shakes his head, sadness fills his eyes. "What are you afraid of?"

"Nothing. I'm not afraid of anything. I just want to help."

"No, you're terrified, and that's why you're running." His chest rises, pulling in a deep breath as he bites his lip.

"I am not scared. Why would I be going to Mexico if I was?"

"You're scared of real life. Getting comfortable. Letting people in."

"That's not true. I let you in."

He scoffs, "No you haven't. Things between us are finally getting good. I've dropped my walls. We're happy, or so I thought. So now you decide you need to leave the country? One doesn't have to be a psychologist to figure you out. You're scared and now you're running. I was stupid for ever thinking you'd stay."

Wyatt throws open the door and steps over Cooper who was waiting right outside it. I follow.

"I'll be back," I say to him as he walks away.

Reaching the kitchen, he takes a glass from the cupboard and fills it with water before downing it all. The glass is set on the countertop. Wyatt leans against the granite surface and crosses his arms over his chest.

"I always knew you'd do this. I'm not sure why, but I felt you would. You were always going to leave."

"I told you that I'll come back," I say softly.

"When?"

I shrug, "I don't know."

"You might be back and you might not. Don't you realize that one of these little adventures of yours is going to get you killed someday?"

"I could walk out of this house and get run over by a car and die. I can't let fear of death stop me from helping, Wyatt. That's not who I am."

"There are countless people, right here, that need help. If you want to help stop human trafficking, Michigan is number two in the country, right behind Nevada. Think of that. Fifty states and you're living in number two. You can help here. You do help, every day. You save lives by rescuing dogs that would otherwise starve or be beaten or mauled to death." He shakes his head, "And that's not enough? Their lives aren't enough?"

"They are and I'm glad I can help, but now Kylie needs me."

Wyatt drags his palms down his cheeks. "I need you. I need you, Peaches. Please." Wyatt isn't one to ask for anything, and I realize how much he wants me to stay, but I can't live my life for him. I have to live my life for me.

"I'm sorry." I step toward him cautiously. I place my hands against his chest, over his heart, and he lets me. "I'm not doing this to hurt you. I love you."

"You can't save everyone in the world," he says, his beautiful blues beg me to see reason. "You can't. It's an impossible task, and you're always going to be searching for purpose, but you'll never find it. You're one person."

"I can try." I raise my shoulders in a shrug.

"You can't save the world, Georgia." His eyes glisten with unshed tears. "You can't save the world," he repeats and lets out a sigh. "But you can save me. Stay. Save me."

Standing before me is no longer the strong Wyatt that I know now, but instead, I see the boy that felt unwanted. I see Wyatt—young and scared—and it breaks my heart. I don't want to hurt him. I don't. But I can't stay for him.

Standing on my tiptoes, I press my lips to his. The kiss is short, only lasting a moment, but I hope he feels my love for him. I hope he trusts that I'll come back. Maybe, it's unfair for me to ask, but I want him to wait for me.

"I'm so sorry." I kiss him again. "So sorry." Holding his cheeks in my palms, I run my thumbs across his cheeks, the short, sexy stubble that resides there tickles my skin.

I'm going to miss this face. So very much.

"I love you," I tell him honestly because I really do. Maybe me leaving isn't the best way to show him that. Yet having to do something for myself doesn't take away what I feel for him. I've never felt for anyone the way I feel for Wyatt, ever.

He doesn't respond, so I say it again, "I love you, Wyatt."

"When do you fly out?" His voice is so low, it's almost a whisper.

"Tomorrow." Regret taints my answer.

He grabs my wrists and calmly pushes me backward, allowing himself enough space to step away from me. He snaps his fingers, and Cooper is immediately by his side. The two of them walk toward the back door. He snatches his truck keys from the counter as he leaves.

Right after he opens the door, he turns to me and says, "Have a nice flight." Then he slams the door behind him.

Grief overwhelms me, and I have an awful feeling that I'm never going to see Wyatt again. Yet my resolve to leave remains.

There's a part of me that hates myself and questions everything. But then there's that part that knows I'll go anyway.

There's a big part of me that misses Wyatt so desperately that it hurts even though I've only been away from him for mere seconds.

There's a part of me that knows I'll never forgive myself if I lose him forever. Then there's a part that recognizes that I will never love anyone the way I love him. And as I drop to my knees and cry on Wyatt's kitchen floor, that's the part that hurts the most.

TWENTY-ONE

GEORGIA

"Traveling the world has always been my therapy."
—Georgia Wright

"I can't believe you're really going," Paige says, standing in my room as she holds Mila.

I'm checking over my suitcase, making sure I have everything that I need. Not knowing how long I'll be there or what exactly I'll be doing makes packing hard. Yet, traveling as much as I have, I know the must-have items. Most things I can buy, but some things are only found in the United States, like my favorite deodorant. I pick up the deodorant in my toiletry bag and check it.

Crap, it's almost out. I rush to the bathroom to see if I have a new one in the drawers.

"Success!" I cheer holding the white container of deodorant over my head like a trophy before tossing it into my suitcase.

"Are you sure about this?" she questions again for the hundredth time.

I ignore her question as I've done the other ninety times she's asked. "So I left lots of food for Mila. I bought her extras of her favorite toys. I stocked up on puppy pads. I got her a new bed, but you know she's going to want to sleep with you," I chuckle. "I left an envelope of cash for you on the kitchen table. It should be enough to cover anything she needs, plus a boarding facility if you have to travel and leave her. And you know that the dog place right down the road will take her during the day while you're at work. It's like a puppy daycare where she can play with other dogs. I know it's an extra stop in the morning for you, so if you don't want to I understand. But there's plenty of money to pay for it, and she'd really love it. She's going to miss going into the shelter every day and playing with the other dogs," I ramble nonstop.

Paige holds up a hand. "Whoa, girl. Take a breath. Mila will be fine. But I want to know about you." She grasps my arm, making me pause to look her in the eye. "Are you sure about this? You don't have to do this."

I sigh, "But I do. I get that no one understands, but I have to go help. Now that I know they need me, I have to. It sucks that I have to leave Mila, and I'm sorry for doing this to you. But I have to go."

"What about Wyatt?"

"What about him?" I shrug, opening the drawers of my side table to confirm that nothing important is being left behind. "He'll wait or he won't. There's nothing I can do about it."

I'm leaning toward the latter considering he wouldn't answer any of my texts or calls after he left me in his kitchen last night. I guess I can't blame him. We've barely dated and now I'm leaving for Mexico for God knows how long. It could be months, a year, I have no idea.

"I'm worried about you, Georgia. London's worried. I thought everything was going well."

"It is or was." I close my suitcase and zip it up. "I'm not running away from anything. I'm simply going to help, to make a difference, that's all."

"I kind of thought you were making a difference here. I know the dogs you rescued sure thought you were."

"They'll be fine. They have Wyatt."

"You know what they say about the grass growing taller on the other side of the fence?" Paige asks, wrinkling her brow.

"You mean, the grass isn't always greener on the other side of the fence?" I correct her expression.

"Yeah, it's not greener on the other side, Georgia. It's greener where you water it."

I pull her and Mila into a hug. "I love you, Paige. I appreciate you looking out for me, but I promise I'm fine. Thank you for taking care of my girl."

I take Mila from Paige's hold and squeeze her to me. She snorts and nuzzles into my neck in that puppy way she always does. I kiss her head.

Tears fill my eyes. "Take lots of pictures of her. She's going to grow so fast."

If I regret anything, it's missing Mila's time as a puppy... well, and the way things were left with Wyatt, and leaving the shelter.

Nope. I can't start focusing on all of this now.

I hand Mila back to Paige. "The Uber driver should be here." I motion toward the door with a sad sigh.

"Okay," Paige responds solemnly.

I grab my jacket, purse, and suitcase. I kiss Mila one more time and hug Paige. "I'll call you and Skype with you and Mila. Okay? Don't worry about me."

Paige nods, and with my stuff in tow, I walk out.

New adventures always bring me so much excitement, but it's different now. As the driver pulls away from Paige's house, I just feel sad and I question everything. I'm leaving more behind this time—a roommate that I love, my puppy, Ethel, the rescue, the friends I've made…and Wyatt. It's a lot to lose. It's only natural that I'd feel blue.

I have to remind myself that the fulfillment I'll receive by helping others will feed my soul in ways that nothing else can. Traveling the world has always been my therapy. Not many people can just pick up and leave whenever they want for a mission trip but I can. It's a blessing—one that I've never taken for granted. I simply need to get there, and I'll feel better.

Frank, my Uber driver, is one of the chattiest people that I've encountered, and on any other day, I would've loved talking with him. But I'm too sad for words, right now. I lied to Paige just moments ago. I am running. I just don't know why.

Everything was going so well with Wyatt and me. He's opened up to me more than I ever thought he would. When I first got here, months ago, he was cold and bitter. Looking at how we were at the beginning of my time in Michigan and how we are now—or were just yesterday, it's unreal.

We both held so much hostility toward one another based on our different versions of history, though neither of us even knew the truth. And now, we're good—or were so good. *Ugh.* I hate thinking about Wyatt in past tense. Hate it. Yet I'm the one putting him there, in my past. No one's making me go. This is totally on me.

I know by going I'm ruining everything, but I can't stop. I thank Frank as he drops me off at the airport. I check my luggage and get my boarding pass. I walk through security. I wait and then I board the plane.

I can't stop.

I have to go no matter what.

Tears roll down my face as the plane takes off and I watch Detroit get smaller and smaller beneath me. I feel my heart shattering in my chest, the grief spilling from my eyes, and I can't stop that either.

I keep waiting for the electrified energy to hit me—the antici- pation, thrill, and nerves that I always feel. It usually starts on the plane, the rapid beat of my heart as I ponder the unknown. The out of place grin as I visualize the good I'll do is also ab- sent.

I anticipate it coming to me as I walk through the Mexico City airport to exchange my dollars into pesos, but it stays away.

The energy that invades my body on these trips fuels my soul. It always has. Growing up in a world like I did, one where I never fit in, always felt out of place, and filled with guilt— wasn't easy. Yet what I've been able to do with my life since leaving my parents after high school graduation has made me feel complete in a broken world.

As I board the small plane destined for Colima, the excite- ment still doesn't come. I'm kidding myself if I thought it would. I knew that this time was different. Even if I couldn't admit it, I knew that I was running away from and not toward my life. The reasons for this trip aren't the same as they usually are, and that's why the joy is absent.

I can't rationalize the internal struggle that's taking place in my heart. It's all new territory for me.

My smile stays at bay as the taxi drops me off at a small market. I run my fingers along the colorful fruit. The owner asks if he can help me, and I inform him I'm here to see Kylie. His lips turn up, and he directs me toward a door in the back of the market.

I tell him thank you and when I grin back at him—it's finally real. I feel so honored to be in the presence of a local man who's risking everything to help children. If anyone found out that he was housing our group, they'd kill him. And yet he looks to me with gratitude.

This man grew up in a country where his options were limited, and he's running his own business and helping save children. My heart swells in adoration for this beautiful human being.

Kylie pulls me into a hug and introduces me to the others. She catches me up on the developments as of late, and I half listen for all I can focus on is the sad blues staring back at me in my mind and I want to cry.

In a world where I can be anything, I've always chosen to be brave and kind. But, as of late, I'm neither. I'm a coward—plain and simple.

I excuse myself from the group and pull out my phone. I need to call my dad.

TWENTY-TWO

WYATT

"Loving Georgia was never a choice—it was a privilege—so ingrained into me that it came as naturally as breathing."
—Wyatt Gates

*M*y truck sits idle; the heater blows warm air into the cab on this chilly spring morning. I've been here in this same spot for over an hour now. There's a little dog in my lap resting his face in the crook of my neck. He's no longer shaking.

I found this little beagle mix this morning huddled in the corner of an alleyway—skinny and alone with tears leaking from his eyes. Some don't believe that dogs cry, but they do. I've seen it many times. I couldn't put him in the crate in the back of my truck. I knew he was scared, so I held him. I'm still holding him.

He's been neglected and abandoned, and it's clear that he's terrified. I want him to know that he'll be fine now. He doesn't have to be afraid anymore. I run my hand down his matted coat, showing him affection, which he probably hasn't felt in a long time. I'll need a shower when I get back to the rescue, but that goes with the territory.

It doesn't matter how long I've been doing this, my heart never ceases to break when I see a dog that's spirit is this shattered. I don't need to talk to a shrink to understand why I chose this line of work. Yes, Cooper was a big part of it. But it runs deeper than that. I see myself in these animals. I was once hungry, alone, and unwanted. My spirit was beaten down so many times that it took a long time to find it again after Ethel took me in off the streets.

Most of my life was spent praying for someone to save me, to protect me, to love me. Knowing what it's like to be truly alone isn't something most have experienced. Everyone usually has at least one person to love them. I know what it's like to have no one. This guy in my lap knows what it's like to have no one. It's not something any person or animal should have to experience.

My phone has been blowing up all morning, but I've since turned it to silent. I just need a moment of silence to breathe. I need to sit here, hold this little guy, and breathe because the truth is, I'm not doing too well either.

Georgia left a few days ago. I honestly thought she would change her mind. I believe that she feels something real for me, the same as I feel for her. Truthfully, I love her—down to my soul love her.

Loving Georgia was never a choice—it was a privilege—so ingrained into me that it came as naturally as breathing. Even now, when I'm so furious and bitter, I can't help but love her. As beautiful, kind, and special as she is—she's broken, full of insecurities, and demons that I don't understand. She's running, and I wish I could figure out why.

But it doesn't matter. She's gone. She made her choice. I asked her not to go. She left. That's that. I wasn't enough to keep her here.

I'm never enough. I feel more alone than I have in a very long time. Ethel's on another vacation. Carrie's in rehab. Xavier is my friend, but I don't feel comfortable spilling my pathetic guts out in the open for him to see. Cooper's here, as always. He listens to me groan and grumble every night, but let's face it—as much as he thinks he's a human, he's still a dog. It helps having him next to me, of course. But he can't bring her back either.

As much as I love Georgia, truth be told, I don't want her to return because I know she'll end up leaving again. I simply have to go back to living without her. I've been without her my whole life. I know that role well. It's sucks, but I can do it.

"What do you think, buddy? Ready to go?" I say to the pup. I set him atop the blanket on my seat. He leans into my side, and I put the truck into drive.

When I get back to the rescue, I take our new addition inside and hand him to Florence, one of our new workers who I came across living on the streets. She's been doing great here. She has a room in the house at the edge of the rescue's property that I use to house anyone who needs it. It's a large house, and many of my employees have a room there.

"You having a good day?" I ask Florence.

She nods and gives me a smile, half of her teeth are missing. I make a mental note to call around to the local dentists and see if any of them are willing to do some work for charity.

"I found this little guy this morning. Can you get a pen ready for him? Fresh bedding, food, water, toys…all the works. And please give him a bath once he's settled."

"You got it, boss man," she replies using the title that Xavier has obnoxiously given me. I wish she wouldn't call me that, but given the fact that every employee here does, thanks to Xavier, I don't bother correcting her.

I thank her and make my way to the office. Cooper greets me on the way, sniffing me everywhere to see where I've been. "I got us a new friend," I tell him, rubbing his big head. "You should go say hi. Florence has him."

Cooper goes trotting off toward the kennels. I know it's crazy, but I swear that dog understands English. Once in the office, I grab some extra clothes from the closet and step into the bathroom, locking the door behind me. I take a long, hot shower getting the smell of loneliness off me. Next time I hold the new dog, which I still need to name, he won't reek of desperation.

It never ceases to amaze me what a good shower and clean clothes can do for a person. Granted, my heart is still shattered. I'm consumed with rage over Georgia leaving, and I want to sink into a deep depression that I don't have time for. But at least I don't stink.

I toss my old clothes into the washing machine, careful to retrieve my phone from my side pocket before starting it.

Looking through my messages, I see an Ann Arbor number that has called several times. They must have an urgent rescue situation. I tap the screen to listen to the voicemail. A woman addresses me through the phone's speaker, but I'm finding it hard to focus on her words. She's stringing words together that make no sense.

Ethel.
ICU.
Critical.

The drive to the University of Michigan hospital seems to take hours when in reality it probably took fifteen minutes as I sped at least twenty miles over the city street speed limits. Finding a parking spot in this god-forsaken structure is literally taking forever, though. I'm on the verge of insanity. I've gone around and around this shitty parking garage for over a half hour trying to find a spot. I'm about to say, screw it, and leave my truck in the fucking aisle. Let them tow it.

Finally, I see the brake lights of a car getting ready to leave, and I put on my blinker. The car pulls out and some jackass in his little Honda Civic starts to pull into the spot. I punch the horn in the center of my steering wheel, holding it down. The sound echoes obnoxiously as it bounces off the cement walls that surround us. The dude looks up toward me, and I give him my *I will fucking end you* stare. Apparently he's not a complete idiot because he puts his car in reverse and vacates my spot.

It takes me a minute to find my way to the intensive care unit, but I finally make it and ask for Ethel at the front desk.

A nurse greets me and informs me that I was the only emergency contact that Ethel had listed. I ask questions, and she answers them. She tells me that Ethel had a double mastectomy, her words so powerful that I feel like I'm going to fall over from the sheer intensity of them.

Ethel had breast cancer?

Why didn't she tell me?

How long has she been fighting this alone?

I'm so angry that I can't see straight. I can't believe I wasn't there for her. My heart breaks for the woman that is the closest person I have to family.

The nurse continues, telling me that Ethel had a post-surgical complication, a large blood clot in her leg which broke off and traveled to her lungs, causing a pulmonary embolism. I don't know a lot about medical stuff, but I know that a pulmonary embolism can kill a person, and from what I remember, pretty easily.

My ears ring and my vision blurs as she talks about medicines, procedures, and complications. I can't focus on any of it, I feel as if I'm going to be sick. I need to see Ethel.

"I need to see her," I blurt out, interrupting the nurse mid-sentence.

She nods in understanding and I ask, "Is she going to be okay?"

"I believe so," she says, "barring any additional complications. She's still very weak and sore. She's on lots of medications that make her drowsy, and she's asleep now. But sleep is good. Her body needs to heal."

"I just want to sit with her."

The nurse leads me to Ethel's room and leaves me alone with her. I stand at the doorway and take her in. She sleeps soundly in the hospital bed. There are IVs inserted into her arms connected to bags of liquid on a pole by her bed. There's a machine that seems to be monitoring her heart rate and various other things that I don't recognize.

I walk over to her slowly, afraid to wake her. Pulling up a chair, I position it beside her bed, and I sit. She seems so different lying here, and honestly, she looks older than she ever has. It's a shock seeing her appear old and frail because that's never been how I've seen her. She's always so strong, full of life, and bold.

She's the hardest working person I know, and it's a childish notion, but I've never stopped to think about her dying, despite her age, because she's so full of life. I've never imagined what it'd be like not to have her. I've taken her presence in my life for granted.

I should've loved her more, stopped her from working so hard, and spoiled her the way she deserves. This woman is more of a mother to me than my own ever was. She loves me without the bonds of blood. She loves me because she wants to. She chooses me and my happiness every time and not out of obligation. She puts my happiness above everything because she truly loves me unconditionally, a feat that only she holds.

I've known this, but I've never stopped to think about the enormity of it. I've yet to take time to send my immense gratitude for Ethel into the universe. Most importantly, I haven't told her. She needs to know how very thankful I am that she loves me. She needs to know that I love her just as much in return.

If she were to leave me now, I don't know what I'd do.

I take her hand in mine. It's cold and almost lifeless covered in wrinkles that I've never seen before. I squeeze it, rubbing it gently to warm it up.

"I'm so sorry," I choke out. "Please get better. Please be okay. I love you."

I drop my head to the side of her bed, and I cry. My body shakes with sobs, and I don't try to stop them. I'm completely overcome with emotion, and I just don't know what to do. I feel so useless sitting here. I want to help her, but I don't know how.

I know one thing for sure. I'm not leaving her. She will wake up, she will be fine, and I will help her every step of the way.

My body grows tired, and I fall asleep with my forehead against her hospital bed, with her hand in mine, and grief weighing heavy on my heart.

TWENTY-THREE

WYATT

"Love doesn't change a thing.
People let you down just the same."
—Wyatt Gates

I've been sitting in this chair for sixteen hours, and she still hasn't stirred. Fear runs wild in my mind reminding me of all the things that could go wrong. I hate that she's not waking up. I've called Xavier to ask him to take care of Cooper and hold down the fort at the rescue while I'm here. He didn't even hesitate with his assurance that everything would be perfect when I got back.

I have to talk to him when I get back and let him know how appreciated he is. Sitting in a hospital room watching someone I love lie here, almost lifeless, has given me a lot of time to think, and I've made some realizations. First, I have to appreciate people in my life more. I always assume that they know how helpful or important they are, but sometimes people need to hear it. Ethel tells me all of the time how much she loves me and how proud she is of me. I've never questioned her love, and I figured she assumed that I felt the same way for her. That's not good enough, and I know it.

I'll do better. I'll be better. Something else I've come to realize is that I had no control over the environment in which I lived and the situations I was forced to go through. I was a child, and I did the best I could with what I had. But I'm not a child anymore. I can't go around sulking at the world because of the ways in which I was wronged. Living in the darkness of my past will never allow me to find the light here and now. The life that I make for myself now is my choice. If I fuck it up, that's on me. No more excuses.

"Why so serious?" Ethel's voice is hoarse and barely audible.

"How are you feeling?" I jump up and hit the nurse call button. "She's awake," I tell the nurses' station excitedly.

I hold her hand and bend down giving her a kiss on the forehead. "You have some explaining to do." I narrow my eyes in her direction, and her lips tilt up in a weak smile. "And I love you. Very much. More than you realize." I sneak in the last sentiment right before the nurse walks in.

I step out of the way as the nurse takes Ethel's vitals, checks her IVs, and medicines. When the nurse has convinced me that everything looks great, she exits the room.

I sit down next to Ethel. "I'm not going to yell at you because, well, I'd be a dick if I screamed at you in the ICU, but why didn't you tell me?" I say, sadness in my voice. "I'm so mad that I wasn't there for you. I'm furious that you've been going through this all alone. You almost died, E, and I didn't even know you were sick in the first place."

She pats my hand. "You've lived through more than enough in your life. I didn't want you to watch me get sick. I didn't want to burden you."

"What do you think family is for if not to burden during your time of need?"

Ethel chuckles softly.

"You should've told me. You have to give the people you love the chance to show up for you because you're worth showing up for. You are so loved by so many, and I know more than just me would've wanted to be here for you."

"I'm not going to be a burden, Wyatt. That's not who I am."

"It's not a burden if I want to help, and I do. I want to. Do you want to know who you are? You are the best thing to ever happen to me. You saved me, E. You saved me." My voice cracks with emotion. "It wasn't until I thought I might lose you that I realized how much. It's not fair of you to take away my choice to love you back. If something would've happened to you and I wasn't there, I would've lived with that guilt forever. You're not a burden. You're family. You're my only family."

Ethel's watery gaze remains on mine as the corner of her lip tilts up. "Okay," she nods, squeezing my hand in hers. "I'm sorry."

"So tell me everything," I urge. "When did you find out you had cancer? What type? What treatments have you been through? I want to know it all."

Ethel explains that she's been receiving chemo for a while. The mass in her breast was small and contained and it hadn't traveled to her lymph nodes. The chemo she was on wasn't extremely aggressive. The mastectomy was a precaution toward future breast cancers since apparently she carries a gene that predisposes her to it. Her prognosis is very good.

"So you're going to be around for a long time?" I ask a question that no one has an answer to. Nobody knows when their last day will be, but I want reassurance regardless.

"I'm going to be a pain in your ass for years to come," she grins.

"Good because I need you to get better and come get your damn cats," I joke with her and she laughs before raising her hand to her chest with a pained face.

"Don't make me laugh," she winces.

"Sorry," I mutter. "But seriously. We miss you. The place has gone to shit without you."

She shakes her head against the pillow. "That's not true. It has you. Everything that is good about the rescue is because of you, Wyatt. It was your vision that you've carried through to fruition. You are the smartest, most caring man that I know. With or without me, you will continue to do amazing things."

"I don't know about that," I argue, "but we miss you regardless. Even if you come back just to prop your feet up and relax on the couch, we want you back. It's not the same."

"How's my Georgia girl?" Ethel's smile is immediately replaced by a frown when she sees my face fall.

"She left," I say coldly, so much bitterness rises within me just at the mention of her name.

"What do you mean?"

"She left a few days ago for Mexico. She's going to help out down there now, apparently." Each word comes out with an air of annoyance.

"For how long?"

"I have no idea, E. The point is, she's gone, and I'd like to forget about her, now."

A low scoff comes from Ethel, and she taps my hand. "She'll be back. She's just working through some things. You'll see."

"I don't want her back. Enough people leave. I need someone who will stay."

"She's a good person, and she's good for you. We've all seen that. Just don't give up on her yet."

"I was stupid," I tell her. "I all but begged her to stay, and she left anyway. I feel like an idiot."

"Well, you wouldn't be in love if you didn't have moments of idiocy. It goes with the territory."

"Did you hear the part where I told you that she left? She's gone. So whether I loved her or not, doesn't matter."

She taps my hand once more and holds me in her stare. "Loving someone always matters. Love matters, Wyatt. Don't you forget that."

I let her have the last word on the subject, considering she almost died and all. Yet I know it doesn't. Love doesn't change a thing. People let you down just the same.

"So let's change the subject, shall we?" I ask her.

She's only awake for a little while longer. In that time, I catch her up on the dogs at the rescue and of course her cats. There's not much to tell her about them. They're cats—they purr, meow, and sleep. I try to get an idea of what type of assistance she'll need when she gets out of here. I have no idea what is needed when caring for a sick loved one, but I want to do it right. She made me promise to go home to eat, shower, and sleep. It's been twenty-four hours since I've eaten anything besides some graham crackers and juice that they have in the patient lounge outside her room.

I'm not ready to leave just yet. I have this irrational fear that if I leave her side something bad will happen, and I won't be here.

Ethel's right though. A shower, change of clothes, and food would do me some good. The nurses say that she's stable and set to be moved from the ICU to a regular post-surgical unit tomorrow if all stays well.

I lean back in my chair. Crossing my arms, I close my eyes. I'll head home in a bit. I'm going to sit here a while longer.

In my dreams, I hear her voice—soft and beautiful, as it always is. She's so real, I can smell the light scent of coconut and lime from her shampoo. I know I should block her out, think of something else. Yet I can't bring myself to. In sleep, I can pretend that she never left. In my dreams I can go on as if she's still here with me. When I wake, the reality that she left will weigh on me so greatly that it will be hard to breathe, like it has been every day since she's been gone. Right now though, I see her and I smile, for in my dreams I still love her. I still have her. I still want her.

When I wake, I'll let her go.

TWENTY-FOUR

*"The downfall about constantly moving
is not knowing how to be still."*
—Georgia Wright

"Wyatt?" I say his name again, softly as to not wake up Ethel. He stirs and for a moment I think he's going to wake up, but he doesn't. A faint smile crosses his tired face, and I wonder what he's thinking about it.

The image of the two of them in this room passed out from exhaustion is enough to break my heart, and the guilt that already consumes me is so great now that I'm not sure how I'll ever recover from it.

I left him. He begged me not to, and I left anyway.

Now, he's here at Ethel's side, and God knows what they've been through. The nurse wouldn't give me details since she couldn't verify that I'm family—as I told her I was—but the fact that they're here in the ICU indicates that whatever is going on, it's not good.

Remorse is a hard one to swallow because had I chosen differently—had I chosen Wyatt—this reality would be altered.

Maybe Ethel would've still gone through what she has, but I would've been here loving them both. Instead, Wyatt's alone. He should never be alone.

I confessed my love to him and then I abandoned him under the pretense of human rights. Yes, there are people in Mexico that need help. There are people all over the world in need. But Wyatt's right, there are people here in this city that need help, too.

I left because I was scared.

The downfall about constantly moving is not knowing how to be still. I've built more connections over the past four months than I have in my life. I've never felt more attached to a place than I do here. And, truth be told, it freaks me out.

I felt trapped, like I was suffocating. In actuality, nothing was caging me in but my own mind. I've never had to work through these feelings because I've never been in a location long enough to have them.

I have more to lose here than anywhere else in the world, and when the anxiety in my mind became too loud and flight or fight kicked in—I fled because I couldn't risk losing the fight. Choosing to leave behind the one I love is somehow easier to swallow than the chance that he'll leave me.

He gave me no indication that he had any thoughts of ending things between us, but I loved him too much to find out. I don't have the coping mechanisms for loss. It's ironic really, the girl that's been given everything doesn't have the strength to gamble on the unknown. Money can buy a lot of things, but clearly security isn't one of them. Love is always a gamble, and I finally realized that I'm never going to truly experience it unless I open myself up to heartbreak.

Wyatt shifts in his chair and briefly opens his eyes before bolting up out of the chair.

"What are you doing here?" he whispers, the animosity in his voice causes me to take a step back.

"I came back. I wanted to see you," I say sheepishly.

"Leave. I don't want to see you," he snaps.

"Listen, I'm sorry...I..."

He takes a hastened step toward me and grabs my arm, leading me out of the room.

"Go," he warns.

Tears fill my eyes. "Wyatt! Let me explain, please."

His stare leaves me to look back at Ethel, and when it returns to me, it narrows. "Be quiet. She needs her sleep, and I need you to leave. I have no interest in talking to you. You made your choice. Now go." He shoos me away with his hands. "Go back to Mexico, China, Russia, Australia, Brazil, or any other place you choose. Just don't stay here."

He walks back into Ethel's room, his footsteps heavy. I watch him as he sits down beside her and adjusts her blanket so that she's completely covered. Tears cascade down my face, and I stand out in the hall looking in. He told me to go, but my feet won't move. They can't move. Two of my favorite people are in this hospital room, and I can't force myself to leave them.

He's right to be angry. I was a coward. He's been abandoned and alone for most of his life and then I do it to him again. I would hate me too. I don't deserve his love, but I want it. I fight for others all of the time. It's as natural to me as breathing. Yet when it comes to standing up for myself, I falter every time, but not today.

I'm choosing to fight.

I'm choosing Wyatt.

I'm choosing uncertainty because the most important things in life are never guaranteed. He's here now, and I love him. If I lose him at some point in the future, at least I will have known what it was like to have him in the first place.

"I'm not leaving," I say into the room, my voice shaky. "I'm not leaving you, again."

I watch as Wyatt's shoulders sag and he runs his fingers through his hair, but he doesn't turn around to face me. He stays focused on Ethel, who's still sound asleep.

"I'm not leaving until you talk to me, Wyatt. Talk to me," I plead as a sob gets caught in my throat. I swipe my fingers beneath my eyes catching some of my tears. "Talk to me," I say again.

His shoulders rise with a sigh, and he stands before turning to face me. In his blues I see brokenness, and my chest aches knowing that I'm the cause of his hurt. My lip quivers and I keep my stare on his, silently begging him to come to me. After many shaky breaths and broken heartbeats, he does.

He walks past me, and I follow him as he leads us down a quiet hallway. He steps into a vacant room and closes the door.

"Talk," he says, defeated.

"Well," I stumble on my words. Now that I have his attention, my brain is completely scattered, and I don't know where to start. I sense him getting agitated. "Um," I say for lack of anything better.

"Well? Um? Good talk, I have to go now."

"Wait." I reach my hand out and clench his forearm. "Just wait. Give me a moment."

Wyatt pulls his arm from my grasp and crosses his arms in front of his chest. I pull in a calming breath.

"I love you," I tell him. "I really love you. And the thing is, you're the first man I've ever felt this way for. This is new to me and really scary. You're right, I ran. I was afraid, terrified. I don't know how to do this," I chuckle sadly.

"I don't know how to open my heart up to someone and be vulnerable in that way. You know what it's like to be abandoned, but the thing is that I've always left before I could be. I love you so much that the thought that I could lose you scared me more than any Mexican cartel ever could." I shake my head. "Moving around my whole life, I'm an expert at talking to and making friends with new people. Put me in a room with anyone and we'll leave as buddies. But I've always known that those relationships were temporary. They were always categorized into the 'here for now' place in my brain, and as soon as I moved to a different place, they were replaced with new people. I've never been afraid of losing anyone, outside of my sister and my parents, because from the second I meet people I know in a matter of time, I'll be gone."

Wyatt takes a breath and his features soften. Hope expands in my chest, and I pray that he's truly hearing what I'm saying.

"Somewhere along the line, you left that 'here for now' category and moved over to the 'forever' place in my heart. You're the first person, outside of my family, to ever reach it. Then I started to think, what if you weren't forever? What if you left me? How would I handle that?" I shrug, "I don't know how I would. So I left so I could make sure that you'd never leave me." More tears stream down my cheeks. "I'm sorry. I wasn't prepared to fall in love with you."

I blink and Wyatt's in front of me threading his fingers through my hair and pulling my mouth to his. The kiss isn't hard and frantic like I thought it'd be. It's soft and sad.

It's a broken boy forgiving a broken girl.

It's two very flawed people coming together in pieces to make a whole.

It's hopeful and scared all at once, and it's everything.

It's everything.

And it's worth the fight.

TWENTY-FIVE

WYATT

*"I truly see Georgia now, and not just her perfections,
but her flaws, too. And I love her even more."*
—Wyatt Gates

*G*eorgia's moan as I slide into her wetness is the hottest sound I've ever heard. It's drives me to the bridge of insanity, like everything about her does. Every. Fucking. Thing.

She's turned away from me, her long blonde hair, still wet from the shower, falls to cover her face, and I continue my assault. My fingers splay across the toned skin of her shoulders, and every time her ass thrusts back to hit me I want to explode.

We're frantic now, our bodies pounding against each other chasing another orgasm that we're desperate for. Georgia slides a hand between her legs, and the image of her touching herself makes me growl loudly into the dark room. She whimpers and cries out as her body starts to shake.

Fuck, yes.

I thrust into her hard sending her body forward, and she throws her free hand out against the headboard to stop from hitting it. Our skin slaps together.

More moans.

Labored breaths.

Slapping skin.

Desperate whimpers.

Guttural sighs.

Sobs of pleasure.

It's the best symphony I've ever heard and it's ours. Only ours.

Georgia collapses to the bed, face down, after we both reach climax. I fall atop her, my chest expanding, desperate for air.

I roll off her, throwing my forearm over my eyes, my body still humming from pleasure. Georgia rolls toward me and kisses my chest, slick with sweat.

"That was amazing," she sighs.

"Fourth time's the charm," I respond thinking about all the other ways we've pleased each other since getting back to my house. We've worshiped each other's bodies. We've reunited. We've made love, slow and sweet. We fucked, hard and desperate. Each time amazing. Each time perfect because it was with her.

"All equally amazing," she says. "Make-up sex is the best. We should do it more often."

"Agreed, but can we have it without doing the shit that comes before it?"

We're both quiet after my reference to the drama of this week.

"Do you really forgive me for leaving you?" she asks softly, laying her cheek against my chest.

"I told you that I did, and I do. I'm not perfect, Peaches… nowhere close. I'm sure I'm going to make lots of mistakes in this. You hurt me, but I forgive you. Of course I do. I love you."

She gasps and sits up. "You said it."

"What?" I ask, confused.

"You said you love me."

"You know that I do."

"But you've never said it out loud. Sometimes, I need to hear it."

I sit up and place my mouth over her exposed breast, pulling her nipple between my teeth. When it releases, I say, "I love you." I kiss the soft skin above her collarbone. "I love you." I place small kisses up her neck. "I love you." I pull her earlobe between my lips and whisper in her ear, "I love you."

I lean back, my face inches from hers. Her eyes well with tears. "I love you, Peaches. I think I've loved you for a long time." I wrap my arms around her back and pull her down to the bed with me. She lays atop me and glides her fingers up and down my arm.

It feels so good lying here with Georgia. When she first showed up at the hospital room, my walls—the ones that have protected me my entire life—shot up, and I just wanted her gone. I didn't want to feel the pain that she would inevitably bring me. I wanted to protect myself and shield my heart from more hurt. She had left me once, and I knew she could do it again. But then she started explaining, and I heard so much of myself in her words. I know what it's like to be afraid of losing someone you love. I know what it's like to let fear and insecurity dictate life choices. Despite the vast differences in our upbringing, Georgia and I are more alike than I ever realized.

The second I started really internalizing her words, I knew the night would end with my lips on hers. I truly see Georgia now, and not just her perfections, but her flaws, too. And I love her even more.

When I'm scared, I put up walls and push people away. When she's scared, she runs. Neither coping mechanism is better than the other, but they're both forgivable. I saw her standing there, her heart wide open as she told me everything, and I fell more in love with her. Now that I know that these worries fester within her, it's my job to make sure that she knows, without a shadow of a doubt, that I'll never leave her. She may not be perfect, but she is one hundred percent perfect for me. I could never love anyone as much as I love her.

"So what happened when you were in Mexico?" I ask.

"Well, I made it to Colima and checked in with Kylie. She told me that the human trafficking ring that had been working with them under the pretense of selling them children got wind that something might be off. So the human traffickers broke off communication with Kylie and her group. They're going to try to pose as different people and set up another exchange down the road, but it will take time. And I didn't have time. I realized what I left behind, and I had to get back to it."

"And you're okay with that? Just leaving before everything was resolved? You're not going to have regrets?" I ask, a small part inside is still afraid she's going to choose to leave again.

"The truth is, it may never be completely resolved. It's a huge problem all over the world. I called my dad, and he gave me the name and number of one of his Mexican business associates that is very invested in stopping human trafficking in Mexico. Kylie spoke to him, and they're going to work together. He has more money and connections than Kylie and her team do, so I think together they can make a real change. And you're right, I can't fix the whole world. I'm only one person. But I regretted leaving you, and losing you would've haunted me forever."

She props herself up on her elbows and runs her fingers through my hair, her gentle hazels gazing into my blues. "This is all new territory for me, Wyatt, and I'm not promising that I won't mess up again. But please try to love me anyway."

I chuckle at her request. "Same. We're like the blind leading the blind here."

"That seems to be a pattern with us." She smiles. "I promise to love you even if you royally screw up," she tells me before kissing my lips.

"And I promise to love you even if you royally screw up," I tell her, and she kisses me again. When her lips leave mine I say, "Those are some crazy-ass vows."

Georgia's eyes open wide. "Vows? Slow down there, buddy," she says with a shake of her head, and I laugh. "We've been good, for what?" She pretends to look at a nonexistent watch on her wrist. "For four hours. Let's get out of the fast lane, shall we?"

"We need time, of course, but I'm letting you know that I'm going to marry you someday, Peaches. You've always been the only girl for me. You don't have to fear me leaving you because it won't happen. I've seen what it's like without you in my life this past week, and I hate it. I will never leave you. Ever." I put emphasis on the last word so that she hears me, down to her soul. I don't want her to live in fear that she'll lose me because she won't.

"Okay," she says softly.

"Okay," I nod.

"When did we do a one-eighty?" she laughs. "I used to be the confident, lovey one, and now you're reassuring me."

"I felt what it'd be like to lose two people I love this week, and it made me realize that only an idiot would keep someone they love at arm's length. Real love is rare, and it's not something everyone gets. So when someone is fortunate enough to be loved, they need to cherish it because it could be gone tomorrow." I run my fingers up her back, pulling her down to me, I kiss her. "I cherish you. And I promise that I will always cherish you."

She sighs contently, "And I promise that I'm done running, Wyatt. I don't need to search the world for happiness. I already have it right here with you."

I tuck a strand of her hair behind her ear. "Georgia Wright, have I tamed your free spirited, world traveling ways?" My lips tilt up in a smile.

She grins back, so much love radiating from her face. "Wyatt Gates, your love freed me, and for the first time in my life, I'm home."

TWENTY-SIX

GEORGIA

"Family is the people that fill your life with joy, have your back, and love you unconditionally."
—*Georgia Wright*

"Do we really need all of this? She's just one person," Wyatt says of the plethora of groceries that's spread across the countertop. He's right. It's enough to feed a large family for at least two weeks.

"We just got what the recipes called for," I shrug. "We can always freeze them in portions so she can use them later."

"I just had surgery. I'm not dead. I'm capable of making my own food," Ethel calls from her recliner in the living room.

"Hush it!" Wyatt calls back. "Watch your *Wheel of Fortune* and pet your cats. We're making you meals."

Ethel grumbles something in retort, but I can't make it out over the clicking sound of the wheel coming from the television.

Wyatt and I sat down last night and planned out a week of meals for Ethel. It was his first experience with Pinterest, and it was hilarious. We laughed hard and had a ball planning these dishes. Scanning this mess of food, I have a feeling that making them all isn't going to be quite as fun.

"We just need to start. Let's pick one of the meals," Wyatt suggests. "You want to go with the pasta?"

"Yeah, pasta is always easy, and she loves it."

Opening my Pinterest app on my phone, I pull up the recipe for the eggplant penne with fresh mozzarella, basil, and a garnish of gremolata.

"Okay, you take the eggplant and slice it in one fourth inch cubes," I instruct Wyatt.

"Like exactly?" He furrows his brow.

"I'm sure close is fine."

He picks up the slice of eggplant. "Do I peel it? This skin is really thick."

"It doesn't say. Google it." I look down to the recipe. "Do you know what a microplane is?"

"No clue."

"We need a microplane for the lemon rind." My hands wet from washing the parsley, I ask Wyatt to Google what a microplane looks like, too. After I dry my hands we spend the next fifteen minutes looking through every drawer and cupboard trying to find the lemon peel device. When I'm certain Ethel doesn't own one, I search online for what we can use instead. "It says a small grater. Did we see one of those?"

"Do you all need help in there?" Ethel yells over the TV.

"Buy a vowel, E, we got this." Wyatt opens a drawer and pulls out a metal object with holes. "Is this a grater?"

I bite my lip. "I think so, but aren't the holes supposed to be smaller?"

"It's going to have to do."

We spend an abnormally long time on every part of the recipe. I pull open the top of the mozzarella balls and some of the liquid they're in splashes out causing me to drop the entire container on the floor. White balls bounce everywhere.

"Shit!" I cry staring down at the floor of wet balls. "I'm going to cry," I say with a sigh.

"Five second rule?" Wyatt questions as he hastily tries to retrieve the balls of cheese.

"Should we? What if cat hair gets on them?"

"We'll wash them. They were in water to begin with. It will be fine." He tosses the cheese into a strainer and begins running them under water.

I grab the mop and clean up the mess I made of the floor. Wyatt looks back at me with his sexy grin. "We should've ordered pizza," he teases.

"Totally," I agree.

What feels like eighty hours later, our first meal is finished. "This should be tonight's dish. I'm starving after all of that work."

"OMG. Me too," I laugh. "I can't believe we have six more to do. We're never going to finish. I thought you could cook," I tell him.

"I never said I could cook. I figured you could. You're a girl."

"Sexist," I huff in mock-offense. "I am proficient at many things, but cooking is not one of them."

"Noted. So takeout for life?"

"Definitely. Or we practice and get better at it?"

"Takeout it is." Wyatt reaches into the cupboard and grabs three plates. We dish up the food. Ethel's too sore to sit at the kitchen table, so he sets her meal on a tray and carries it out to her. I grab both of our plates and follow him.

"Dinner is served," he sets the tray down on her lap and kisses the top of her head.

"Looks and smells delicious," Ethel grins.

Wyatt and I sit with our plates on the sofa next to her, and the three of us start eating. I almost gag on my first bite. The lemon flavor is so strong that I feel the tart fumes shoot through my nostrils. I place the back of my hand to my mouth and swallow hard, reaching for my glass of water to wash it down with. I turn to look at Wyatt and Ethel and gauge their reactions. They're both silent, their lips pressed in a line, and their faces scrunched up.

"It's so bad," I say with a chuckle.

"Horrible. God awful," Wyatt agrees.

"It could be better," Ethel says in a kind voice.

I throw my head back in laughter and Wyatt and Ethel laugh hard along with me. I can't believe we just spent hours making something that tastes so horrible.

"Did we zest the peel or just chop up the whole thing and throw it in there? The after taste of the rind is vile," I say, raising my eyebrows and looking to the others.

"I don't know, but we shouldn't be allowed in the kitchen anymore," Wyatt states.

"Agreed, but we still have to feed her," I say.

"I'm not dead. I can feed myself," Ethel snaps.

Wyatt waves his hand. "Hush. Pet your cat."

As if angels descended from heaven, there's a knock at the door followed by Xavier's loud voice and the smell of pure bliss.

"Hey! Hey! We come bearing gifts." He walks into the living room with metal trays stacked in his arms. Luciana follows behind him with big bags in hand.

"Oh my God…I love you," I tell them both, almost squealing with happiness. Nothing is better than a friend whose family owns a restaurant, especially a Mexican one.

"Thank you so much," Ethel tells them. "Thank your parents, Lucy. They are too kind."

"It's our pleasure," Luciana replies with a tilt of her lip.

"We can't possibly eat all of this ourselves. Wyatt, text the rest of the guys and see if any of them can make it over. Georgia, why don't you invite your roommate to eat."

Wyatt furrows his brow. "You just had surgery, E. I don't think hosting a party is wise."

Ethel scoffs, dismissing him with a wave of her hand. "I'm not hosting anything. I'm going to sit here and eat. It won't bother me a bit. I don't want any of that food going to waste. Invite them over."

Wyatt and I grab our phones and send our texts. Then, I take each of our plates of uneaten crap and carry them to the kitchen.

"What happened here?" Luciana asks.

"Wyatt and I attempted to make dinner," I snicker as I dump the contents of our plates into the garbage disposal. "It didn't go well."

"What's all of this?" She motions toward the piles of food on the counter.

"Ingredients to meals that will never be made." I shake my head with a grin.

"I can make them," she offers.

"No, we wouldn't make you do that."

"You wouldn't be making me. I'd love to. I enjoy cooking. I've been preparing dinner for my family since I was very young. It would be my pleasure, really."

I quirk up an eyebrow. "Only if you're absolutely sure."

She giggles and shakes her head. "Help me put everything away, and I'll come over tomorrow and prepare it all."

The two of us put away the food that Wyatt and I purchased and set up a Mexican buffet with the items she and Xavier brought. She opens the lid to the pan on the stove. "Is this your dish?" she asks, curious.

"Yes, but don't try it unless you want to vomit," I warn.

She grabs a wooden spoon and gets a mouthful. "You're silly. I'm sure it's not that bad." She closes her mouth around the pasta and her eyes immediately bug out before she spits her mouthful into the sink.

She waves her hand toward me. "No more cooking for you." She holds back a gag.

"I told you!" I laugh.

Wyatt and Xavier pull the table and chairs from the kitchen into the living room so that we can all eat together with Ethel. Workers from the rescue and Paige show up, and we all dish up our food, filling the living room.

"I promise to only feed you takeout or Lucy's cooking from now on," Wyatt says across the table to Ethel, to which she smiles.

"Yeah, we're sorry. We weren't trying to kill you earlier. We really do love you." I shoot her a wink.

She chuckles, "And I love you. I appreciate the sentiment. It's the thought that counts."

"Yeah, but our thoughts are no good. Our attempt would have you starving to death, so we need to let that go," Wyatt says before tossing a freshly made corn chip topped with salsa into his mouth. Luciana's parents make the best tortilla chips and salsa in the world. I could live off them.

The room is filled with noise—laughter, voices, dishes clanging, and forks scraping against plates. There's so much commotion, and yet it's oddly peaceful because it's incredibly joyous. I look to Ethel and notice the content smile across her face as she takes in the craziness in front of her, and I know she's happy.

I'm happy. I love these people. I love this place. No one here is related by blood, and yet every single one of them feels like family. Family is the people that fill your life with joy, have your back, and love you unconditionally. Wyatt's wrong when he says that he only has Ethel. He's created a beautiful family with these people, one that's stronger than most conventional ones. He's very fortunate, and so am I because they love me too.

TWENTY-SEVEN

"I want Wyatt—today, tomorrow, and always."
—Georgia Wright

Wyatt and I walk into the rescue the next day hand in hand. I don't offer to release our grasp and neither does he. He officially doesn't mind public displays of affection, and I couldn't be more thrilled.

Who are we? This happy, well-adjusted couple with all of our hopes and insecurities laid out on the table. Our relationship seems so mature now. What a difference a week makes. It may have taken losing Wyatt, flying to another country, Ethel getting sick, and tear-filled apologies, but we're exactly where we need to be.

We spent the weekend helping Ethel get adjusted and, of course, attempted to kill her yesterday with our poisonous pasta. She's still in pain from the surgery. I can see it in her face when she moves. But it was major surgery, a mere week ago—some pain is to be expected. Overall, I think she's doing great after her blood clot scare. Luciana is heading over there today to cook and package up the rest of the meals we planned for her this week. So she'll be fed, and of course we'll stop by every day to check in on her.

I talked with Wyatt last night, and I'm going to start transitioning my belongings over to his house. We've only just gotten back together, but it's different this time. There are no underlying fears and insecurities. For the first time in my entire life I feel settled. I know exactly what I want, and I don't need to jump on a plane to search for it. I want Wyatt—today, tomorrow, and always.

I want this life, with these people—in this place. I want to go to bed every night in Wyatt's arms and wake up each morning beside him. I want to go to work every morning to do one of the most devastating jobs I've ever done. I want to help these precious babies, even if it breaks my heart to do so, because I can. I can make a difference. I can save lives every day and, I can do it here with the only man I've ever loved.

Rescue work isn't for the faint of heart, there's no doubt. I've seen tragedy firsthand in many places all over the world, but there's something about these animals that breaks me more than I thought was possible. Yet the moment a beaten down dog realizes that he's safe for the first time, the moment his scared tail wags, his desperate eyes find mine, and his forgiving spirit extends a tongue to kiss me in gratitude—it's worth all of the tears because I know that this precious animal is safe. He will be happy, and he will be loved.

This place mirrors life in a way. Some don't come by a happily ever after easily. Some have to fight hard for it, and some never get one at all. The ones that hold out for it the longest appreciate it the most.

Cooper passes us as we walk through the kennels, prancing like he owns the place, and Mila struggles in my grasp. I let her down so she can chase her best friend, Cooper. I swear, that girl loves me and Wyatt—but that chubby, big-mouthed, long-tongued pittie is her absolute favorite. She would follow him anywhere.

I turn to Wyatt. He releases my hand from his grasp and brings both of his hands to my cheeks, holding either side. He kisses me, and I sigh into his mouth. He pulls his lip from mine. "Have a good day, Peaches."

"You too."

"I love you," he tells me, and my heart begins to race. I will never tire of those words coming from his mouth.

"I love you," I tell him back and then he's off to his office, and I just smile as I watch him go.

Our days here are busy. The list of things to finish seems daunting, but we get it done—each playing the parts we're best at. We make a good team.

Mila's at my feet playing with my shoe. "Do you want to help Momma? Come on. Let's go see your friends."

She starts off toward the kennels like a pudgy bucking bronco, and I laugh, my heart completely full.

Regardless of what happened yesterday or what will occur tomorrow, I have my happily ever after today. Each breath I pull in will be one of gratitude, each smile I make will be one of happiness, and each kiss I give will be one of love. I'll cherish every second of this crazy life because it's the one I choose, the one I want, the one I need.

TWENTY-EIGHT

"Living a good life—knowing how to fill one's soul with joy—is the true gift, money is just a bonus."
—*Wyatt Gates*

I dry off the last dish and put it away in the cupboard after our big Sunday meal. Our weekly gatherings have continued since the one at Ethel's house right after she came home from the hospital last spring.

It's hard to admit that I look forward to these meals, but I do. We're the biggest group of misfits—the world-traveling rich girl, the ex-nurse turned crazy cat woman, a heavy dose of ex-homeless people with varying odd personality traits, the ex-sorority girl that despite her good job in the business world always seems to use phrases that make no sense, and me with more baggage than them all. Despite our vast differences we all have one thing in common, and that's our love for dogs, and I've found that dog people are the best people.

Entering the living room, I find Georgia sitting crossed legged on the floor amidst a scattered mess of papers. We've been together for a solid six months, and she was working at the rescue a couple of months prior to us dating, so I figured it was time to elicit her help with the never-ending paperwork in my life. Running a rescue comes with lots of paperwork, and I'd much rather be out on rescues or working with the dogs. Thankfully, Georgia saw my request for help as an exciting challenge and not as me passing off my shit work onto her, which shamefully, I feel it was.

She holds a piece of paper in her hand, her mouth open as she scans it. Her head raises when she hears me enter. "Wyatt Gates, you're loaded," she says in astonishment. "How did I not know this?"

I shrug with a chuckle, "It never came up."

She pins me with a stare. "My money comes up all of the time and yet this," she waves my bank statement in the air, "somehow hasn't been mentioned."

"It's not important. You know I don't care about money."

"Clearly, but this is a big deal. It should be invested correctly. It could be used to do some amazing things in your life if you manage it correctly," she states.

"Well, that's why I solicited your help," I respond.

"First of all, where did it all come from?"

There's a giant chew toy in front of my foot. Bending down, I begin to gather up the dog toys and toss them into the toy bin. "Apparently, my dad had a separate account set up with a substantial sum that had a high interest rate. The only thing the account was used for was to pay for my parents' excellent life insurance policies. I never knew it existed until Ethel helped me go through some boxes that my mom had stored in her garage when we lost our house and moved to the apartments in Ypsilanti. I guess my mom was too high to find time to go through all of my dad's things when he died. She never knew this money existed or that she had so much money coming to her from his life insurance policy."

"That's so sad. All of that time, you could've had more than you did. You suffered for nothing."

"No," I shake my head, surveying the room to make sure I picked up all of the toys before stepping closer to Georgia. "I'm glad she never knew about it. She would have wasted it away on drugs. I don't regret my childhood. Yeah, it was hard, but I made it through. It turned me into the man that I am today. Looking around at what I have now, I can't regret my past because I wouldn't have all of this without it."

She shakes her head slowly, obviously still getting used to this new information.

"Money doesn't buy happiness. You know that's true. It's what one does with money that does. I've done a lot of good with that money. Believe me, that sum used to be a lot higher," I chuckle. "A person running a nonprofit animal rescue doesn't make much, if anything. That money bought this house, my truck, the shelter, paid off Ethel's bills, and the house that the employees stay in. I try to get the rescue funded as much as I can through donations now, but if the dogs or employees need something and I haven't raised enough money to afford it, I have that." I nod toward the paper in her hand.

"Wow. I had no idea. I guess I never thought about where you got the money to open the rescue in the first place. You know if you invest it that you can do more good with the earnings from the interest on this amount of money."

"And that's why I have you," I tell her with a smile.

She sets the paper down on the floor beside her and stands. She walks over to me and drapes her arms around my neck.

"You're a really good man, Wyatt, and that's why I love you so very much."

I kiss her lips softly.

"Not everyone in your shoes would've done the same. I'd say most wouldn't have. You were without money your whole life, and when you get it, you spend it to help others. I mean, that's incredible."

"Have you seen my truck? It's pretty sweet," I joke.

"You know what I mean, Wyatt. You're special, in here." She places a hand on my chest.

"You're the same," I tell her. "Your heart is beautiful, and that's one of the main reasons I love you."

She stands up on her tiptoes and kisses me. "I can't believe I'm dating a rich guy. My dad's going to be so excited!" she teases, causing me to laugh.

"I don't know what you're talking about," I chuckle. "I'm as poor as they come, in here." I point toward my head. "I'll always feel like that kid with nothing, and I'll never want fancy extravagant things."

There are two types of people with money—those who worship it and those who don't. Of no fault of her own, Georgia was raised by the kind of people that worship money. They feel that money not only brings happiness but status and worth. I know that it doesn't. It's nice to have, no doubt, and I'm grateful that I can do the things I want without worrying about where I'll get my next meal. Yet money will never bring true fulfillment, it will never make me better than anyone else with less, and it won't make me more important by merely having it. Living a good life—knowing how to fill one's soul with joy—is the true gift, money is just a bonus.

"That's fine by me. I think our life is perfect just the way it is." Her lips tilt up in a smile.

"You know, had my mom found this money when I was younger, it wouldn't have made a difference. I never cared about where we lived or what I wore. I truly didn't miss not having the latest video game. All I ever wanted was to be seen and to be loved by the woman I loved the most, and she was so stuck in her own personal hell that she could never do either of those things. She never saw me, and she never loved me. Money wouldn't have changed that."

A tear falls down Georgia's cheek. "She loved you, Wyatt. She may not have been able to show you, but she loved you. I know it because you're impossible not to love."

I kiss her forehead. "Want to go sit out on the deck for a bit? Maybe start a fire. I can make you a cappuccino?" I quirk an eyebrow up, knowing how much she loves cappuccinos from our new coffee maker.

She claps her hands together. "Yes!"

"You might want to put your…" I look down to the complete chaos on the floor, "…piles on the table before Thing One and Thing Two wake from the couch and go scattering them everywhere." I nod toward the slumbering fur babies.

"Hey, you may not see it, but there's an order to this madness." She waves her hand over the floor.

Pressing my lips into a line, I raise both eyebrows. "I'm sure," I say, shooting her a wink.

It's a beautiful autumn day in Michigan. The bright, colorful leaves blow in the warm wind. The sun shines through the trees making the yellow, orange, and red leaves almost twinkle as they dance.

I'm a grump by nature—or I was before Georgia—but even on my darkest day, a day like today would bring me joy. I always saw perfect fall days as rewards for making it through the rest of the not-so-great ones. Everything around me—the vibrant view, the touch of the soft breeze, the autumn smells, the sound of rustling leaves that create a soothing symphony—all come together in a sensory paradise.

I've started a small fire in our pit on the deck. Cooper and Mila run around the yard playing keep away with a stick. Mila's really good at it as she whips her head around right before Cooper grabs it. He does have a good seven years on her though. It's hilarious how Cooper refuses to just pick up another stick. Instead, he'll chase her around until he needs a nap.

Georgia sits in the swing on the porch. She's in yoga pants and a T-shirt, her hair pulled up into a messy bun without a stitch of makeup. She's smiling as she watches the dogs play, and she's more beautiful than she's ever been. God, I love her.

I still can't believe she's mine.

Most days feel like a dream because they're so incredible. I've never believed in true love or soul mates because the concept was so foreign to me. If one's mother doesn't truly love him, who else will? I believe now. No one on this planet is more suited for me than Georgia. She's everything I've wanted but was too insecure to hope for. Life taught me a long time ago not to wish for miracles, not to pray for perfection, but to settle with okay. Life doesn't know a damn thing because Georgia is my miracle. She's the perfection that fills me up with absolute love every single day.

She envelops me in a sense of security that I never knew existed. I'm no longer fearful of the future. I'm not waiting for the bottom to fall out beneath me. I have Georgia today, and

I'm secure in the fact that I'll have her always. She loves me in a way that only she can, and it happens to be the precise way I need to be loved. She is my soul mate—my forever. I've stopped questioning why I deserve her, why I'm so lucky—instead, insecurities have been replaced with gratitude, and I give thanks by loving her with everything I have, every second of the day.

I hand her a mug of warm coffee. She pulls the cup up to her nose and sniffs. "Mmm," she says. "It smells like heaven in a cup. Thank you." Her hazel eyes shine up to me with a kaleidoscope of colors mirroring the landscape surrounding us—flecks of green, tan, gold, and gray—all uniquely beautiful and mesmerizing.

"You're welcome," I say, before returning to the house to grab something. I was going to save it for our first Christmas together, but I can't wait any longer. It's the perfect day, with the perfect girl, in this perfect life.

Today's the day.

I come back with a big silver box wrapped in a large pink satin bow. Georgia's eyes widen when I emerge from the house with her present. She places her mug down on the table and sits up.

"What's that?" she asks, clapping her hands in front of her.

"Well, I got you a gift. I was going to wait until Christmas to give it to you, but I'm weak, and I want you to have it now."

"Oh my gosh, I love presents," she says, giddy with excitement.

I place the large box on her lap. She runs her palms over the smooth paper and looks up to me, her lips turning up into a wide smile. She pulls the bottom of the ribbon; her eyes sparkle as they dart up toward me again. The fabric falls to the side, and she pulls off the top of the box. After removing the tissue paper, she gasps.

"You kept this?"

"Yeah, I kind of stole it."

"You did not!" she laughs.

"What were they going to do, come after me? Ruin my credit score?" I shoot her a wink.

She shakes her head, "This is where it all started, didn't it?" She runs her hand over the cover of my old biology textbook from high school.

"It sure did," I tell her. "There's a note."

She picks up the small note and removes it from the envelope.

"Read it aloud," I ask her.

Her eyes fill with tears, and she swallows, "This is when I started falling for you, and I've never stopped. I'll continue to fall for you for all eternity because my love for you has no end. I love you—Wyatt. P.S. Open me." Her beautiful face looks up from the card. "Open the book?" Her voice trembles.

"Open the book."

Her hand shakes as she sets the card down. Grabbing the corner of the textbook she opens the cover; her hands go to her mouth as she stares wide-eyed at the diamond ring placed neatly in a hole cut out of the center of the book's pages.

I grab the ring and get down on one knee. "Georgia, there was a time in my life when you were the only reason that I got up in the morning. Seeing you for one hour, every day, made my existence matter. At the darkest point in my life, you were my light. Now, you're my favorite reason to get up in the morning, and you're still my light. Life works in mysterious ways, and I'm so grateful that you came back to me. I was put on this earth to love you and only you. I promise to love and cherish you with my whole heart for the rest of my life. Will you marry me?"

Georgia sobs across from me and throws her arms around my neck. She peppers my face, her kisses wet with tears. "Yes! Yes! Yes!" she cries. "I love you! Yes!"

We make out like two seventeen-year-olds finding love for the first time. The truth is, every day I discover more ways to love, more ways to be loved. Georgia heals a piece of my heart each day with the way in which she loves me.

"I can't believe you stole that book," she giggles between kisses.

"Yep, you're marrying a criminal."

"And I can't wait." She pulls my mouth to hers before stopping the kiss abruptly. "You have to put it on!" She grins.

"What?"

"The ring," she squeals, her gaze dropping to my hand.

"Oh yeah." I lift my hand, holding the diamond ring between my fingers. She extends her left hand, and I slide it on.

"It's perfect." She holds her hand out in front of her swaying it back and forth allowing the light to catch the diamond. The ring I had designed looks completely stunning on her finger, as if it were always meant to be there. The two carat oval cushion cut diamond sits atop a rose gold halo band. It's unique, classic, beautiful, and one of a kind—just like my Peaches. "I can't believe we're getting married. How did I get so lucky?"

"I could ask the same thing."

"Do you ever wish that we didn't have that misunderstanding in high school? Maybe we could've gotten together sooner? I could've gone to college in Ann Arbor, like London did. We could've been together all of this time."

I shake my head, "It wouldn't have worked like that. I think we needed to be apart so we could grow together. We had to discover who we were and what we wanted in life. So that when we saw each other again, we'd know without a shadow of a doubt that this is the life we want, together."

Georgia nods thoughtfully. "Yeah, maybe you're right. I can't imagine a life more wonderful than ours. I can't believe this is all real." Her stare leaves me to look down at her ring.

"It's real, and it's forever. I hope you're ready," I tell her, running my hands up and down her waist.

She bites her bottom and lip and inhales through her nose. Her gaze holds mine. "I've been running my whole life, desperately seeking some unknown that was always just out of my reach. All this time, I was running to you." She shakes her head, tears slide down her rosy cheeks. "I never knew it was you that I needed all this time. It was always you, Wyatt." She brings her hand up to my face, her palm cups my cheek.

I cover her hand with mine, holding her grasp against my face. "I've been waiting my whole life for you to find me. It's always been you, Peaches."

I lay my lips against hers and smile. The outlying fragments of my heart, shattered when I was young, come together, and I'm finally whole. Georgia tamed my broken heart with her love, and I'll spend the rest of my life loving her with everything I have.

EPILOGUE

"Fairytales are real. I live in one every single day."
—Georgia Gates

I set the Minnie Mouse cake down next to the Lightning McQueen cake and smile at the cuteness. Disney is single-handedly responsible for my children's current obsessions. I know every word to all of the *Cars* movies and *Mickey Mouse Clubhouse* episodes. When one is the parent of a two- and one-year-old, one learns quickly that Disney saves lives—or at least Mommy's sanity.

Our first little miracle came less than a year after our wedding. We named him Asher, which means fortunate or blessing. We tossed around the idea of naming him after a place like my parents did with London and me, but it didn't feel right. I've been all over the world and never felt at home anywhere, until Wyatt. For me, it's the people that make a place a home—not a spot on a map. Asher's unofficial name is Asher Wyatt Stanley Cooper Gates, his three middle names after three souls that played a part in this amazing life in which I now live.

I think back to Stanley, the homeless man that I met as a child who single-handedly changed my views on the world. He was a chance meeting that changed the course of my life from what was expected to what was right. Meeting him made me think about everything—what I wanted to be and what I didn't. Our encounter starting me on the search for more, which ultimately led me to Wyatt.

The four-legged Stanley that accompanied Mark, the homeless man I met running when I first moved in with Paige, played an essential role in my happily ever after as well. For he and Mark directed me to Cooper's Place and Wyatt.

Then there's Cooper, my first fur baby, who Wyatt says saved his life. I never knew I could love an animal so much until I met Cooper. He's an amazing breed ambassador, showing everyone what a pit bull is. He loves every creature he comes across, both two- and four-legged alike. He's seen the worst that humans have to offer, and he loves us just the same. He is the inspiration for Cooper's Place, which once again, brought me to Wyatt.

After baby Asher was born, Wyatt convinced me that three middle names were a bit excessive and persuaded me to choose one. Truthfully, it wasn't hard to narrow it down because as important as both Stanley and Cooper were to my life—Wyatt's my miracle. He's the soul mate I didn't believe existed, the love of my life. He's my home.

So our little love—Asher Wyatt—carries his father's name, and it's perfect. He's a two-year-old, rough and tumble, little miniature of his father. My heart opened more than I knew possible the day Asher was born. The love I have for Wyatt is all-encompassing, but the love I have for Asher is indescribable.

There really are no words to portray a mother's love for her children. It's an astonishing gift that I'll forever be grateful for.

Then, almost a year to the date later, our baby girl came. It's clear now that when people say that one can't get pregnant while nursing, they are in fact lying. Having two babies so close has been a lot of work, but I wouldn't change a thing. We named our girl Mirielle Ethel Gates. Mirielle is a French name meaning miraculous, which she is. Anyone in Michigan that sees it written automatically mispronounces it. The French pronunciation is "Meer-ay," which has turned into RayRay, her ever-so-fitting nickname. RayRay is a little blonde spitfire. Besides her beautiful blue doe eyes, which are all her father, she's my mini-me. She's loud, bossy, and full of attitude in the most adorable way ever. She's only one, but I can tell that she's going to change the world someday. It's written all over her soul.

Wyatt comes up behind me and places his hands against my round belly. I lean back into his chest, a content sigh leaving my lips. He kisses my neck. "Cakes look good, babe."

"They're cute, aren't they?"

"Very."

"How's Happy treating Mommy today?" he asks of the baby growing inside my belly, which we're currently calling Happy.

Wyatt and I decided after RayRay that we were content being a family of four. Fast forward to six months later when I was in Target buying a shirt with a quote from the late Bob Ross that said, "There are no mistakes, just happy accidents," I got the urge to buy a pregnancy test as I was feeling off. I presented the positive pregnancy test wrapped in the T-shirt to Wyatt that night. Baby number three has been lovingly referred to as Happy since then, though I've told Wyatt the name is temporary. I have no qualms about naming my child after a dog, but I draw the line at the seven dwarfs.

"Good," I sigh with a grin.

"You are so beautiful," he whispers against my neck between kisses causing goosebumps to erupt over my entire body.

"Yeah, right. I'm fat," I tease because truthfully I do feel beautiful in spite of my huge belly. I love being pregnant. I feel so fortunate that my body will carry a little life inside it until he or she is ready to come into the world. The fact is, all babies are miracles, and we're not sure what we're going to name Happy, but I'd guess the name will mean miracle.

"Isn't it weird that I've had a belly the majority of the time that we've been together?" I ask with a chuckle.

Wyatt turns me around so that I'm facing him and kisses me on the lips. "If by weird you mean fucking sexy, then yes." His eyes darken as he scans my body because he's serious when he says that my pregnant body turns him on. We've had the hottest sex with this big ball protruding from my middle.

My arms wrapped around his neck, my thumb traces the short hair at the base of his neck. "You going to show me how sexy you find me tonight?" I ask coyly, my lips against his.

Wyatt growls and captures my mouth, kissing me like only he can. "Hell yeah. I can't wait." His voice is husky with need.

Suddenly, Wyatt's face morphs from need-filled to uncomfortable as he winces. I look down to find Asher smashing a Lightning McQueen matchbox car against Wyatt's pants, specifically his groin area.

"Keen, Dadda! Keen Dadda!" Asher whines.

Wyatt bends and picks him up. "You have McQueen in your hand," Wyatt says sweetly.

"Keen! Dadda!" Asher repeats.

"Which McQueen do you want, baby? The blue one? The big one?" I start listing off the different versions of Lightning McQueen that Asher possesses.

He doesn't seem to know what he wants. "Hey, birthday boy." I press my finger against his nose. "Daddy will help you find the car you want, okay? But do you want to see your cake first?"

Asher's eyes widen at the mention of cake, and his car drama is forgotten for the moment. "Look." Wyatt shows him the cake that's set up on the outside table.

"Keen!" Asher points to the cake, a huge smile on his face.

"Just for you, buddy," Wyatt tells him.

"A McQueen birthday cake just for you." I lean in and kiss his cheek. "How old are you today?"

Asher raises three fingers because he hasn't quite mastered bending his ring finger down yet and yells, "Two!"

"Good job. You are two! You're a big boy," I tell him.

"WayWay," Asher says and points to the Minnie Mouse cake. He also hasn't mastered his "r" sounds yet.

"Yes, that's RayRay's cake."

"WayWay baby," he says knowingly.

"Yeah, Ray's still a baby. She's one now."

"My two," Asher says.

I giggle, "You are two." I look to Wyatt. "By the way, where's Ray? I want to show her the cake."

A smirk finds Wyatt's lips as he holds in a laugh. "Last time I saw her she was running, bare-bottomed, away from your mother. You'd think your mom has never changed a diaper."

I laugh at the vision of my mother chasing a half-naked Ray around the house. "Well, she did have nannies with London and me, but she has to know how to change a diaper, right?" I scrunch up my nose.

"You would think, but I didn't step in, figuring she could figure it out," Wyatt grins.

"You're so mean," I chuckle, hitting his chest lightly. "You know Ray's giving her a run for her money."

"That's our girl," he nods, "determined like her momma."

"Okay, well, I'll go rescue my mom. Can you take him to his room, to his toy chest, and figure out what car he's talking about? The guests should be arriving soon."

Just then Mila and Cooper come ambling out of the house, and Asher points, "Miya! Coop!"

"You want to play with the puppies?" Wyatt asks as Asher struggles to climb down Wyatt's body. "I guess the car is forgotten," Wyatt chuckles as he walks over to Cooper who stands patiently as Asher hugs his neck.

I watch for a moment as my boys throw tennis balls for Cooper and Mila. Asher giggles every time he pulls the slobbery ball from one of the dogs' mouths. Cooper's definitely a senior dog now, at twelve, but it doesn't show besides the extra white fur on his snout. He's still as active as he ever was for which I'm thankful. I pray that he breaks records for the amount of time a dog lives. Pit bull breeds usually live to fourteen or fifteen, but we have a friend whose rescue dog lived to nineteen. So I'm hoping for at least seven more healthy years for Cooper.

I make my way inside to find my mom holding Ray, looking more than a little exhausted. "You okay, Mom?"

"Oh yeah, we're fine." She lets out a tired breath.

RayRay holds her arms out to me, and I take her, setting her on my hip. "Are you being good for Mimi?"

"She's perfect. She's just like you were at that age," my mom says. "Just perfect."

"I'm so glad you and Dad could make it up," I tell her. "Where is Dad?"

She waves her hand. "He's on a business call. You know how it is."

For the first time, I see a hint of sadness in her expression. My mom has always gushed over how hard my dad works. She's never complained about the lack of time she spends with him. I suppose it was their example that led me to question soul mates in the first place because I couldn't fathom loving someone the way that I love Wyatt and spending so much time apart. It's never seemed to bother my parents, though, but now if I'm wondering if it upsets my mother more than she lets on.

"Where are you headed after this, again?"

"Somewhere in Arizona. You know I can't even keep track half of the time," she chuckles.

"Well, Mom, you know you're always welcome to stay here for a while if you want to visit longer."

"Really?"

"Really," I tell her honestly. Placing my hand to my belly, I say, "I could use your help around here."

"I'll talk to your father about it." Her expression softens as she smiles.

"Now, I don't have a housekeeper, a nanny, or a cook," I warn her, quirking up an eyebrow.

She chuckles, "What must you think of me?"

"I don't judge you, Mom. I just want you to be happy. Also, London and Loïc's new house is very close, as well. I'm sure London would love for you to spend more time with Lindi, too."

"What about me?" London walks in with her two-year-old daughter, Lindi, on her hip.

"Hey!" I give her and Lindi a hug. "Mom's thinking about staying a little bit. I told her she could spend some time here and with you."

"I'd love that, Mom," London says excitedly.

Guests start arriving, and the almost serene ambiance of the morning preparations are replaced by loud laughter, lots of people, and a handful of dogs playing in our large fenced-in yard. As much as a quiet morning is needed, an obnoxiously loud afternoon feeds the spirit, and I love it.

Ethel and Luciana are finishing the buffet set-up, and I can't help but laugh as RayRay tugs at Ethel's leg chanting, "Nana!" There are few people that our little girl loves more than her Nana Ethel.

All of our friends from Cooper's Place are here, including past and present employees. Paige and her husband are chatting with Wyatt's friend Carrie and her man over under the colorful maple tree. I was hoping we'd get a perfect fall day for the party, and we did.

I grin wide when I see my dad in his three-piece suit sitting on the porch swing with Gus Gus, one of our newer, elderly and toothless employees. The two of them are the polar opposites of each other, and yet they're rooted in conversation. It makes my heart swell with happiness seeing all of the people that I love here to celebrate our two little miracles.

I catch London glance at my hand that absentmindedly rubs my large belly, and my heart hurts for my sister. She just finished her third round of in vitro fertilization with no luck. It's not fair how I can get pregnant so easily and she can't.

"I'm sorry," I tell her.

She tilts her head, the sides of her lips tilt up. "Don't be." She places a hand on my arm. "I am so happy for you and Wyatt.

I'm okay," her stare finds her husband Loïc, who is in the yard playing with their daughter, and her smile widens, "we're okay. If we're only meant to have Lindi, then that's more than enough. Or we can adopt again. It will all work out."

"So just one more round?" I ask her.

She nods, "Yep, we're going to try in vitro one more time and call it good—no matter the outcome. I want more than anything to feel what it's like to carry my own baby, but I can't keep doing this."

"Yeah," I tell her as if I understand, but honestly I have no idea what it's been like for her. I pray that this last round works for her. London deserves to have a baby. She's a fantastic mom. "You know, my offer still stands," I tell her. "It would be an honor to be a surrogate for you. I'm serious. I'd love to help you, if I can."

She tilts her head and rests it on my shoulder. "I know," she says softly. "And I love you for it. We'll decide what's next after this last round. Who knows? Maybe the fourth time will work?" She raises her head and pulls in a steady breath. "So you're really not finding out with this one?" she asks, changing the subject.

"Nope," I shake my head. "Our last is going to be a surprise. We have our girl and our boy. This baby is our bonus baby, and we don't care what it is. We just want Happy to be healthy."

"I get that you'll be pleased either way, regardless if it's a boy or a girl, but how can you wait nine whole months to find out? That would drive me crazy."

I chuckle, "It's kind of fun, reading the old wives' tales, trying to guess if it's a boy or girl based on the heartbeat or position. It's great."

"If you say so." She raises her eyebrows. "If I get pregnant someday, I'm finding out."

"When you do, you should do one of those gender reveal parties. I'll throw it for you. It will be awesome." I grab her hand that rests between us and squeeze it, letting her know how much I want her dreams to come true.

"Will Lucy's parents cater?" She puckers out her lips in question.

"Of course, the Rubio-Reyeses are the official caterers of the Gates household." I let out a chuckle.

"Thank God Wyatt hired someone who married someone whose parents own a Mexican restaurant," she says dramatically.

"Right? How lucky did I get? Us Wright girls need tacos."

"Agreed." London nods her head.

"I'm so glad you moved back to Michigan," I say to London as I wrap my arms around her. There's nothing better than living by your sister and raising your kids together. Asher and Lindi are best friends. I know in a year, or so, RayRay is going to join them, once she gains a little more language.

"Yeah, me too. It just seemed right. Ann Arbor has a great VA Hospital where Loïc can work with veterans and I can write from anywhere. We've never really had a home base with Mom and Dad constantly moving. I'm so glad the two of us are now settled and can raise our families together."

"Me too," I agree. "Maybe someday Mom and Dad will move here for good, once Dad retires."

"Maybe," London says thoughtfully.

"Can you even believe our lives?" I ask, my voice thick with emotion.

London shakes her head, "No, we're so lucky. It's pretty amazing."

"It is."

Ethel walks over to us. "Everything's ready, babe."

"Thanks, Nana," I tell her, now calling her what my kids do. I'll never get to know Wyatt's birth mother, but his surrogate one is the best that there is. We're so fortunate to have her.

RayRay runs to me, and the little Minnie Mouse ears with a bow that I had pinned to her fine blonde hair have slipped down and are now hanging by her ear. I snatch her up in my arms and spin her. Her giggles are infectious.

I unclip the Minnie ears. "Your hair's not quite ready for bows yet, I'm afraid. Soon you'll have thick hair like Mommy, just not yet."

Ray's little pudgy hands slap against her hair as she attempts to repeat the word, hair.

I nod, "Yep, soon you'll have long hair, birthday girl. How old are you today?"

She raises her whole hand and smiles wide, proud of herself. We've been working with her all week, teaching her to show one finger, but she's set on raising her whole hand, and that's fine, too.

"Are you one hand old?" I ask in a silly voice and nibble at her cheek, eliciting another round of giggles.

Wyatt steps beside us with Asher in tow. "Are we ready to eat? Do the birthday babies want some tacos?"

"Big boy," Asher interrupts.

"You're right. Do the birthday girl and big boy want some tacos?"

RayRay claps her hands excitedly. She's obsessed with tacos. She's definitely my girl.

We eat, have cake, and open presents all the while smiling and laughing with our family. One thing's for sure, my kids are never going to know what it's like to not feel loved. I don't know two kids who are more loved than they are, and it will be just the same for the third. Family are the people we choose, and we've chosen well.

"I don't think so," Wyatt grumbles toward Ethel, and I hold my belly while I laugh. Both kids just opened their present from Nana, which happens to be a four-foot-long plush cat for each of them.

"Raising them right." Ethel shoots Wyatt a wink.

Meanwhile, RayRay climbs atop the stuffed animal and wraps her little arms around its neck chanting, "Kiki! Kiki!"

"Did Nana get you a kitty cat? Awe, do you love it?" I can't stop smiling at the cuteness before me.

"I swear E, if there are more presents with obnoxious cat shirts," he shakes his head, "I don't even know."

"Well, you'll just have to wait and find out. Won't you?" Ethel shoots him a smirk.

"I don't know, babe. I think our kids are taking after their Nana with their love of cats," I tease him.

"No. We are dog people. The Gates family are dog people." He enunciates each word a little slower than usual as he narrows his eyes toward Ethel in mock-annoyance.

"They can be both, dogs and cats," I say.

"Of course people can like both, but one always edges the other out. No one is equally as much a dog person as they are a cat person. One is always preferred, and we prefer dogs."

"Kiki!" RayRay is now jumping on the back of her sizeable plush cat.

Nana bends down closer to RayRay. "My baby girl is a cat person, isn't she? Do you love the kitty cats?"

"Kiki!" RayRay says again.

Ethel claps her hands together in front of her as she stands. "Well, I believe my work here is done," she says, causing us all to laugh at Wyatt's expense.

The party for my babies is absolutely perfect. I find myself in awe on more than one occasion with just how happy I am. When the family has gone and it's only the six of us, our two fur babies included, I look to Wyatt and him to me and we just smile.

Asher and Ray fall asleep the second their heads hit their pillows, both worn out from such an incredible day.

Wyatt draws me a bath, and as I step in, my aching feet feel relief.

"Ah, this is heaven," I tell Wyatt as he gets in behind me. I lean my back against his chest, and he runs his soapy hands up and down my arms.

We chat about the day as he lovingly washes my body. My husband is the greatest man I've ever known. He's a giver. He would do anything for anyone, both human and dog alike. He loves the kids and me so profoundly that thinking about it makes my chest ache.

Who would've thought that years ago when I first stepped into the office at the rescue to meet the boss and saw his dark blues glaring back at me that we would've ended up here? It's crazy how life works out sometimes.

I'm so different than the girl I was when I met Wyatt in biology class. Wyatt's right when he says that we came together precisely when we were meant to. The seventeen-year-old version of myself wasn't strong enough to fall in love then. I didn't know who I really was, so I couldn't give my heart and soul to another.

Truthfully, I didn't fully find myself until I returned to Wyatt after my three-day escape to Mexico.

When I was young, I thought that true love and fairytales were a lie, but I was wrong. Fairytales are real. I live in one every single day. A real-life fairytale is the support that my husband whispers in my ear before an important doctor's appointment when I'm nervous. True love is when he massages my feet before bed because they're swollen from pregnancy even though he's had a long day and is exhausted. A prince is one who gets up to change the baby in the middle of the night and rocks her back to sleep so I can stay in bed. A knight in shining armor is someone who comes home early from work to clean the house while I'm visiting my sister so that I don't have to when I get back. A hero is someone who holds me when I'm sad, tells me that I'm beautiful, and loves me with everything he has.

Wyatt is my one and only. Maybe not everyone finds their true love, but I'm so grateful that I found mine.

Someday, when my daughter asks whether true love exists, I'll let her know that it does. I'll tell her that she needs to find herself, love herself, and be true to herself, and when she's done all of those things, her prince charming will come—not because she needs him, but because she wants him.

If anyone had to search the world until he could find me to return my shoe—it would be Wyatt. If anyone's love for me was so incredibly powerful that with one kiss he could wake me from the darkest sleep—it would be Wyatt's lips that saved me.

If life were a fairytale, in a storybook, Wyatt would be my prince charming. There's no question. He was made to love me, and I to love him.

Yet I have it so much better than all of the princesses combined because my version of happily ever after is real, and I get to live it each and every day.

Dear Readers,

I hope you loved reading Georgia's story as much as I loved writing it. I feel I did London's sister proud. It was fun checking in with our favorites from the *Flawed Heart* series. Stay tuned for other spin-off books that may include reader favorites Paige and Maggie.

Taming Georgia is near and dear to my heart, and if you follow me on social media you already know why—I'm a huge advocate for dogs.

We currently have four pittie-mixes, including two pups that we fostered and proceeded to adopt. I love all dogs, but if you've ever been loved by a pittie, then you know why they hold a special place in my heart.

Cooper was the first pit bull I owned. I didn't know anything about the breed or stigma they carry when I got Cooper. It was a huge wake-up call when my neighbors in Ypsilanti told me to never leave him outside in our fenced-in yard unattended because someone would steal him to use him for a bait dog.

Cooper lived for eleven years, until he passed away from cancer. He was the best dog I've ever had, and I miss him every day.

There are so many great dogs in shelters around the United States that are in need of homes. If you're looking for a companion that will love you more than anyone else and are able— think about adoption, and save a life.

Thank you so much for reading.

Make your journey beautiful.

Love,
Ellie

ACKNOWLEDGMENTS

To my beta readers, blogger friends, author friends, and readers who message me—You all are so awesome. Seriously, each of you is a gift, and you have helped me in invaluable different ways. I love you all so much. XOXO

This book especially wouldn't have been what it is without a few incredible women—Kylie, Amy, Jen, Kim, and Tammi. Thank you so much for everything.

I would love to thank the people that spend their lives saving animals. Thank you to all of you who've adopted, or shared a dog on social media that needs a home, or donated to a rescue organization. You are all heroes. A special shout-out goes to the Detroit Pit Crew and Cober's Canines for rescuing our boys, Bo and Tucker, and their six siblings from Eight Mile in Detroit. Also, I couldn't write a story about dog rescue and not thank Tia Torres and her family for being my idols for years. If you want to see her giant heart in action, check out *Pit Bulls and Parolees*—our family's favorite show.

To the bloggers—I adore you! Out of the kindness of your hearts, so many of you have reached out and helped me promote my books. There are seriously great people in this blogger community, and I am humbled by your support. Truly, thank you! Because of you, indie authors get their stories out. Thank you for supporting all authors and the great stories they write.

Lastly, to the readers—I want to thank you so very much. Thank you for reading my stories and loving my words! I wouldn't be living this dream without you. Thank you from the bottom of my heart!

You can connect with me on several places and I would love to hear from you.

Find me on Facebook: www.facebook.com/ EllieWadeAuthor

Find me on Twitter: @authorelliewade

Visit my website: www.elliewade.com

Remember, the greatest gift you can give an author is a review. If you feel so inclined, please leave a review on the various retailer sites. It doesn't have to be fancy. A couple of sentences would be awesome!

I could honestly write a whole book about everyone in this world whom I am thankful for. I am blessed in so many ways and I am beyond grateful for this beautiful life. XOXO

Forever,

Ellie ♥

ABOUT THE AUTHOR

ELLIE WADE resides in southeast Michigan with her husband, three young children, and four dogs. She has a master's in education from Eastern Michigan University, and she is a huge University of Michigan sports fan. She loves the beauty of her home state, especially the lakes and the gorgeous autumn weather. When she is not writing, she is reading, snuggling up with her kids, or spending time with family and friends. She loves traveling and exploring new places with her family.

CPSIA information can be obtained
at www.ICGtesting.com
Printed in the USA
BVHW080014260419
546424BV00001B/1/P

9 781635 765687